A HERO FOR HER

BAYTOWN HEROES
BOOK THREE

MARYANN JORDAN

This book is a work of fiction. Names, characters, places, and incidents are either products of the author's imagination or are used fictitiously. Any resemblance to actual persons, living or dead, events, or locales is entirely coincidental.

Cover: Graphics by Stacy

ISBN ebook: 978-1-956588-21-7

ISBN print: 978-1-956588-22-4

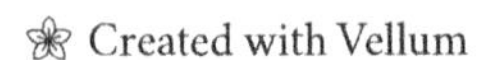

Author's Note

Please remember that this is a work of fiction. I have lived in numerous states as well as overseas, but for the last thirty years have called Virginia my home. I often choose to use fictional city names with some geographical accuracies.

These fictionally named cities allow me to use my creativity and not feel constricted by attempting to accurately portray the areas.

It is my hope that my readers will allow me this creative license and understand my fictional world.

I also do quite a bit of research on my books and try to write on subjects with accuracy. There will always be points where creative license will be used in order to create scenes or plots.

1

The early morning mist hung over the Chesapeake Bay. Gulls, terns, ospreys, and black pelicans swooped over the water in their search for breakfast. Snowy egrets and blue herons stood in the shallow waters with their long, stately necks stretched out as they waited with infinite patience for a fish or crab to come within their reach.

The sunrise illuminated the sandy shore, giving evidence of the breeze blowing the sea grasses on the dunes. The lush pine tree forests joined the fall colors of red, orange, and yellow from the oaks and maple trees beyond the dunes in the distance.

The sky morphed from black to a glimmer of pale blue in the east, then, with each passing moment, pink and yellow oozed across the horizon to mingle with the various blue hues. The light breeze was not strong enough to cause waves, and the water gently undulated.

The autumn air was cool as the boat sliced through the ghostly mist. The only sounds were the boat engine, water slapping against the sides, the call of seabirds, and in the distance, the sound of oyster fishermen talking as they stood hip-deep in the water, their rakes digging the oysters off the beds.

It was one of Jared Dobson's favorite times on the water. Out on patrol, he stood in the wheelhouse of the thirty-three-foot special-purpose craft of the Virginia Marine Police. He wasn't alone since they always traveled with partners, and today he was with Callan Ward, grateful for the other man's desire to enjoy the peace of the early morning as well.

Jared kept the speed low until the rising sun burned off the last of the mist. Callan stood on the bow of the boat, helping to direct through the low visibility. They called out greetings as they came upon boats filled with local fishermen. Callan had grown up on the Eastern Shore of Virginia, part of a group of men often referred to as the original Baytown Boys, the moniker for the high school baseball team. An early career with the Coast Guard had resulted in Callan's assignment back to his hometown, and when he left the Guard, he eagerly came on board with the VMP.

Jared had also served in the Coast Guard, but their similarities ended there. Callan's parents still lived in Baytown, and he'd reunited with and married the beautiful love of his life. He and Sophie had a baby several months ago, living near both sets of parents who doted on them. Jared sighed, scrubbing his hand over his face. He'd seriously be jealous if Callan weren't such a good officer and friend.

Jared's father had attended the Naval Academy and

served as a career officer in the Navy. He could still hear his dad's response when he came home after joining the Coast Guard. *"The least you could have done is go to college to become an officer in the Navy instead of pissing away your career in the Guard!"*

His parents now lived in Florida, and he'd visited them for the obligatory holiday for years until his mom had a cancer scare about three years ago. She'd battled and won, and in the process, Jared's dad let go of past disappointments, finally deciding that life was too short not to hold tight to family. Jared had been shocked at his dad's turnaround, but now the visits were more celebratory and not times to be avoided.

"Hey, Chuck!" Callan called out, signaling for Jared to slow their progression.

Callan's shout jerked Jared back to the task at hand, and he expertly maneuvered their craft to the side of the old but well-kept fishing trawler. Paint was chipped from the once white-painted sides, and the fishing lines were worn and dark, but Chuck kept his boat in excellent working order. Jared grinned, throwing his hand up in greeting as the older fisherman smiled in return.

"You boys are out awfully early, aren't you?" Chuck asked, pulling off his ball cap and wiping the brow of his weathered face, the creases from years of working outdoors deepening with his smile. Wearing a plaid shirt and yellow fishing bibs, he was ready for the autumn weather. His hair was shot with silver, but his body belied his age. The daily grind of being a fisherman honed his lean body, but arthritis slowed his movements.

"We have to get up early to keep up with codgers like you," Jared called out, earning a hoot from Chuck's grandson, who moved around their deck with the ease of a young man who'd spent time on boats since before he could walk.

Chuck laughed, shaking his head. "Codger, huh? I can still outmaneuver most of these young 'uns on the water!"

"I'm sure you can," Jared agreed with a smile.

"I have something for you," Callan said as he leaned into the wheelhouse and grabbed his backpack. Jared watched with curiosity as Callan unzipped the pack and pulled out a plastic container. Walking back over to the edge of his boat, Callan handed it to Chuck. "My Sophie appreciated the soup your wife dropped by when she was sick a few weeks ago. When I told her I was going out early this morning and would probably see you, she wanted me to give you these cookies to take home."

Chuck's grandson grinned and leaned forward, but Callan pulled them back slightly. "Now, you better make sure your grandmother gets at least a few of these."

Jared shook his head and chuckled as Chuck slapped the back of his grandson's head and reached out to take the plastic container. "You tell your wife I'll make sure my Anna gets these."

"How's the haul this morning?" Jared knew Chuck and his grandson had already been out for at least two hours.

"Rockfish and drum aren't too bad." Chuck's gaze moved out over the water, his chest heaving in a sigh. "I can still get a decent price to make a living. God knows that's not always easy."

Jared knew the words were true. It was hard, back-breaking, sunup-to-sundown work to eke out a living from the bay. "Take care," Jared called out as Callan pushed away from the fishing vessel's side. Steering away from the boat, they continued their patrol near Baytown. He maneuvered through open water and inlets, checking on the fishermen hauling crab pots and the oyster farmers working in the private oyster beds.

As the sun rose higher in the sky, the crystal waters of the Chesapeake glistened like diamonds underneath a cloudless blue sky. The jacket he'd worn when they left the station was no longer needed, and he shrugged it off, tossing it behind him.

The morning was peaceful compared to the summer months when the vacationers were out in kayaks and boats, some without the proper licenses or training. Summertime rescues were much more prevalent than in the less trafficked times of the year. "I know the town needs the tourists, but I don't mind telling you that I like it when they go home," Jared said, his gaze moving over the water as he steered.

Callan joined him in the wheelhouse and nodded. "You've got that right. The teens are back in school, and hardly anyone is out on Jet Skis. And for now, it looks like the only fishermen we've come across are those out here legally."

As he maneuvered through another inlet, they passed several small piers and boat docks belonging to the people who owned property along the water's edge.

VMP Chief Ryan Coates and one of the other officers, Joseph Newman, lived nearby. It seemed as though those who worked on the water wanted to live there, too. *God knows I do, too.*

"How's your house coming along?" Callan asked as though reading Jared's thoughts.

He grinned, thinking about the property he'd bought recently. The small house backed up to the water of an inlet that led to the bay and was a fixer-upper. But that was fine by him, considering it was the only way he could afford it when it went on sale. "I was thinking about when the work on the house is complete, and I can have a dock built."

"I know Ryan and Joseph love theirs." Callan nodded. "I wouldn't mind living on the water, but I don't think Sophie would ever want to leave our house." Callan and Sophie lived in a big house in town, not too far from their parents.

From the broad smile on Callan's face, it was evident his friend would never deny his sweet, beautiful wife anything. Thinking about their new baby, Jared teased, "Or your parents."

"You've got that right. With both my parents and Sophie's parents nearby, Phillip is spoiled. He grinned. "And we have babysitters anytime we need to get away."

The radio sounded, and the dispatcher's voice broke through his thoughts, sending the coordinates for a stalled boat nearby. Jared steered them in the opposite direction, and they headed farther out into the bay.

The oyster-shell driveway crunched underneath the tires of Jared's older model SUV as he parked in front of his house. Climbing down, he stopped and sucked in a breath of air, appreciating the view. The home had seen better days, but that was a part of its charm. Built in the early 1900s by a railway worker, it had served as a home to a number of families over the years.

The two-story wooden structure was held together with good bones. The real estate agent explained that the original house had three small bedrooms and a bathroom upstairs, with one being about the size of a walk-in closet. A previous owner had taken the space to enlarge the bathroom and make two bedrooms instead of three. A living room with a fireplace and built-in bookcases, a small dining room, a kitchen, and a half bathroom with a stackable washer and dryer completed the first floor. Before purchasing, he'd hired a top-notch inspector and had been assured the only work needed was cosmetic. *A lot of cosmetics.*

So far, he'd managed to knock a few items off his to-do list. The original floors were sanded and refinished. New drywall was up on multiple interior walls, and new insulation filled the attic space. With winter coming, he wanted to ensure the heat stayed inside and didn't escape through the roof. While he appreciated the large bathroom upstairs, it needed updating, so he'd tackled that project. He'd removed the floral wallpaper in the larger bedroom and painted it a neutral soft gray.

He was halfway finished with the kitchen, having upgraded the appliances, cabinets, and countertop. Those jobs required long nights, off-duty weekends, and the help of some friends. He hired out having the roof and windows replaced, not afraid to admit when he was in over his head—lacking the time or skill to make sure the job was complete and up to code.

But he still had a lot to do. Updating the downstairs bathroom, finishing the kitchen, fixing the front porch, installing new stair rails leading to the second floor, continuing to paint the interior and exterior, and then planning an addition to the house down the road. *Yeah, a fuckton of work to do.*

Walking through the front door, he smiled in spite of the disarray presented to him as a loud woof greeted him. He braced himself as his dog jumped up on him. "Hey, Daisy girl," he murmured, rubbing her black fur. "You ready to go out?" If her prancing in circles was any indication, he assumed she was busting to get outside.

They moved through the kitchen, and he tossed his take-out bag onto the counter before he opened the back door to let her into the fenced yard. She bounded off the steps, racing around, sniffing, barking at birds, and taking care of her business. She trotted to the back steps, now eagerly awaiting their nightly game. Bending, he snagged a ball from the bucket near the door and tossed it, watching as she raced to snap it in her jaws, trotting back for a repeat performance. As she darted back and forth, he cast his gaze around his yard.

The fence had been in a state of disrepair when he bought the property. Since he wanted Daisy to be able to run safely, he'd torn down the remnants, re-dug the post holes, and put up a new picket fence. He'd thought of painting it white, but for now, the natural wood would do. The fence encompassed a large part of the backyard, and just outside its boundaries was the one-car garage located to the side. It had once been a small barn, but a previous owner had used it as a garage. Like much of the house, it had seen better days. Jared used it to house his lawnmower, tools, extra building supplies, and anything else he could store out there.

The best part was that it had a full room over the garage. Another former owner had turned the upstairs into a small efficiency apartment, complete with a mini fridge, stovetop, and microwave. A tiny bathroom that contained a sink, toilet, and minuscule shower completed the space. It wasn't fancy, but it was functional. He'd been glad for the apartment because he'd lived there while he refinished the downstairs floors and had the new roof and windows installed in the house.

Now, he hoped to find someone to rent the studio apartment, giving him a modest amount of rental money to offset the cost of the work he was doing on the house. He'd contacted a local real estate agent, given a list of conditions, and hoped they might send a renter to him. *I need a quiet guy, someone who keeps to himself and doesn't trash the place.*

His attention fell back to Daisy as she tired of her game and dropped the ball at his feet, walking to the back door.

"You hungry?" His question was unnecessary, considering he could read her expressive face. Once back in the kitchen, he filled her bowl with dog food before placing it on the floor.

Ready to have his own dinner, he opened the take-out bag and pulled out the wrapped sandwich. Grabbing a beer from the refrigerator, he settled onto a kitchen stool and devoured the BLT he'd gotten from the pharmacy's diner in town. He groaned with pleasure, wiping his mouth as the condiments dripped off his chin. *Extra bacon. Perfect.*

Leaning down, he gave his last bite of bacon to Daisy, who gently took it from his fingers, then turned and trotted back into the living room. After cleaning the take-out wrappers, he glanced at the prioritized list he kept on the refrigerator, giving a mental fist pump at the number of items crossed off.

The drywall hanging on a few walls downstairs was taped and mudded but not painted. Drop cloths covered the furniture and floors in the living room. He had no dining room furniture, so he ate each meal at the kitchen counter.

Deciding to tackle the living room walls, he shook the paint can, popped open the lid, and poured a generous amount into the roller pan. It didn't take long to get into the rhythm, and the pale blue-gray paint soon covered the back wall.

Hearing his phone vibrate from the other room, he climbed off the ladder and jogged into the kitchen, finding it lying on the counter. Seeing the local real estate agent on caller ID, he quickly answered. "Hey, Joanne, what's up?"

"Sorry to call so late, but I thought I'd get ahold of you this evening. My partner, Larry, found someone who seems perfect for your efficiency. It's someone who's looking for cheap housing. Are you still interested?"

"Yeah, sure. I was just thinking about that a little while ago. Do you know anything about them? They need to know it's a small apartment."

"Larry said he went over the specs with them, and they were very interested. You know how hard it is to get a small place around here for a reasonable price."

He opened his mouth, but she kept talking.

"Let's see. I have a sticky note around here somewhere. Oh, phooey, where is it? Anyway, his name is Bill, and he's filled out the application and already paid the deposit and first month's rent."

"Any idea where he works?"

"I believe Larry said he's from Norfolk… or maybe it was Chesapeake."

"Well, if the guy doesn't mind roughing it, there's a bed in there, a bathroom, and a way to heat some food."

"Well, Larry indicated Bill was contemplating a camper, so it sounds like he would consider this a step up."

Jared snorted, glancing out the window at the garage. *Hell, a camper might be better.* "Listen, I don't want to take advantage of him. We can rent month to month from the beginning in case he hates the place."

"Excellent!" Joanne enthused. "I'll let Larry know, and Bill can contact you when he's ready to move in."

Disconnecting, Jared shoved his phone into his pocket and walked back to the living room. An hour later, with one coat of paint covering the walls, he stood back and nodded in appreciation. "What do you think, Daisy? Like it?"

She lifted her head from the cushion on the floor, offered a baleful expression, and then lay back down.

"Hmph," he grunted. "Well, I like it." It took another half hour to clean the roller brushes and pan, secure the paint lid, and pick up the area. After letting her out for a final run, he secured the house, and they climbed the stairs. It didn't take long to shower, and when he walked into the bedroom, Daisy had already claimed her space on the king-sized bed.

"Move over, girl." He pretended to grumble, but in truth, he didn't mind sharing his space. They'd only been together a few months, but she'd caught his eye from the first moment he'd walked into the shelter. When he knelt, she raced over, sat in front of him, and nuzzled his hand. From the moment he'd first brought the retriever-spitz-shepherd mix home, she'd plastered herself to him. Climbing into bed, he glanced out the window, saw the garage out of the corner, and sighed. He liked his privacy and would have preferred not to rent. *But the extra money will be nice. And as long as he's not a criminal, I can put up with just about anything for a few months.*

2

The special-purpose craft expertly cut through the water as Jared and fellow VMP officers Joseph Newman and Andy Bergstrom headed out on their patrol. Today, Andy stood at the wheel, and he and Joseph checked the licenses of some of the area fishermen. Commercial licenses were required for all fishermen specific to what they caught. Considering the size of Chesapeake Bay, it wasn't unusual to see fishing vessels they didn't recognize. Verifying the licenses was an everyday duty as well as checking the catches at times to ensure the fishermen abided by the licenses they owned.

Passing by one of the small sandy islands near the coastline that formed when the tide was out, Jared lifted his binoculars to his eyes. Spying a single-person red tent near the dune and a small single-motor boat anchored in the shallow water, he lifted his hand and gave the indication to bring them closer to the island. Joseph moved next to him and stared out as well.

"Campers?" Joseph mumbled.

He didn't see any signs of anyone around, but Jared couldn't imagine the tent had been there long. "Let's check it out."

Andy brought them close to the shore, and he and Joseph hopped into the shallow surf, walking toward the tent. Inside was a rolled-up sleeping bag secured in a plastic bag for protection and a small chest with a lock on it. Footprints were around the outside, but the surf had taken away any indication of where the camper had gone.

Snapping pictures of the area, they walked toward the trees and seagrass but saw no more evidence of anyone.

Back in the boat, they continued their patrols until an emergency call came from the dispatcher. Andy turned them around, and they raced toward the location of a capsized boat. Another VMP vessel and a Coast Guard crew were just behind them as they came to the upside-down center console boat with four people clinging to the sides.

While Andy slowed to keep the waves from rocking the already dangerous situation, Jared was relieved to see all the visible men wearing life jackets. "Are you all here? Anyone missing?"

"N-No," one of the men answered. "There w-was only four of us."

The water temperatures cooled with the autumn weather, so hypothermia would set in quickly. He and Joseph leaned close and tossed a life ring and rope to the nearest one. "Grab hold, and we'll pull you over."

The closest man caught it easily and handed it to the older man next to him. As soon as his arms were looped around the flotation device, Jared gently pulled him to the side of their vessel with ease. Joseph did the same with one of the other men. It took both of them to assist the men over the sides and into the VMP boat.

Casting his practiced gaze out on the scene, he observed as Callan and Ryan in the other vessel performed the same rescue with the other two men. Once secured, they moved away to allow the Coast Guard to deal with the capsized boat. They would need to tow it into the harbor for examination and to ensure the vessel didn't leak any more chemicals into the water.

"How long were you out there after the boat capsized?" he asked as he wrapped the older man in a thermal blanket.

"About tw-twenty minutes," the man replied, still shivering.

"Was that your boat?" Accepting a bottle of water from Joseph, Jared unscrewed the top and handed it to the man.

"No, my s-son rented it for the day. He's in the other boat," he said, inclining his head toward the second VMP boat. Holding Jared's gaze, he swallowed deeply as tears leaked down his cheeks. "I'm sure glad you came along when you did. It was hard to feel my fingers after a while."

"We'll get you checked out once we get back to the harbor," Jared assured.

He looked over his shoulder toward Joseph, and they

shared a look. This was the third rental boat that had taken on water in the past two months, and he wondered if it was from the same owner. Turning back, he aimed his smile toward the two men sitting on the deck. "We'll be at the harbor in about ten minutes, and an EMT will be waiting to check you out. Hang on, and we'll get you there safely."

Standing, he walked into the wheelhouse where Joseph was already huddled with Andy. "You thinking what I'm thinking?"

"George Mooney?" Andy asked.

"If so, we need to go check out his rental boats. Ryan will have his operating license jerked faster than old George can blink if this was another one of his boats."

As soon as they pulled into the harbor behind the second boat carrying the other men, they were met by Zac Hamilton, the captain of the Baytown Rescue Station, and one of his volunteers. The four men were taken inside the warm VMP station while the medical team evaluated them. Only the older man agreed to be transported to the hospital, and one of the others went with him.

As soon as he could, Jared headed directly to Ryan to find out about the boat and to see who the men rented it from. The look on his chief's face gave him the answer. Ryan Coates was in his mid-forties, married with children, an easy boss to work for, and one of the best men Jared had ever met. But right now, Ryan looked like he wanted to spit nails.

Speaking cautiously, Jared held his gaze. "George, right?"

A muscle ticked in Ryan's jaw.

"I'll head over to his dock now. Who do you want to go with me?" Jared asked.

"Me." Ryan's one-word response was definitive.

"Okaaay." Jared drew out the word as his brows lifted.

Because Ryan wanted to have the rest of George's fleet examined, he called out for Andy to go with them. Andy had been in maintenance in the Navy and had expertise in examining watercraft for safety.

Soon, the three of them occupied one of the smaller vessels and headed to the location of George Mooney's business at a dock north of town. He had a fleet of small center console boats for rent, and today's incident made the third one with issues recently.

Pulling up to the dock, Jared leaned over the side and secured the boat. Glancing at the small building at the end of the dock, he spied George already walking toward them. The gray-haired, barrel-chested man had gotten thicker and slower with age but still loved to sit and talk about his glory days in the Navy when he was at the pub, hoping someone would buy him a drink.

With his hands up in a placating manner, he called out, "Yep, I know why y'all are here! Already heard those dumbasses wrecked my boat!"

Jared and Andy deftly jumped onto the dock, quickly followed by Ryan. Stepping back to let his chief speak, he scanned the other boats docked nearby.

"We're here to check your licenses and inspect your fleet," Ryan announced. "And just to let you know that the Coast Guard is hauling the capsized boat into their station where it will be evaluated."

"I don't know why it needs to be evaluated," George said, puffing out his chest and planting his beefy fists on his hips. "It's not my fault if dumb shits don't know how to go out in the water. I'm the one who'll have to take the financial hit!"

"You have insurance," Jared said, his head swinging back around to pin the belligerent owner with his gaze.

"Of course, I have insurance. That's not a crime. In fact, in my line of work, insurance saves me from the people who rent and don't know what they're doing."

"Three boats in just as many months," Ryan said. "Your insurance company must be tired of paying out."

"They can drag their feet all they want, but my boats are fine. And if the insurance companies don't pay, I'll sue!"

"Well then, you're in luck," Ryan added. "'Cause we're going to take a look at your boats today and make sure that the ones you have left are seaworthy."

While Ryan spoke, Jared kept his gaze on the other man, easily spotting the unease that crept through George's eyes.

"You ain't got no warrant. You ain't gonna go snooping around my boats," George said, jutting out his chin.

"As the Virginia Marine Police, we don't need a warrant to inspect your watercraft."

George's hands flexed into tighter fists. "I'm telling you, Chief Coates, you get near my boats, and I'll call the law on you."

Ryan turned toward Jared and Andy and offered a chin lift. Jared hid his grin as he and Andy moved around George toward the other boats docked nearby. He could still hear George arguing with Ryan when the chief reminded the old blowhard that they were the law.

He'd often examined vessels before, but acknowledging Andy's expertise, he waited to see the list of items they should check.

"If we were doing a full inspection, we'd look for everything on these lists, but I think Ryan just wants to make sure that as soon as we find something, we can possibly pull his license."

Nodding, Jared agreed. "So what's first?"

"If you'll look at the hull for any serious scrapes and dents, I'll look at the engine connections and steering cables. You can also look at the propeller, anchor, and mooring lines. Ryan will look over the certifications, licenses, and documentation, or if George gives him any trouble, he may call the sheriff for backup while we look at them."

He took the rubber mallet Andy gave him and began tapping along the hulls of the two boats out of the water. Just as he suspected, it didn't take long to discover that the fiberglass was delaminating in several places. The Coast Guard could do a more precise exam, but he determined water may have been gathering, or it could have rotted on the inside. One of them also had serious scratches and large dents in the hull, possibly making them susceptible to taking on water.

Andy looked over and called down, "I'm already finding violations up here. What have you got?"

"The same thing. Enough to give Ryan reason to shut him down until these are looked at and remediated."

Ryan walked over, his jaw still tight, but Jared could detect a slight twinkle in his boss's eyes. "The boat involved in the accident last month is already back on the rental list, but there is no paperwork of repairs or inspection."

"Three of these four don't pass our basic inspection either," he said, handing his checklist to Ryan as Andy hopped down onto the dock from the deck of the boat.

Moving back to George, who was on his phone, he looked up to see a deputy car pulling next to the small building at the end of the dock. Grinning, he asked, "You call in reinforcements?"

Ryan shrugged, but his lips curved slightly. "I'm writing him up for violations and want the sheriff's office to witness that I've shut his business down until he's rectified them." Jared couldn't help but chuckle as they walked toward George, who was already arguing with one of the deputies.

As Ryan explained the violations, George continued to bluster, trying to talk over him. Finally fed up with George's continued interruptions, Jared shook his head. "Just stay quiet, man. Close your mouth and listen if you want your business to open up again."

"Fuck you!" George yelled, his face red as he lashed out with his fist, landing an unexpected glancing blow on Jared's chin.

He staggered back under the punch, stunned for a second before pain caused him to squint. Then red-hot fury fired his blood as he stood straight, his body tight as he nearly lost the battle to return the punch.

Andy grabbed his shoulder to keep him from reacting, but before he had a chance to do anything, the deputy had George in handcuffs.

"You okay?" Ryan asked.

Jared could tell his boss was barely holding on to his shit. Working his jaw from side to side, he nodded. "Yeah. It was more of a glance than a direct hit. Fuckin' asshole."

"I'll stay and deal with this," Ryan said. "He just added assaulting an officer to his list of transgressions. The deputies can drop me back at the station. You and Andy head on back."

He hesitated for a few seconds, then nodded, adrenaline still firing through his blood as anger made him almost reckless. He stalked back to their boat and climbed aboard, grateful Andy didn't try to fill the silence. Finally, back out on the water, he let the rush of the wind cool his heated body and sucked in a lungful of crisp air.

Casting his gaze over the vista, he spied the red tent they'd stopped at earlier. Only this time, he watched as a lone figure walked in the distance. Calling out for Andy to stop, he wasn't in the mood to deal with a wayward camper who didn't have enough sense to get off the island before dark.

"You still look pissed, man. You want me to talk to them?" Andy offered as he anchored their vessel just off shore.

Shaking his head, he stepped to the side of the boat

before jumping into the shallow surf and stalking inland. “Thanks, but I’m in the mood to kick some ass, even if it’s just verbal.”

3

By the time he'd made it to the figure walking along, he could see it was a woman in spite of the oversized hoodie and jeans. Her feet were stuffed into rubber boots as she made her way toward the tent.

Her attention was elsewhere, and he was almost upon her before she was aware of his presence. By the time she lifted her head, he was close enough to clearly see the surprise in her ice-blue eyes. Wisps of pale-blonde hair had escaped the hood, waving across her face. For a second, his feet nearly stumbled to a halt as her ethereal beauty struck him. She was a fairy waif wandering along the deserted beach.

Her gaze held his, but she didn't appear alarmed, perhaps due to the uniform he wore that kept her from being frightened of an approaching man. Whatever the reason, he now found himself pissed that she had little regard for her personal safety.

"Ma'am, it's getting too late for you to be out on this island. You'll need to pack up your gear and leave." His clipped words came out much harsher than he normally spoke.

She cocked her head slightly to the side as her blue eyes looked over his shoulder toward his vessel and then back to him. "Excuse me?"

Her voice was soft, almost fragile. He refused to let it wrap around him. Instead, it irritated him more. "I said you need to pack up your gear and leave."

"I have no plans to leave. I'm going to—"

"I don't care what you're doing out here, but wandering around alone with nighttime falling is a pretty stupid thing for a woman to do."

Her head straightened, and her gaze pinned him to where he stood. "Stupid in general for anyone, or particular to my sex?"

He opened his mouth to retort, but she wasn't finished.

"If it's a comment aimed at my sex, and you kick me off this island while saying that you wouldn't if I was a man, that means that I'm afforded less protection in the eyes of the law simply because I'm a woman."

His jaw flexed, reminding him of his earlier hit. Squaring his shoulders, he ignored the sharp pain. "You don't need to question my understanding of the law," he fired back, disregarding the quick inhalation from Andy, who was now standing next to him. "All you need to do is follow my directions."

"Well, without any other indication of why I should do so, I'm not in the mood to acquiesce to your demand."

Still smarting from the confrontation with George,

he sucked in a deep breath and let it out slowly, trying to maintain his usual calm. "Ma'am, can I see your driver's license?"

"May I pull it out of my bag without being afraid that you're going to shoot first and ask questions later?"

The earlier gasp from Andy was now replaced by an attempt to choke back a chuckle. Glancing to the side, Jared speared his friend with a glare before aiming it back toward the obstinate woman. If he'd been less angry, he would have acknowledged that his body was reacting to her beauty and was sure Andy felt the same. But considering all he could see was a smart-ass trying to push a policeman's buttons, he ignored his baser instincts. "Just hand over your driver's license," he growled.

She slung the backpack from her shoulders and bent over to unzip the side pocket. Digging around, she stood with a wallet in her hand. Once opened, she pulled out her license and handed it to him.

He glanced at the picture and then up at her, then back to her name. Blinking, he said, "Wil... Wil-hee-ma?" Even knowing it made him an asshole, he scoffed. "Your parents stuck you with that name?"

If looks could kill, he'd be eviscerated on the sand from the glare she sent his way. Andy whispered a warning, "Man, be cool."

"Will-a-mee-na," she pronounced slowly, then lifted a single brow, offering a searing glare. "Wilhelmina. For your edification, its origin is German, although it is prevalent in Dutch and Yiddish. Its meaning is protection, or if you want to be specific, Wil means desiring, and Hel means protection. Mina is the feminine version of the name. There are many notable women, royalty, and even fictional characters with the name Wilhelmina. But for me, the most important one is the woman I was named after… my maternal great-grandmother. And in case you need to know how to pronounce my last name, it's Schmidt. Is there anything else I can help you with today, *Officer*?"

Andy lost the ability to keep his amusement in as his chuckle bubbled forth, adding to Jared's ire at her attempt to make him feel stupid for making fun of her name. An attempt that was successful, he had to admit. "The only other thing you can do, Ms. Schmidt, is to pack up your things and leave the island."

"Then I'll sleep on my boat if I'm unable to camp here tonight."

His chin jerked back. "Why?"

"Why? Why *what*?" she asked, her hands spread out to the side.

"Why would you put yourself at risk by staying in your boat tonight? That's just not smart."

Her hands landed on her hips as she lifted a brow. "Not smart for just *me*? Not smart for a *woman*? Or not smart for anyone? Once again, I'll bring it to your attention that if you're giving me different information just because I'm a woman, then you're making assumptions that I can't take care of myself or that society demands that women not place themselves at risk when, in truth, men shouldn't prey on women, to begin with. And if you're directing your comments just at me because, for whatever reason, you've decided that *I* don't belong, then as an officer of the law, you're being discretionary at whom you give directions."

Jared felt a nudge from the side as Andy stepped forward, obviously feeling the need to mitigate whatever the fuck was going on between him and this woman who was getting on his last nerve. *Despite the fact that so far, everything she said has been right.*

"Look, Ms. Schmidt," Andy began. "Camping on these islands isn't illegal, but we advise anyone who tries it to be aware of the dangers. Plus, you need to respect the ecosystems in place that are vital to the bay."

Jared's lips curved upward. *Pulling out the ecosystems —good one. Wish I had thought of that!*

"The ecosystem," Wilhelmina said, nodding slowly, tapping her forefinger on her chin as though giving great consideration to Andy's statement.

Jared braced as she once again lifted one brow, adopting the scholarly expression from earlier. He'd only been in her presence for a few minutes but was quickly learning that she was as smart as she was beautiful. *Shit...*

"The ecosystem you're referring to must be the complex food webs in the bay based on the plants, algae, and plankton that not only clean the water but also offer food for the fish, crabs, and mollusks that, in turn, are food for the larger fish, birds, and mammals. This doesn't include the fact that the bay provides fisheries, recreation, and tourism that all must coexist. This creates the natural resources of the country's largest estuary. When you add in the adjoining farmland and developments, the runoff creates a major risk to the precious ecosystem. Much more than a single camper for one night."

A wide, very fake smile graced her beautiful face. "Gee, officers, do you think I have any of that right?"

Jared's chin jerked back in surprise again, and glancing to the side, he could see that Andy's wide-eyed expression mirrored his own. "Just who are you?" he asked, turning to face her fully once again. "What are you doing here?"

"Now, that would've been a smarter question for you to have led with before we got off on the wrong foot, which ended up in your mouth." Reaching into her wallet again, she pulled out another card and handed it to him.

Taking it from her, he felt a tingle as his fingers moved over hers but ignored the feeling. Looking down, he let out a long sigh.

Wilhelmina Schmidt. National Oceanic and Atmospheric Administration employee. She also handed him another identification. Chesapeake Bay Foundation Water Analysis Evaluator. It was her job to be in the area.

A growl rose from deep in his chest. "Why the hell didn't you say this, to begin with?"

She tossed her blonde hair, swiping it behind her ear before pinning him with her hard stare. "First of all, you didn't ask. Second of all, you had already made your own assumptions. Third, I found it much more amusing to spar with you than to give you the satisfaction of giving in to your pompous tirade."

"You're here testing the water in the bay? I didn't

think the foundation's testers usually spent the night," Andy said, having looked over Jared's shoulder at her identification.

"Normally, we wouldn't, except I've been tasked with checking the water levels along a ten-mile area and making comparisons at various times during the day. Very early, as in pre-dawn. Midmorning. Midday. Midafternoon. Dusk. Even at night. And I need to do this for at least a month, possibly longer, depending on the results. In order to accomplish this without losing my mind, I decided it made more sense to camp here." Shifting her gaze back to Jared, she lifted one brow again. "I can sleep in the boat just as easily as in the tent. I certainly wouldn't want to break any laws or, for that matter, any random rules that someone wants to place on me."

He handed back her ID and threw his hands up. "All right, Ms. Schmidt, you've made your point. You have a job to do, and so do we. I'll let the other officers know you'll be spending a couple of nights out here. That way, no one else will bother you. If you have any problems or need assistance, you can call emergency."

Without waiting for Andy or her to say anything else, he turned and walked over the beach toward their boat, trying not to stomp as frustration filled him. Or rather, frustration battled with irritation which battled with fatigue that came from a shitty day at work. *I want nothing more than to go home and crash.* He waded through the surf and climbed back onto their vessel. By the time he made it to the wheelhouse, Andy had hauled himself to the deck as well.

Pulling up the anchor they'd dropped, Andy started the engine and steered them out into the bay. Jared told himself he wasn't going to look back at the infuriating woman yet was unable to keep from turning his head to see her slowly recede into the distance. *Fuckin' hell... she's packing up, which means she'll sleep in her goddamn boat!*

He dropped his chin to his chest, and his anger turned inward as he snorted. Their shift over, Andy headed back to the station, and both were silent for most of the trip.

Wondering when Andy was going to give up the pretense of not questioning, he wasn't surprised when his coworker finally asked, "You want to talk about what went on back there?"

It was on the tip of his tongue to deny that anything had gone on, but he knew he couldn't get away with such an inadequate response. Rolling his shoulders and twisting his neck to relieve some of the tension, he sighed. "You mean why I was an ass back there?"

"Yeah, pretty much."

"I guess the day just kept getting worse, and after George took a cheap shot at me, I was in a pissed-off mood. While I admit to being high-handed with her, it would've been a hell of a lot easier if she'd identified who she worked for when we first approached. It's almost like she wanted us to make the wrong assumptions."

Andy didn't say anything, and he sighed heavily again. "And I suppose you're going to tell me that that was my fault, too."

"Let's just say that you didn't exactly give her time to give you any information. You pretty much jumped down her throat from the minute you walked up. I figured something must be going on because that's not like you. Hell, you're always Mr. Easygoing."

He nodded, not saying anything else, grateful he didn't have to. He hated being seen as unprofessional. *And I lost my professionalism with that one little slip of a woman.* He snorted, thinking of her sharp tongue and quick wit.

By the time they landed at the station, he felt the pull of fatigue settling in. Securing their vessel, he stepped onto the dock. Staring out over the bay as the sun set beyond the horizon, he thought about the woman alone on the island. Or in her boat. Scrubbing his hand over his face, he winced as his fingers grazed over his bruised jaw. As they walked into the station, he decided to go back to the island and check on her tomorrow. *And, maybe, apologize. Yeah... an apology is definitely in order.* Plus, seeing the beautiful Ms. Schmidt again wouldn't be a hardship.

Wilhelmina stomped over to her campsite and began packing her few belongings to take them to the boat, then stopped. Hands on her hips, she glared out over the water and then back to the small tent. *What an ass! What an unmitigated asshole!*

Sucking in deep breaths of fresh air, she struggled to clear her mind. In the service, she'd known men who automatically assumed women, especially someone as diminutive as she, weren't as capable or as smart. *And that's why I like to work by myself!*

Glancing toward her small boat rocking where it was moored in the surf, she knew if she tried to sleep there, she'd probably lay awake all night.

Dammit! She normally didn't have to collect samples numerous times in forty-eight-hour intervals, so camping out somewhere was never an issue. *Only a few more days.* Looking up and down the beach of the small island, she felt her anger at the policeman fade away with the beauty of what greeted her eyes. Sandy beach. Sea grass waving on the dunes. Tall pines in the distance. And quiet. No cars. No people. Nothing but the call of sea birds and the lapping of the barely-there bay waves on the shore.

Fuck it... I'm staying! If he comes back, he can kiss my ass! An image of him kissing something else snuck into her thoughts. *Ugh! Why couldn't he be ugly instead of cute?* As soon as the word cute hit her, she knew it was wrong. "Cute is for little boys and puppies." She spoke aloud, knowing no one could hear her but the gulls. "That jerk was drop-dead gorgeous." Tall, built, and muscular. *Not to mention the tats covering one arm that disappeared beneath his sleeve.*

"Okay, girl, get a grip!" She secured the area, making sure her tent was tucked behind the dunes for protection from the surf and wind. Opening the chest, she doubled-checked her water samples and the early tests she'd completed. Locking the container, she crawled into the small tent but kept the flap open to watch the sun sink into the horizon over the bay while she ate her sandwich and drank from her water bottle.

The sky's ever-changing color palette captured her attention as it had since she was little. The blues changed to oranges and reds before giving over to pinks and yellows streaking across the sky. Her favorite childhood memories included the sunset over the water with her father on his fishing boat. And when the sun finally dropped beyond sight into the horizon, she smiled. She'd traveled to many places, but the Chesapeake Bay always called her home.

Zipping the tent flap, she pulled on her extra clothes expecting the autumn temperatures to drop during the night. Sliding down into her sleeping bag, she closed her eyes, thinking of the duties she needed to attend to tomorrow and everything on her to-do list for the next week. But no matter how many items she placed on her mental list, the blue eyes of the policeman still crept into her restless dreams.

4

Jared let out a long sigh of relief, thrilled it was Friday. The week had been hellacious, but then it wasn't too hard to put up with the shit days when, overall, he loved his career.

His plan to go back to find Wilhelmina the next day after having met her, despite their auspicious verbal sparring, fell by the wayside as soon as he arrived at work. Immediate call-outs had taken precedence, and she was gone by the time he'd made it back to the island. He'd kept his eye out during the week, but the evidence indicated that she'd completed her work and had returned back to wherever she came from. He knew the Chesapeake Bay Foundation had an office in Virginia Beach, but the CBF also had offices all along the bay, including Maryland and Pennsylvania. Plus, she was a NOAA employee, so he had no clue where her home office might have been. *Yep, she's long gone.* As he walked out of the station toward the Seafood Shack for lunch, his feet stumbled as a thought hit him. *She's long gone, yet why the fuck can't I forget about her?*

During the rest of the week, she'd popped into his mind at random moments. When he spotted a small boat in the bay. When he spied a blonde on the shore. When a new report on bay water quality was posted on the board in their workroom. And his nights were now spent with the image of the beauty filling both his thoughts and his dreams.

"You coming?"

Jerking out of his thoughts, he looked up to see Joseph, Callan, Jose, Bryce, and Andy waiting for him to head to lunch. "Yeah, sorry," he mumbled as he jogged to catch up. Entering the restaurant near the station, he grinned as Joseph walked over to greet his beautiful fiancée, Shiloh. Their relationship hadn't been easy for his friend. *Easy.* He coughed to cover his snort. Joseph, like most of the singles he knew, had been used to *easy.* A one-night stand with someone who understood the rules of a one-and-done. Then Shiloh showed up in town, and she was complicated—wonderful and kind but definitely complicated. And Joseph was a changed man.

Jared was pleased for his friend, but so far, he hadn't met anyone who had given him reason to change from his occasional hookups with someone not from Baytown. Someone who wouldn't overstay their welcome if they came home with him. Someone who wouldn't expect him to show up for Sunday dinner after he'd left their place. No morning-after chats. Just sex.

The last hookup ran through his mind. He'd met

Stephanie several months ago at a local brewery when she'd traveled through town for work. They'd ended up at his apartment, and while she'd been fun the couple of times they'd gotten together, he was glad they'd clearly agreed on the terms. But the last time she'd spent the night at his apartment, she'd indicated that she would love to see his new house when he bought it. *As long as she doesn't want to change our easygoing hookups.*

Sliding into his seat, he pushed that thought down. After work, he and the other singles were heading to a bar just north of Baytown, where Stephanie was meeting him. *It'll be fine,* he thought, convincing himself that she wasn't getting clingy. *A night out is just what I need.* A chance to drink, dance, and then come home for a night of horizontal fun only. *It'll give me a chance to knock the infuriating Wilhelmina out of my thoughts!*

"Heard you've got a renter for your garage efficiency," Callan said after they'd placed their food order.

"Yeah, the rental agency found some guy who needs a place. I got a text earlier that he was moving in this weekend. I told the agent that I had plans tonight, so she'll give him the key."

Andy's brows lowered. "You don't know anything about him? Age? Job?"

"I don't have time for that right now. The agent is handling it all so I don't have to. They had him sign a lease that clearly stated what my rules were—no noise, no parties. Hell... basically that I don't want to know they're there."

Joseph laughed and rolled his eyes. "That makes you sound like the worst landlord in the history of rentals!"

His shoulders slumped. "Yeah, well, if I didn't need the money to finish the renovations, I'd rather not have someone rent the space."

"Man, the work you're doing on your place is really good," Andy said, reaching for the appetizer of nachos they were sharing.

Catching the shared look of agreement among his friends, he grinned. "I've been making my own way for a long time, so the help you all have given is really appreciated. I'll get it all done eventually."

Bryce lifted a nacho chip and then waved it toward Jared. "How do you know this guy isn't a serial killer? Or a bomb maker? Or—"

"Jesus, Bryce, how many crime shows do you watch?" He laughed.

"Hell, we're in law enforcement. You know some seriously fucked-up people are out there, and I just don't want to find your body somewhere when you don't show up for work."

Shiloh delivered their food, effectively stopping the conversation. As he ate, he thought of his coworkers' concerns. He was still looking forward to his Friday night with friends and hoped for some recreation afterward. But tomorrow morning, he'd be ready to meet Bill when he moved in. Nothing like laying his eyes on his renter to make sure he didn't get any serial killer or bomb-making vibes from the guy.

By the time the day was over, he showered in the men's locker room and changed clothes. He and the others going out each took their own vehicles to the bar, making it easy to leave when they wanted, especially if post-bar activities were on the horizon.

As soon as they walked through the doors leading inside the bar, music, laughing, conversation, and the clink of glasses met his ears. It was a newer business, one of many on the Eastern Shore, where entrepreneurs were hoping to pull in off-season tourists making their way along the coast. So far, the weeknights were slow, but with a small band playing in the corner, wings on the menu, and Friday night drink specials for the ladies, the owner had discovered a way to pull in a small crowd.

They found a table large enough to hold their group, and he noted the interested glances tossed their way from some of the women already dancing or at the bar. Offering chin lifts to a few of the North Heron deputies that he knew, they soon settled with food and drinks, enjoying the time away from the stresses of work. The band was decent, and it didn't take long for Andy and Bryce to find dance partners. A woman had slid into one of their abandoned chairs and chatted with Jose.

"Damn government types always sticking their noses where they ain't got any business. Got to where a man can't hardly make a living."

Jared casually looked over his shoulder to see who was complaining. He didn't recognize all the men sitting at a nearby table, but spied a few fishermen he'd met before. They continued their collective grumblings, but his attention was snagged in a different direction as Stephanie arrived.

She sashayed along, her hips swinging. Her gaze

moved from side to side, checking out the men around who were obviously staring at her. He wasn't jealous. In fact, if she found someone else she'd rather be with tonight, that was fine by him. But he was struck by how desperate she appeared to be with attention. As she neared, her gaze landed on him, and a predatory gleam appeared in her eyes, making him shift uncomfortably in his chair.

Squeezing the back of his neck, he tried to sort out his random thoughts. Stephanie was pretty, but over time, he'd realized she had little to add to any discussion. Granted, at first, he'd just been looking for fun between the sheets, not conversation. While convenient, he had the uncomfortable inkling that she expected more from their relationship than he'd ever offered. Suddenly, the idea of sharing their night seemed less palatable.

What he really wanted was for the stress of the week to fall away. A pang of disappointment hit as the image of the beautiful Wilhelmina and her cool blue eyes moved through his mind once again. *And she could certainly hold her own in a conversation or debate.* His cock twitched at the thought of the enigmatic woman.

"Jared! I'm here!" Stephanie called out loudly, her arms spread wide. He winced, wishing she'd spend less time needing the spotlight. He stood to greet her as she leaned in for a kiss. "I've been waiting to make it back to the Eastern Shore just to see you!"

They took their seats, and she turned to him, brows lifted. "Well?"

"Um… well, what?"

"Seriously?" she snapped.

"I can't read your mind, Stephanie."

She huffed, sweeping her hand down her body. "Aren't you going to tell me how good I look?"

His gaze followed her hand. Heavy on the makeup and teased-out hair. Dressed in clothes that left little to his, or anyone's, imagination. It was on the tip of his tongue to say that, but considering she was aware of the attention she'd gained as she walked through the bar, he hardly needed to add to her ego. Keeping his smile in place, he simply nodded. "You look nice."

As soon as the words left his mouth, she blasted him with a white-toothed smile, exuding, "I know!"

For the next hour, he tried to enjoy himself with his friends as they found women to join them at the table, sharing platters of wings, pitchers of beer, and laughs. Glancing to the side, he was painfully aware that Stephanie made no attempt to get to know his friends, and from the narrow-eyed glare she sent to a few of the women, he realized she viewed them as competitors. This made the fourth time they'd hooked up when she'd come to the area, and the handwriting was on the wall… it needed to be the last.

"I'm bored," she said, whispering in a loud enough voice to be heard by the others around. Leaning close, she dragged a nail over his chest. "I want to go back to your place. You promised to show me your new home."

He almost declined, but the thought of her making a scene didn't sit well with him. He pushed his chair backward and stood, frustrated with his decision. *Christ, when did I become such a pussy?* With her clutching his arm, he offered a chin lift to his friends and tried to ignore their expressions of sympathy. She followed him to his house, and during the short trip, his mind ran over the list of house projects he wanted to accomplish the next day as soon as she left.

He'd left on his porch light, and as he pulled up to the front and parked, he couldn't help but smile at the soft glow it provided over his house. Stephanie parked next to him and walked over the shell path, her gaze moving over the area. "Oh… it's small. Like *really* small."

Sensing her obvious disappointment, he felt the need to justify and retorted, "Yes, but it's mine." He unlocked the door, bending to corral Daisy, who anxiously awaited his arrival.

"God, please get this dog off me," Stephanie huffed, her hands waving dramatically about.

"She's not on you, Stephanie. She's just sniffing your boots."

"Do you know how much money I paid for these boots, Jared? The last thing I want is dog drool on them."

He walked into the kitchen and poured a glass of wine for her, knowing it would go a long way to appease Stephanie. Just as he suspected, she grinned as soon as she saw the bottle of expensive red that he had bought at one of the little shops in town.

"Oh, honey, just what I wanted!"

"I'll run Daisy out, and you can look at what I've done in the living room."

Stephanie took a healthy gulp of wine, then laughed. "It just looks like all you've accomplished is to move your mess from the sides of the room to the middle. Not exactly what I'd call progress."

He stepped out into the backyard, watching as Daisy ran, did her business, then pranced in the dark, wanting to chase the ball. Jared enjoyed the ball toss with his dog more than the thought of going back in and facing Stephanie. He turned and glanced through the window into the kitchen, seeing her gulping the wine as she looked down and tapped into her phone, probably complaining about the state of his house to one of her friends.

Blowing out a long breath, he wasn't sure why he hadn't canceled their plans for tonight. *Well, that's not exactly true.* He'd hoped the sex would be the stress reliever he needed.

She had expressed excitement when he first said he was buying a house, but he'd mistaken her emotion for someone who cared. She'd once referred to them as friends with benefits, but in truth, they weren't even friends.

The back door opened, and she popped her head out with a pout. "Are you coming?" Then giggling loudly, she said, "At least I hope that's what we're going to do, but I'd rather do it in bed!"

Walking inside, he questioned his sanity. He might be Mr. Easygoing, but the idea of being Mr. Easy didn't set well with him, and she'd already managed to get on his nerves. She plastered herself to his front, so with her arms wrapped around his neck and her breasts pressed against his chest, his cock finally twitched. As she palmed him through his jeans, he responded as any red-blooded male would. Once upstairs in his bedroom, he let his body take over, giving his mind a break. It wasn't phenomenal sex, but they'd both gotten off before she'd rolled over, almost instantly falling asleep.

He lay awake, knowing for sure this would be their last time. Squeezing his eyes shut for a moment, he let the embarrassment and shame wash over him for sleeping with her this time. But he contented himself with the knowledge that they'd always been clear about it being only a physical relationship. Finally, rolling away from her, he eventually found a restless sleep.

Waking up early the following morning, he looked down at the open-mouth, snoring woman sprawled naked on the other side of the bed. Her teased-out hair now looked like two squirrels had battled while trying to build a nest there. The heavy eye makeup resembled raccoon circles around her eyes. Her lipstick was smeared around her mouth, and even the memory of the blow job she'd given him the night before wasn't enough to make up for listening to her complain about the state of his "run-down house" in the light of day.

Rolling onto his back, he sighed heavily as his forearm rested on the pillow over his head. Acknowledging they wouldn't be back for a repeat performance made him breathe easier.

Her phone vibrated, and she suddenly jerked, sitting up with her arms flinging out to the side, one hitting him in the chest. Grunting, he looked over to see her blearily staring around the room.

"What the fuck?" he asked, rubbing his chest.

"Oh God, I set my alarm because I need to get out of

here this morning. I'm meeting some friends for coffee, and then we're going into Virginia Beach to do some shopping."

Thrilled that he wouldn't have to encourage her to leave, he murmured, "That's good. Hope you have a nice day."

She twisted and placed her hand on his chest, her nails dragging along his skin. "I'd much rather stay here and fuck you again."

"Yeah, well, I have things to do, so this is for the best."

She looked as though she wanted to say something, but then her phone vibrated again, and she jumped out of bed. She pulled on her blouse but only buttoned the button between her breasts. She grabbed her bra and panties, shoved them into her purse, and slipped into her miniature skirt. Without looking into the mirror, she wiggled her fingers and said, "Can't wait for a repeat performance. Maybe your house will look better the next time I'm around."

He ignored her as he climbed from bed and pulled on his boxers and jeans, left them undone in haste, then padded barefoot as she walked downstairs and out the front door. She turned and kissed him quickly before she stepped onto the porch and walked to her car. He waved, thrilled that she was leaving, his mind already on the day's projects.

"When can I see you again?" she called out as she stopped near her car.

Though he hated to get into what could be an unpleasant conversation, he knew he needed to be honest. *Hell, I should have been honest last night before we left the bar.* "Stephanie, I think we've run our course."

She blinked, a crinkle forming along her forehead. "Huh?"

"Look, we were just having a good time. That's what we both said. I think to keep seeing each other would be taking us in a direction that's not right for us."

"You're breaking up with me?" she screeched, her eyes flying open wide, now looking like a pissed-off raccoon.

"I'm not breaking up with you because the only thing between us was the occasional hookup."

She threw her purse into the passenger seat of her car, then turned back to shriek, "You've just been using me for sex?"

"I'd say we both got something out of our times together—"

"Oh, don't flatter yourself. It wasn't that great!"

He pinched his lips together, determined not to lose his temper. Nodding slowly, he said, "Then it'll be easy for you to walk away."

She stomped over and poked his chest with a long red fingernail that looked more like a weapon than an accessory. "How dare you use me! I don't care what we said when we first got together. We've seen each other at least four times now. Ask anyone! That makes us more than a hookup!"

And this was exactly why I should have my head examined for ever going back a second time. Christ, I need some coffee. Refusing to argue more, he simply stared at her until she finally turned and stomped back to her car.

She yanked open the driver's door and looked back. "I must have been crazy to think you were worth it. As soon as I saw this shitty house, I should have known you were a loser!" She turned to climb into her car, then stopped and jerked slightly. "Oh, who are you?"

His gaze shot past her to the person standing at the bottom of the stairs, leaning against the garage doors with a cup of coffee in their hands.

"I'm no one. I just rent the apartment above the garage."

His heart jerked in his chest. His mouth fell open. His eyes blinked several times. And he stared dumbfounded at his renter, Bill.

Wilhelmina?

5

Billie woke with the autumn sunlight streaming through the window closest to the bed. While she loved the light, she added buying curtains to her list of things she would need. When the real estate agent met her at the garage the previous day, she could tell the woman was nervous. After all, most people would look askance at the rough garage and wonder what the apartment above would be like. But she knew she could make any space livable. It wouldn't be the first time.

They had climbed the wooden stairs on the side of the garage, coming to a small landing at the top. It wasn't large enough to be considered a deck, but she could set a small chair there to enjoy coffee. Stepping inside, she'd walked to the middle of the room and turned around slowly, her gaze taking in the entire space. A double bed was pushed into a back corner. The mattress appeared clean, but she would need her own linens. A small chest of drawers was next to it, also serving as a nightstand with an older lamp sitting on the top.

In the front was a short counter with a sink, a microwave, and a double-burner electric stove top. A dorm-sized refrigerator was squeezed between the counter and the two-seater table. The other corner held a small settee, a chair, an end table with a lamp, and a bookcase just large enough for a small TV perched on top. She'd walked to the only other door and peered inside to find a minuscule bathroom containing a shower, sink, and toilet. There was no closet, but a metal bar hung under one of the eaves near the bathroom door, and she realized it could serve to hold clothes.

Meeting the real estate agent's anxiety-riddled gaze, she'd nodded. "It's good." She'd almost laughed at the woman's audible sigh of relief and hasty retreat as though Billie would change her mind. She'd spent the next few hours bringing in her meager belongings and making a run out to the grocery and market to purchase a few cooking supplies. She'd splurged on a toaster oven and air fryer combination, figuring she would get full use of the simple kitchen. There was no place to put it, so purchasing a small counter-height movable island would be next on her list.

By the time she'd finished setting up the room, she'd taken a shower, grateful for the hot water, and climbed into bed. Falling into a dreamless sleep, she was glad to be in a bed and not in her sleeping bag.

Rising early with the autumn chill seeping into the room, she'd dressed quickly. Running a brush through her long hair, she pulled it up into a sloppy bun, then donned an extra sweatshirt hoodie. After making a steaming cup of coffee, she'd wandered down the outside stairs to take in the surroundings, knowing there would be a view of a bay inlet through the back-yard once the mist lifted.

What stunned her was the woman stomping toward a car that hadn't been there the previous day. It was her understanding that her landlord was a single male. The woman's eyes were rimmed with smudged mascara, giving the appearance of a raccoon caught with its paw in the birdfeeder. The red lipstick that probably had been sexy the night before was smeared around her mouth. Her hair was tangled wildly about her head, and Billie assumed she was staring at a classic description of sex hair. Before she had a chance to think about what activities the woman may have engaged in to achieve that level of teased-out hair, the screeching began.

"You're breaking up with me?"

"I'm not breaking up with you because the only thing between us was the occasional hookup."

"You've just been using me for sex?"

"I'd say we both got something out of our times together—"

"Oh, don't flatter yourself. It wasn't that great!"

Billie's grin over her sex-hair musings quickly dropped as she pressed her back against the garage door, not wanting to hear their private argument. But walking around the side to go back up the stairs to leave the lovers to their spat would only make her more visible. Staying very still, she watched as the wild-haired woman sputtered and fumed. The man was still in the shadow of the porch, so she couldn't see who had caused such ire.

"Then it'll be easy for you to walk away," he said.

Billie nearly spat out her coffee at that comment, already knowing the raccoon lady wouldn't like that at all. She watched with awe as the woman stomped back to the porch and poked the man in the chest.

"How dare you use me! I don't care what we said when we first got together. We've seen each other at least four times now. Ask anyone! That makes us more than a hookup!"

The man didn't say anything, and Billie wondered if she could sneak away. Seeing her landlord have a lover's blowup in front of her was not how she wanted to start her morning.

"I must have been crazy to think you were worth it. As soon as you bought this shitty house, I should have known you were a loser!"

The woman headed back to her car, and glad that the too-early-in-the-morning argument was almost over, Billie halted her breath when the woman's gaze landed on her. Unable to hide her presence, she sighed.

"Oh, who are you?"

Uncertain of what to say, she sure as hell didn't want to get pulled into the battle. "I'm no one. I just rent the apartment above the garage."

The woman sneered. "Well, enjoy this dump. Whatever you're paying, it's too much!"

The woman started her car and backed out of the drive so quickly that oyster shells flew out from beneath her tires. Billie stared at the retreating vehicle before she looked over to see the man had now walked off the porch, and his open-mouth, wide-eyed gaze was pinned on her. *Well, shit... it's Officer Dick.* And fucking hell, he's even more gorgeous half dressed. His muscular torso was on glorious display, trailing down to where his unfastened jeans hung on his hips. His biceps were not only massive but without a shirt, his mouth-watering sleeve of tattoos was also clearly visible. His hair stood on end as though his fingers had just run over his scalp, although the spitting-mad raccoon lady might have done that, in which case Billie's fingers were jealous. And his now narrowed eyes were the most tantalizing shade of blue.

"You?" he sputtered. "You're Bill? Why the fuck did you put down a fake name?"

All thoughts of his over-the-top gorgeous looks fled her mind in the face of his once again nastiness. Pushing away from the garage door, she held her ground. "Billie. I go by Billie."

"The real estate agent said your name was Bill."

"Well, that's not my fault if she can't read. Check the lease agreement."

"Your name is Wilhelmina."

"Yep… and here's another little lesson for you. Wilhelmina is the female version of William. If I was a male and my name was William, but I told you I went by Bill, would you be out here complaining?"

His mouth opened and closed a few times, and it was all she could do to keep from commenting on his fish-like appearance. *Stay quiet... after all, he's now my fucking landlord.* Biting her tongue, she watched as his gaze dropped to the cup in her hand. Sucking in a breath, she forced a little smile on her lips. "So after the way your day started with your girlfriend—"

"She's not my fucking girlfriend!"

"O...kay. So after the way your day started with your side piece... beneficial friend... fuck-buddy, whatever the hell you want to call her, would you like some coffee?"

"She's nothing. Certainly not to you. You might be renting the efficiency over the garage, but that's it for your involvement. Got it?"

Straightening her spine, she narrowed her eyes as she held his gaze. "Absolutely, *Officer*." Turning, she seethed while forcing her steps to slow and not race as she ascended the stairs and disappeared into her new home. Setting her cup into the sink, she gripped the edge and stared out the window, glad the view was on the opposite side and she couldn't see the house or her infuriating landlord. "Fine, Officer Dick," muttered to herself. "I'll stay out of your way, and you sure as hell will need to stay out of mine!"

She'd initially planned on enjoying her new space today by cleaning, putting everything away, and resting. But after the early morning's bizarre turn of events, she showered, changed, and climbed into her car. Deciding to spend the day exploring Baytown, the beach, and the surrounding areas, she breathed easier as she pulled out of his driveway.

Fury rose in Jared as he stormed back inside his house, only calming when Daisy jumped up on him, quivering in excitement. She sniffed him, caught between wanting to make sure her owner was okay and desperate to go outside. Walking through the house, Jared opened the back door and let his antsy dog run into the yard. He started to step outside as well, then halted, glancing toward the garage. Only one window and the door in the apartment had a view of the backyard, but he hated to be seen by *her* until he had a chance to settle his racing thoughts about the morning's events. *Crazy, unexpected, and fucked-up morning events.*

Swiping his hand over his face, he sighed heavily as Daisy stared up at him with hopeful eyes and a ball in her mouth. "Okay, girl, I'll stop being an ass and play." Stepping outside, he tossed the ball, giving her a chance for morning exercise. And as much as he promised he wouldn't look over, his gaze wandered to the garage. More specifically to the window over the garage.

When Daisy was finally tired, they went back into the kitchen. He flipped on his coffee maker and poured a bowl of cereal after putting the dog food down. At the counter, he shoveled in the cereal, barely tasting anything. Disgusted with Stephanie, himself, and now, Billie, he thought about going back to bed. Snorting, he shook his head. Looking down at his dog, he said, "I really am a fucking ass."

Determined to do something to get the churning thoughts out of his head, he washed out his bowl and spoon before walking upstairs to his bedroom to change into old pants and a T-shirt that had seen better days. *No time like the present to get the living room walls finished.* Needing noise to drown out the thoughts clashing through his brain, he turned on the music, cranked up the sound, and began painting.

By lunchtime, he'd painted a second coat of pale blue-gray on the walls and trimmed the windows in white. He'd chosen a deeper gray for the accent wall behind the built-in bookcases around the fireplace. Stepping back, he found it easier to breathe with what he'd accomplished. But while the music had been enjoyable, it hadn't quieted the voices in his head.

He assumed he wouldn't see Stephanie again, and that was fine. He hated that their parting had turned ugly but recognized that once she began to see them as more than just an occasional hookup, it was always going to end ugly. He just wished he'd realized her intent sooner.

Then his mind whirled to her. *Wilhelmina. Billie.* Dropping his chin to his chest, he sighed. *Bill.* He snorted, shaking his head, still in disbelief that the one woman immune to his charm and who had undoubtedly seen him in the poorest light was now living practically in his backyard.

He wished he could keep her out of his thoughts, but she crept in no matter how many times he tried to push the image of her away. She could not have looked more different compared to Stephanie this morning. No makeup. Straight, silky hair she'd pulled up effortlessly. Blue eyes, clear and bright. Dressed for the weather in a hoodie and jeans tucked into the rubber boots she'd been wearing the other day. Casual. Unaffected.

Beautiful. The kind of beauty a man would give anything to wake up to each morning, just knowing the day would be a little better with her to return to at night. His chest heaved with an invisible weight pressing upon his lungs, and he swallowed deeply. *Jesus, what the fuck is wrong with me? Waxing poetic about a beauty with a smart mouth?* After the disastrous scene with Stephanie this morning, thinking of another woman didn't make any sense.

Rinsing out his brushes and rollers, he cleaned the paint mess and pulled off the furniture covers. Once the walls dry, he'd finally be able to have his furniture appropriately placed in the living room. Glancing up at the ancient light fixture, he put that on his mental list of things to get to.

After fixing a sandwich, he let Daisy back outside and couldn't help but look toward the garage. After Stephanie had stormed off this morning, he'd noticed the small car barely peeking from the other side that he now knew was Billie's. But it was gone, and he battled a grimace, thinking she was off somewhere just to be away from him. *It's her place now, too.*

He dropped his chin and stared at his work boots for a long moment. *I've always been so easygoing, and she did offer me coffee. Okay, I owe her an apology for the rude introduction she got from me as her landlord. I'll apologize, and then that will be all.* But as the afternoon continued into the evening, her car never reappeared. And by the time he went to bed, he wished he knew why that bothered him so much.

6

"Rita, you've seen the readings. There's something there. I have to get closer and figure out where. I just wish David had sent the rest of his reports before he decided to take a vacation!"

Billie was frustrated, having driven across the bay to the CBF office. The foundation had numerous full-time employees but relied heavily on volunteers. A previous water analyzer assigned to take water samples had indicated possible pesticide runoff from a local farm on the Eastern Shore, but then sent a message that he had a family emergency and would have to take an extended leave from his job duties.

Billie had already been assigned to the Eastern Shore in the Accawmacke area, but with the loss of an employee, she'd been reassigned to the North Heron County coastline near Baytown. The change was nice, but it was her reason for looking for cheap lodgings to save on gasoline and wear and tear on her old car.

"I know it's frustrating, but I need you to continue

analyzing," Rita said. "I'll report this to Douglas at NOAA, just to let him know we're staying on top of it." Looking up from the report, Rita held Billie's gaze, then asked, "Did you find a place to live?"

Rolling her eyes, she nodded. "Yes, the cheapest place I could find, which is just an efficiency apartment over an old garage."

Rita's brows scrunched together. "Is it nice enough? Is it safe?"

Billie smiled, tucking a strand of hair behind her ear. Rita had not only been a supervisor but had also become a friend, something Billie didn't have an excess of. Since on loan from the NOAA, Rita had been her supervisor, and Billie felt lucky. The other woman was friendly, a good manager, understood the procedures, and encouraged Billie to get out more. Rita always appeared more polished than Billie, but her boss could get down and dirty with the rest of them when it was time to tromp through marshes and out on hot beaches or boat through mosquito-infested inlets.

"It's fine, Rita. Just a one-room efficiency with a bathroom, but it's clean and safe."

"Yes, but what about your landlord?"

"As it turns out, he lives in the house next to the garage."

Now Rita's brows lifted to her hairline. "He lives right there? What do you know about him? Is he creepy?"

Officer Dobson. Seeing his name on his uniform and deciding that continuing to refer to him as Officer Dick was not appropriate, she shook her head. "Believe it or not, he works as an officer for the Virginia Marine Police."

That pronouncement obviously shocked Rita as she widened her eyes even further and jerked back. "Oh, wow. Well, I guess that makes it as secure as it can be."

Billie leaned back in her chair and felt her back crack. For the past week, she'd risen early, making sure to leave before Jared. It had finally dawned on her to look at her copy of the lease, where she discovered his first name was Jared. But even with that tidbit of knowledge, she had no desire to run into him, even if he did fill her nights with sparks of imagination. Piercing blue eyes. Bulging biceps. And tats that she'd feasted her eyes upon when he'd walked outside without a shirt.

Billie shrugged, struggling to push those thoughts to the side. "Well, since I'm going to be on the Eastern Shore for an extended period, it just makes sense to rent something small and cheap. And believe me, that's really hard to find over there."

Rita nodded and sighed, tapping her pen on the desk. "I'm sure. And for what it's worth, I'm sorry. But you are our best analyzer, and since NOAA has loaned you to us, I know you'll get the job done."

"I'm not trying to be a bitch because I totally get why David had to leave for a family emergency. Hell, I've been there, too. But I just wish he'd sent his preliminary reports. I feel like I'm starting over."

"I know," Rita agreed, tucking a strand of dark brown hair behind her ear and then pushing her reading glasses up on her head. "But I didn't want to say anything to him since I don't know what's going on. I assume he went to Texas, where he's from originally."

Placing her hands on the arms of the chair, Billie pushed herself to a stand. Smiling at her supervisor, she said, "I know I was a mess after… well, I can hardly blame him. Anyway, the Eastern Shore is a nice enough place to spend some time."

"I'd really like it if you could make some friends there," Rita said, standing as well, her gaze warm. "I feel like you spend too much time alone."

Billie laughed and shook her head. "There's nothing wrong with being alone, Rita. Sometimes I think my company is just as good as spending time with people I don't have anything in common with."

"You won't know if you have anything in common with someone if you don't spend any time with them."

Scrunching her nose, she nodded. "I have discovered an American Legion chapter in Baytown. I overheard someone talking about it in the grocery store and went online to check them out. While I hate walking into a room full of people who all seem to know each other and I don't know anyone, I decided I'm going to give them a try."

Rita clapped her hands, then walked over and hugged her. "I'm proud of you, Billie. You're smart, tenacious, and one hell of a person. I've been thrilled to have you as part of my team ever since you joined us."

Returning Rita's hug, she tossed her hand up in a wave as she walked out of the office. Stopping by the desk that she used when she was in the home office area, she shoved several things into her backpack and then made her way down the hall to the lab.

Pushing her way through the swinging door into the equipment room, she grinned as she walked over to one of the men working there. "Hey, Bart! How's it going?"

The tall redhead grinned in return. "Hey, gorgeous! Did you need some equipment?"

She rolled her eyes at his easily tossed-out compliment. "Yes, because I'm going to be working on the far side of the bay for a while and don't wanna keep running back over here. I know the foundation pays the bridge toll, but my old car can't take the wear and tear."

"You still have your junker?"

"Unless you see me getting a big raise, that heap of junk will have to keep working!" She walked over and handed him the list of equipment that she needed.

It didn't take long for him to pull together the testing strips, beakers, colorimeters, DO meters, ORP meters, and whatever else she might need. Filling a box, she waved off his offer of assistance, signed for the equipment, and carried it out to her car.

As she drove over the Chesapeake Bay Bridge-Tunnel, she thought of her findings. With the Eastern Shore being mostly agricultural, there was also a downside. Over-irrigating farmland, over-tilling soil, and over-applying fertilizers and pesticides that cause runoffs are some of the largest sources of pollution going into the bay. Many farmers work to keep this from happening, while others only give lip service to what they do and often cut corners to make their farms more productive at the cost of the waterways.

She had already identified several areas where the nitrate levels were high and wanted to pinpoint exactly where the runoff came from.

By the time she arrived home, she had pinched her lips together when she spied Jared's vehicle parked at the side of his house. Leaving her lab equipment locked in her trunk, she climbed out and started toward the staircase.

His dog caught her attention as it raced toward the fence closest to her, barking, wagging its tail, and doing every doggy trick in the book to get her attention. She felt horrible not acknowledging the dog, but with Jared standing on his back patio, she couldn't figure out how to greet the dog and ignore the owner.

Oh, fuck it! She turned toward the backyard and greeted the excited animal. "Hey, girl." Then without getting any closer, she started toward the staircase.

"Her name is Daisy," Jared called out.

She turned and looked as he faced her while standing on the patio. Navy-blue pants with a matching long-sleeved, navy-blue shirt. She recognized his uniform and remembered their auspicious first meeting. He wore sunglasses, so she had no idea what he might be thinking. Having no desire to enter a conversation that would undoubtedly devolve into the unpleasant banter of their last two encounters, she offered a slight wave and chin lift. Hoping that would suffice for a more friendly greeting, she continued climbing to the top of her stairs and walked through her door, glad to make her escape inside.

But as though her feet moved of their own volition,

she walked to the window closest to his house and peered down through the slit in the curtains that she'd recently bought. She knew he couldn't see her from a distance, yet his gaze remained pinned on the window. Blowing out a long breath, she had to admit she wished they'd met under better circumstances and had gotten off to a less hostility-laden beginning. Flirting wasn't her forte, but she wouldn't be opposed to a friendly conversation. Maybe even talk about the bay, considering he must love the water as much as she did.

She hadn't seen raccoon-eyes since the first night, nor did anyone else spend the night. But it was only a matter of time before a guy as good-looking as Jared brought his dates back to his house. Jerking away from the window, she stomped over to the kitchen and began pulling out something for dinner. She wished she didn't care who he might bring back to the house. A little snort slipped out. "Yeah, right… you do care," she whispered aloud, gripping the counter. *What would it be like to be surrounded by such a gorgeous man?*

She grumbled again, "Fine, he might be unforgettably good-looking, but he's still a rude, obnoxious prick!" In all honesty, she wasn't sure he was, but it certainly made it easier to keep him in the mental box with the lid closed when she thought of him like that.

Billie stood outside the Methodist Church where the American Legion met. She'd sat in her car for several minutes watching as most men and a few women entered a side door. She hated walking into a group of people who all knew each other when she was the lone outsider. Finding small talk to be torturous, she'd always been envious of people who entered social situations easily.

Watching another group of people go through the side door, she sucked in a deep breath and blew it out. *Get a grip, girl.* Throwing open the door, she climbed out and wiped her sweaty palms on her jeans, pleased to see that the others were just as casually dressed.

Moving inside, she walked down the stairs into a large basement community room, where rows of chairs sat facing a stage. The meeting hadn't been called to order, and most people were milling about, talking to others, or over at the coffee and snack table. Having no idea what to do, she decided to grab a cup of coffee.

"Hello!"

She twisted around at the voice next to her and smiled at the dark-haired woman reaching for the creamer. "Hi."

"Are you new here? It's just that I haven't seen you before. I'm Sam. Samantha."

"I'm Billie." Seeing Sam's brow lift, she chuckled. "It's short for Wilhelmina."

Sam threw her head back and laughed with her. "Okay, you win. Everybody thinks I'm a male, but Sam is pretty easy to figure out from Samantha. I love the name Billie, but Wilhelmina is such a beautiful name!"

She grinned, accepting the cup of coffee from Sam. Glancing around, she said, "And, yes, this is my first time here. To be honest, I was pretty self-conscious about coming in."

"Well, it couldn't be worse than my first time! A guy I'd met had made a crack about my name. He saw me walk in and thought I was here by mistake. I'm a veterinarian, and he came over and said that this meeting was for veterans, not veterinarians. I informed him that I was both!"

Eyes wide, Billie laughed. "What is it about these guys around here and our names?"

"What? You, too? Oh, you've got to tell me!"

Realizing she'd said too much in case he had friends in the American Legion, she shook her head. "Oh, it was no one important. Just someone I ran into. But out of curiosity, what happened with the guy who asked you why you were here?"

Sam's eyes twinkled. "Oh, him? He's now my husband!" She pointed toward a good-looking, long-haired, rather stoic man. "That's him over there."

Sucking in a hasty breath, she turned back to Sam, feeling the heat on her cheeks. "Oh, I hope I haven't insulted you."

Waving her hand, Sam shook her head. "Not at all. You'll get used to everyone the longer you're here. Oh, there's someone else you should meet." She waved toward another woman who immediately walked over. "Ginny, I'd like you to meet a newcomer. This is Billie. This is Ginny, one of the police officers for Baytown."

Standing with Ginny and Sam, Billie breathed easier, no longer feeling so self-conscious since she had found two fellow female veterans to chat with. Looking around as a few people started moving toward their seats, she said, "This is a lot more people than I imagined."

"Mitch Evans, Baytown's police chief, grew up here, and when he returned after his FBI career, he started the Baytown chapter of the American Legion. Through his leadership and the subsequent presidents, it has really grown. We're involved in so many activities and community service projects. I really hope you'll come back," Ginny said.

"I will, thank you."

Sam smiled. "Everyone is friendly around here."

Billie grinned but scoffed. "Well, then I must have met the one unfriendly person out here."

"That sounds like another story!"

"Just my landlord," she said, scrunching her nose. "I'm afraid friendly is *not* a word that describes him!"

"Oh, hey, Jared!" Ginny greeted, glancing over Billie's shoulder.

Her stomach dropped, and her cheeks warmed as she held her breath for a second, then glanced over her shoulder to see Jared standing nearby. Now in jeans with a flannel shirt stretched across his chest and arms, she had to admit he was just as attractive casually dressed. But as her gaze moved to his expression, her breath stuck in her lungs. With his lips pressed together in a tight line, he lifted his coffee cup in a silent salute before turning and walking to one of the seats. Closing her eyes, she sighed heavily.

"Why do I get the feeling there's another story there?" Sam said, her eyes sparkling even more.

"You don't want to know."

Ginny and Sam laughed, both nodding. "Oh, yes, we do. We'll exchange phone numbers, and let's get together soon!"

Before she had a chance to think of an excuse, the meeting was called to order. She slipped into a seat near the exit, keeping her eyes on the back of Jared's head. He sat several rows in front of her. She enjoyed the meeting and was stunned at the number of activities offered to the members. Glad that she came and happy she'd met Ginny and Sam, she hated that she'd mentioned her landlord. *And this is why I suck at small talk!*

With that in mind, she made sure to slip out as soon as the meeting ended, not wanting to take a chance she'd run into him after her blunder. She drove straight home and raced up to her apartment before he arrived.

Peeking through the slit in the curtains, she watched as he parked out front and walked into the house. As was his habit, he popped out the back door with his dog a moment later. And it also didn't miss her attention that he stared up at her window while he was outside.

7

Jared spent the morning on the water, first patrolling and then an hour helping to settle a dispute between an established oyster farmer and one of his employees that had started his own business. He didn't realize he was zoning out until Joseph finally called his name loudly.

Jerking, he looked over to see Joseph and Andy grinning at him. "What?"

Joseph was bent over, coiling the ropes on the deck. He straightened up and grinned. "Man, I've been talking to you for five minutes, and you haven't heard a word I've said."

Grimacing, he mumbled an apology.

"I would ask if it was a woman, but you're always so cool and laid back. I can't imagine it's woman trouble, especially since you got rid of Stephanie. By the way, I could have told you that she'd be trouble the first time you hooked up with her. She's the kind who goes along with fun but expects more." Andy steered the vessel expertly but managed to pin him with a curious stare.

"You got something on your mind? 'Cause you've been out of it all morning."

He hesitated, warring with the same frustration and irritation that he'd carried around all week. "It's my new tenant."

Andy's eyes shot open wide. "Shit, what's the fucker doing?"

"Listen, if you need to evict him already, let us know. We'll go over and back you up," Joseph offered.

A snort erupted. "Uh… no. That won't be necessary." Bending, he worked on the deck rope that Joseph had abandoned, wishing he'd kept his mouth shut. The silence from the other two let him know they were waiting. Glancing up at their lifted-brow expressions confirmed his suspicions. Standing, he planted his hands on his hips and looked out over the water. "You know the woman we found camping a couple of weeks ago? The one from NOAA and the Chesapeake Bay Foundation."

"Yeah," Andy confirmed. He turned to Joseph and said, "It was the day Jared took a punch from old man Toomey and was in a fightin' mood. We ran across someone from the CBF, but Jared didn't give her a chance to explain." Barely holding on to a laugh, he added, "And she gave as good as she got. In fact, I'd have to say she handed him his ass!"

Joseph threw his head back and laughed, much to Jared's chagrin. Glaring at Andy, he said, "Well, it gets worse."

"This I gotta hear," Andy said, slowing the vessel to give Jared his attention.

"Christ, the whole thing is a fuckin' disaster." Shaking his head as a hefty sigh blasted from his lungs, he said, "I agree that I was pissed at ol' George taking a sucker punch at me, then this woman was being evasive—"

Seeing Andy's glare, he amended, "Okay, I felt like she was being evasive. Then her name was something I couldn't pronounce, and she began a dissertation on the origins of her name. Wilhelmina. Hell, I'd never met a Wilhelmina before! Then when we finally got out of her what she was doing and who she worked for, she then gave another mini rant on why her job was important to the bay. I mean, Jesus, all I needed to know was who she was and what she was doing."

"Well, she did tell you—"

"Eventually!" he growled. "I actually went out the next day to apologize, but she was gone." Then with another sigh, he said, "The night we went out, I was already sure that Stephanie and I were at the end of our… our… oh, hell, I don't know… our fuck buddy status since she was expecting more than we'd agreed on. But I took her back to my place for a last night together. She wanted to see the house, but that was a fucking disaster. She was not impressed with my fixer-upper, and I made sure she understood we were at the end of our hookups. She blew up at me in my driveway the next morning. Half dressed, looking like a hooker, screaming at me… and in front of my new renter."

"Holy shit," Joseph and Andy groaned at the same time.

"And…"

"Christ, there's more?" Andy asked, unable to hide his incredulity.

"Oh, yeah. It turns out that my new renter isn't Bill. It's Billie. That's Billie with an *i-e* at the end. Short for Wilhelmina."

There were a few seconds of silence when only the boat engine could be heard. Then Andy and Joseph erupted in howls of laughter. Jared grimaced and shook his head. "Glad you're amused at my situation!"

"Come on, Jared, you have to admit this shit is priceless! You're always the easygoing one. Mr. Laid-Back-Nothing-Bothers-Me. For you to get sucker punched, which by the way, sucks ass and should never have happened, but then to roll into meeting the one woman who isn't impressed with your charm, and then to have the same woman see Stephanie in all her glory pitching a fit… damn, bro. And she's your fuckin' renter! Living practically in your backyard! You need to stay away from gambling 'cause with your bad luck, you'd lose your shirt right now!"

Jared dropped his chin to his chest and stared at his boots for a moment. As much as he hated to admit it, Andy was right… his luck sucked. And he wasn't finished with his story.

"Come on," Joseph prodded. "I know your expressions… there's more."

When he lifted his head, a rueful chuckle erupted. "Yeah. Well, I didn't handle the surprise very well, and my mouth continued to get me in trouble as I accused her of lying on her application. Now, after she avoided me for a week— always getting home before me or late afterward so that I never see her, she turns up at the AL meeting last night. She was talking to Sam and Ginny. Guess she's a veteran, and when I walked up to take the opportunity to finally apologize, she was telling them that her landlord was the most unfriendly person she'd met in Baytown."

At that pronouncement, he expected the other two to continue their amusement at his expense, but they both stood still, their expressions sympathetic.

"That sucks," Andy finally said, shaking his head. "She just hasn't seen the best of you."

"Hell, all she's seen is the worst of me. But then, she hasn't been Ms. Congeniality herself," he groused. Even as those last words left his mouth, he knew they sounded pitiful.

"What are you going to do about her?" Joseph asked.

Shrugging, he said, "She's just here for a couple of months. We've avoided each other this long. I figure we can just keep avoiding each other. Before I know it, she'll be gone. But I sure as hell won't rent the apartment again without vetting the person myself. No more surprises!"

Their conversation was halted with another call out. Andy revved the engine and steered them out into the bay as Jared put Billie out of his mind– or tried to.

Billie sat at the back of her boat with her hand on the single-tiller engine. She'd clipped the safety lanyard to herself, then pulled on the cord to start the engine. Glad it started on the second pull, she sat down and guided her small boat out of the marina's dock. The marina was on the north side of Baytown, opposite the town harbor where the marine police station was located. She'd continued to do whatever it took to avoid seeing Jared again.

She stayed close to the shore as she motored north for about five miles, then turned in toward one of the inlets. Passing a few residential docks, she quickly came to the farmland along the waterway. She observed where some trees and plants lined one side of the water's edge, a good way for natural buffers to slow the runoff of potential pollutants. But the other side and farther down showed signs of erosion leading to the visible crops.

Slowing her boat, she cut the engine and opened the case containing the water analysis kits. It didn't take long to gather the samples, take pictures, and make notes about each sample location.

"What are you doing?"

The barking male voice from the bank caused her to twist around. A man was standing near the water's edge. He was dressed in jeans, heavy work boots, and a plaid shirt with a brown jacket and a ball cap pulled low over his head. All she could determine was that he had a stocky build. And with his arms crossed over his chest, he didn't seem happy to see her.

"I'm taking water samples for the CBF… the Chesapeake Bay Foundation."

"Why?"

"To determine the health of the bay." She watched as

he lifted the cap from his head and wiped his brow, giving her the first look at his face. Younger than she'd thought, she still didn't miss his scowl. Knowing the reaction of some farmers who viewed anyone near their land with suspicion, she added, "I'm not regulating anything. I just take samples to see if the water has the right nutrients for marine life."

"Seen your kind before," he countered. "Then someone around here goes snooping and throws out a warning that the farmer could be fined. Makes me suspicious of anyone coming around."

"I understand, but it's not my job to send those notices or try to regulate what you do. Like I said, I'm just here to check the water."

"Humph," he grumbled, then turned and walked away.

He stopped at an old, rusty truck parked in the field and talked to an older, similarly dressed man leaning against the door, a rifle prominently displayed in his hands. After a moment, they climbed inside, and the vehicle roared to life and rumbled away.

She blew out a long breath and then leaned over the side to dip more water into the sample jar.

"Must get irritatin' to be greeted that way, huh?"

Jerking her head around to look behind her, she observed another man dressed in a heavy denim jacket and worn jeans tucked into work boots. Tall with a wide smile, he appeared more at ease than the other two men. Returning his smile with one of her own, she nodded. "Comes with the territory."

"I'm Tim Belvedere."

She inclined her head to the side. "This your land?"

"Nah. I'm just the farm manager here for the Harpers. That was JC Harper that you just met. His daddy owns the farm. Been around a long time."

Nodding, she offered a slight smile. She preferred to work alone, once again hating small talk. Leaning over the edge again, she continued to collect water samples, glad when he took the hint.

"Well, nice to meet you," he called out.

She waited a moment to give him a chance to leave, then looked up, breathing a sigh of relief. She knew some farmers were proud of their nutrient management, and others became angry when they saw someone testing near their farms. Glad to be alone again, she used the various testing meters and made sure to keep track of all her results.

Chewing the piece of gum she'd gnawed on for the past hour, she sighed at her findings. The levels of herbicides were too high, and at this level, the aquatic life in the inlet would soon start dying. And it would only be a matter of time before it reached the short distance to the bay. Packing her samples and testing equipment back into the case, she secured it before cranking the boat motor again and maneuvered farther along the inlet to her next testing site. A sensation hit the back of her neck, and she twisted slightly to look over her shoulder. There, in the trees, was JC Harper, his gaze pinned on her. Blowing out a long breath, she looked forward, determined to push his angry glare to the side. Wondering if his dad had given instructions to have her watched, she kept testing. *I have a job to do, buddy, so suck it up!*

By the time she got home, Jared's SUV was parked in front of his house, along with two other vehicles. She pulled to the far side of the garage and dragged her case from the back seat. As she climbed the stairs, the call of a hot shower, writing up her report with a glass of wine, and then crawling into bed while knowing she could sleep late the next morning put a smile on her face.

As soon as she stepped into her apartment, the sounds of hammering, sawing, and drilling filled the air. Walking to the window, she looked over, curious about Jared's house. With all the work he seemed to do on his days off, she wondered if it was an entire gut job. *Not for the first time, she wished they'd gotten off to a better start so she could see the inside.* It reminded her of… *nope, not going there.*

After a shower and a hastily prepared dinner, she refilled her glass of wine and headed to her sofa when the sound of laughter reached her ears. Looking down from the window again, she carefully pulled the curtain back just enough to peek outside. Jared stood in his yard with three other men, all smiling. He wore jeans and a T-shirt in spite of the cool air. Her gaze snagged on his thick arms and tattoos again. In the waning sunlight, a glow filtered through the trees, landing on him. Her breath caught in her throat as she looked at the easy smile on his face and the obvious camaraderie he had with the others. A little sigh escaped from her lips at the sight. *He's not an asshole to everyone… great… it's probably just me.*

Suddenly, his face turned up toward the window, and a little smile crossed his lips. She jumped back, dropping the curtain, hoping he hadn't seen her peering down. Grimacing, she aimed a narrow-eyed glare at the now-covered window even though he could no longer see her.

Stomping over to her sofa, she fought the desire to unceremoniously fall heavily onto the cushions as the need to not waste a drop of her wine won the battle. Clicking on her TV, she settled on the familiar home renovation show and couldn't concentrate on anything other than her infuriating landlord.

8

Jared glanced through the open back door as Daisy amused herself by sunning on the patio while he worked inside the house. The day was so mild in temperature, and with her in sight, he didn't mind the door staying open for a little while. Yesterday after work, several friends came over, and they'd managed to get the new kitchen island that he'd bought in place. After he'd torn down the wall between the kitchen and small dining room, the new island provided storage and counter space while still making the area seem so much larger. Now, he was ready for a couple of smaller projects he could handle alone.

He'd dragged the stepladder from the garage earlier, uncertain if the noise disturbed Billie. But since she hadn't made an appearance, he figured she was either asleep or possibly still ignoring him. That thought stuck with him, causing a grimace to move over his face as he set up the ladder in the dining room. He'd never met a woman who affected him like she did. He didn't think he was God's gift to women, but he'd never had a problem getting a date or having fun conversations with his friends' women. Sighing heavily, he had to admit he'd never taken the opportunity to apologize to her after their initial meeting.

A woof drew his attention back to his task at hand. "You want me to get to work, girl?" Daisy walked into the kitchen, drank from her water dish, and then padded back into the sunshine to lie down.

After positioning the ladder under the light in the dining room, he glanced back at Daisy, easily seeing her with the kitchen door open. He also noticed that he could see the garage apartment window from where he was. *Hell, does everything make me think about my tenant?*

Climbing up, he was determined to keep his mind on the task at hand, which was changing the light fixture. The one in place when he'd bought the house was an old rectangle fluorescent light, matching the one in the kitchen. They were ugly as hell and gave off glaring illumination. He'd already had an electrician install recessed lighting in the kitchen, but now he was ready to replace the one over the space where he'd have a dining table. *Once I purchase a dining table, that is.*

He managed to get one side of the light unfastened with little problem, but as with most household projects that always seemed to take more effort than it looked like it should, the other end was stuck. Refusing to climb back down the ladder, he was sure that if he leaned over just enough to reach the caught end, he could pull it the rest of the way down.

Stretching out his arm, he grasped the metal that

had been painted over at one time. Pulling with force, he found the edge was firmly stuck. Finally jerking as hard as he could, the metal gave way, but he realized too late that the ladder was tipping. The light fixture dropped to the floor with a clatter, and he barely had time to throw his hand out before he landed on his shoulder with his head smacking against the wood floor.

"Shit," he moaned as a blinding pain shot through his head as well as his shoulder. Daisy raced inside, incessantly barking as she ran circles around him lying on the floor. Her barks echoed in his head as he tried to push himself upward, immediately falling back down. Drops of blood appeared on the floor. He lifted his hand and swiped at his face, cursing again as his fingers came away covered in red.

"Daisy, shhhh," he whispered, trying to push up again.

"Hang on! Stay still."

The female voice cut through the barking and the pain in his head. He tried to push upward again, now feeling hands on his arms.

"Oh shit, you're bleeding."

Woozy, he blinked at the sight of two women in front of him, mirror images of each other. "Billie?"

"Yeah, I have you."

He felt hands move over his torso. "Why're there two of you?" he slurred, wondering why two white-blonde Billies kept swimming across his vision.

"Jesus, sit still."

Her voice was farther away, but he couldn't see

where she went with Daisy pushing her way onto his legs as he lay on the floor.

"Move, Daisy," she ordered, reappearing.

A cloth was held against his head, and he winced. "How did you know I fell?"

"I could see you from the top of my stairs."

Her reply made sense, but amid the pain, the fact that she must have been watching him to get over to his place so quickly made him smile.

"What the hell are you smiling about?" she asked with suspicion.

With one eye covered by the cloth pressed to his forehead, he could ascertain there was only one of her now. "You. You make me smile," he admitted, throwing a wobbly smile her way.

"You look like a drunken sailor with a sloppy grin." She pulled the towel away and shook her head. "Jared, this isn't too bad, but I think you need stitches. Plus, you may have a concussion. Do you hurt anywhere else?"

"My shoulder. I landed on it."

"I need to get you to the hospital."

"No. I don't want to go to the hospital. It's just a stupid cut—"

"Well, we don't always get what we want, do we?" she snapped. "Come on. Let's get you up. I'm taking you to the hospital."

He wanted to protest, but with her hands on him, the words couldn't seem to form in his head, much less come out of his mouth. She gently pulled him upward, but his legs felt like Jell-O, and he slumped onto her. Hearing an "oomph," he managed a mumbled, "Sorry," as her body wavered underneath his weight.

Barely aware of what she was doing, they somehow managed to get out to her car, where she unceremoniously poured him into the passenger seat. He tried to wipe the blood away from his forehead, but the towel was turning red, so he kept the pressure applied. She was gone for a moment, then he felt the car wobble slightly as she climbed behind the wheel.

"I put Daisy inside and closed your door. I grabbed your phone, keys, and wallet from the kitchen counter."

He was still processing what she said about Daisy when a soft touch landed on his arm, and he rolled his head to the side to see a worried crease marring her forehead. He gave voice to the first thing that popped into his mind. "You're so pretty."

An indelicate snort erupted as she turned away to start her car. "Okay, Romeo, just concentrate on your face for now."

Her melodious voice made him smile. "I like listening to you."

"Well, that's a first for us," she replied.

"Oh." He hadn't realized he'd spoken aloud. She was soon on the highway, and he closed his eyes, knowing it would take almost forty minutes to make the drive.

"I don't think you're supposed to sleep if you have a concussion," she said. "Talk to me."

"Huh?"

"Talk to me. Jeez, I've seen you talk to others, so I know you can do it. Just pretend that you don't hate me and talk."

"I don't hate you," he muttered. "I wanted to apo… apolo… I wanted to say I was sorry."

She glanced toward him, and he tried to smile again, thinking it might make her more amenable to his words.

"Apologize?" she asked before turning her focus back to the road.

Feeling the loss of her attention, he kept going. "Yeah, I was an ass. I'm never an ass. Well, unless I have to be. You know, like if I was in a need-to-be-an-ass sort of situation." She snorted, but he pushed through. "No, really. I'm not an ass. Well, I was with you. Twice. But I didn't mean to be."

She remained quiet, and he continued. "But you were kind of assy, too."

"Oh really? Please tell me how I was *assy*?" She made a sound close to a chuckle, so he was encouraged.

"You were all snobby about your name and then about the bay. I don't know. I was assy. You were assy. We were both assy."

"Christ, how hard did you hit your head?" she bit out, shaking her head.

"Hard…" he breathed, closing his eyes. He'd apologized and now just wanted to rest. He had no idea how much time had passed, but it felt like he'd barely closed his eyes when she shook his knee gently.

"We're here, Jared. You need to wake up."

She pulled into an ER parking space, where someone pushing a wheelchair met them. She shoved his wallet into his hand before he was whisked away while she drove off. He sighed heavily, hating that she was leaving him. *She's probably got better things to do than hang out with me.*

"No, man, she's just parking her car in a regular lot," the aide said as they wheeled him into the ER. "Don't worry. Your girlfriend will be able to come back and sit with you once they know what's going on."

Realizing he'd spoken aloud, he was immediately rolled to the reception desk. Hearing coughing and hacking, he glanced toward the waiting room, hating for Billie to come into the germ-infested area. He looked behind him, hoping to see her, but she was still outside when hospital personnel took him back to a triage room, where a doctor examined his cut while he explained the accident.

"The laceration is deep but not long. A couple of stitches will take care of it. We'll just numb it quickly before we proceed. And I see on the intake information that you also landed on your arm?"

The numbing injection was already taking effect, the ease from pain making it easier to think. "My shoulder. It's okay, though. My head hitting the floor is what did me in."

"Okay, well, I'm ordering a cranial MRI as well as an x-ray of your shoulder."

He endured the quick sutures, feeling stupid for all the fuss when the cut was small. His gaze wandered to the door of the ER bay, wondering if Billie was coming back or if she was stuck in the waiting room. As much as part of him wanted to see her to thank her for coming to his aid, humiliation raced across his face.

Christ, I fell off a fuckin' ladder. And then I accused her of being assy when I was supposed to apologize.

Before he could process the embarrassment, another aide came to roll him to the imaging department for his radiographs and MRI. Just before the swinging doors closed behind them, he thought he caught an image of Billie at the end of the hall, staring after him. Her pale hair was pulled away from her face, showing off her slightly turned-out ears. With her unearthly light-blue eyes pinned on him, she gave off a beautiful elvish look. *I never noticed that before.* Sighing, he closed his eyes. *No way she'll wait. Hell, what does it matter? I'll find her at home and thank her. And offer another apology. Then she'll probably go back to ignoring me again. Yeah… that'd be best.*

Yet the thought of her ignoring him made him feel worse.

Billie stood at the end of the hall watching as Jared rolled through the swinging door that led to somewhere in the hospital. Filled with uncertainty, she wondered what she should do.

"Hey, you came in with Mr. Dobson, right?"

Turning, she recognized the man who'd met them at the ER door to wheel Jared inside while she parked her car. "Um… yes. But they took him somewhere, and I wasn't sure where to go."

"He's gone to imaging. I realized I hadn't put his bag of personal items on the gurney with him. Here, I'll give them to you." He thrust them into her arms. "It might take an hour or so before he'll be back. You can wait in the waiting room. They'll bring him back here when he's done, and someone will call you to come back."

"Well… I'm not sure he'd want me to hold on to these."

"A pretty girlfriend like you? Believe me, he'll want to see you just as soon as he gets out."

"Oh, I'm not his—"

A hospital cell phone beeped, and the aide grabbed it and answered. He offered a chin lift to her, then headed down the hall, leaving Billie little choice but to head into the ER waiting room, the plastic bag in her hands. Peeking inside, she spied his wallet, phone, keys, and shirt. She had no intention of leaving unless he had someone else to call, but since she had his phone and he was off getting examined, she figured the odds of that were slim.

Someone coughed next to her, and she looked to the side, seeing an elderly couple. The woman was obviously ill, and her husband held her hand. Leaning forward, she asked, "Would you like me to get some water for you?"

"Oh, thank you, my dear," the woman said between coughs, "but our daughter is getting some tea in the cafeteria for me."

Nodding, she leaned back in the hard plastic chair and blew out a long sigh, holding Jared's items in her lap. *I'm probably the last person he'd want to have his personal belongings.* Glancing at the clock, she closed her eyes. She hadn't made any plans for the day, but being stuck in a hospital waiting room for someone who'd made it clear she wasn't their favorite person wasn't ranked high on her Saturday list of things to do.

A flash of the morning's memory hit her. She'd just stepped out onto her outside landing with a cup of coffee when she'd spied Daisy lying on the patio in the sun and realized Jared's back door was open. She'd had a perfect line of sight into his kitchen, where he was setting up a stepladder. Curious, she'd watched for a moment and had just looked away when the sound of a crash met her ears. Daisy had begun barking, racing wildly in and out of the house. Jared was lying still on the floor.

She'd almost tripped in her haste to run down the steps outside the garage, then vaulted over the back fence, now grateful she hadn't face-planted in the process. Daisy's excited jumping had nearly knocked her down, but she'd rushed past the dog and into the kitchen, where Jared was attempting to push up, blood dripping down his face and onto the floor.

Now faced with nothing but time in an empty ER waiting room with the sounds of hacking, coughing, and sniffling all around her, she wondered if she had done the right thing. *Maybe I should have called for an ambulance instead of driving him here myself.* Dropping her head forward, she stared at the plastic bag sitting on her lap. *He might really hate me now.* And for some reason, that thought made her feel worse.

9

Billie was startled as the curtain to the ER bay suddenly jerked to the side. The young man who she'd talked to earlier had come to retrieve her from the waiting room, placing her in the bay he said Jared would be returning to.

Her spine snapped straight in her chair, and her gaze darted to where an aide rolled Jared into the small room. The cut on his forehead held two stitches, but as his gaze landed on her, he appeared much more clear-eyed than he had earlier. She even imagined there was a whisper of relief on his face.

"What are you doing here?" he asked.

Scoffing, she shook her head. *I guess that wasn't relief on his face.* The last thing she wanted to do was upset someone who'd already had an upsetting morning. Standing, she plastered the most pleasant look on her face. "They called me in from the waiting room. I just wanted to make sure you were okay. They gave me the bag of your personal effects, and I wanted to hand them to you. Do you have someone you'd like me to call? Someone you'd like to come for you?"

"Oh, uh… no." He licked his lips while furrowing his brow, then winced as he lifted a hand to barely touch his forehead. "I guess you have to go, don't you?"

At his bewildered expression, she jerked slightly, pressing her lips together. "No… I don't have anywhere to be. I was going to stay, but only if I can help." He hadn't reached out for his bag. "Your phone is in here if you need it… or someone… or, um… whatever. But I'm here. I can stay. I'll take you home unless you want to make other arrangements." She knew she was babbling but seemed unable to stop.

"If you really don't mind, I'd be grateful if you'd take me home."

Her shoulders hefted in a shrug. "Well, we are going to the same place."

He smiled, his lips curving, and for the first time, his blue eyes seemed to sparkle instead of crackle with irritation. "Yeah, we are." He looked down at the hospital gown he was wearing. "I guess I should be glad I have my pants on. They cut off my shirt to x-ray my shoulder."

"That shirt was pretty bloody."

He chuckled. "And that was my favorite shirt." At her lifted brow, he added, "One of my first Coast Guard T-shirts. Old, worn, washed a million times, and comfortable."

Uncertain what to say at their first true, congenial conversation, she was saved when the curtains ripped back, and the aide who'd given her Jared's bag of items walked in.

"Oh, I see you got back to your pretty girlfriend," the aide said with a wide smile. "The doctor will be right in, and we'll get you discharged." He turned to Billie and winked.

Before she could explain she was only the neighbor, the doctor walked into the room. He immediately began going over the results of the imaging. Billie wanted to excuse herself, but the space was too tight. She was unable to get around the aide to make it out the door.

As she tried to press by, the aide stayed in her way and said, "You're fine where you are. The doctor will also review some aftercare instructions with you."

"Oh, but I'm not—"

"Because of the concussion, you'll need to check on him throughout the rest of today and tonight. You don't have to wake him every two hours but definitely check on him. We'll give you an aftercare packet to review."

With the doctor and the aide both staring at her, she did the only thing she could think of and nodded. Keeping her eyes on them, she refused to look down at Jared. The heat rolling off her cheeks let her know her face was flaming. *It's fine. I can just get him home, and he can call a friend to come stay with him. There's no need to make a big deal about this now.* "Yes, that's fine. He'll have someone with him to keep an eye on things."

Once he was discharged, they wheeled them out after she'd hustled to get her car from the parking lot, and they were finally driving away from the hospital. His shoulder wasn't seriously injured, just bruised, but he held himself stiffly. Glancing to the side, she tried to think of something to say. "You were lucky." As soon as those words left her mouth, she winced. "Well, not lucky to have fallen off a ladder, but lucky you weren't hurt any worse."

He turned his head toward her. "Believe me, I know it."

She felt his gaze on the side of her face but kept her focus on the driving. Wishing he'd close his eyes and sleep, she was surprised when he appeared intent on keeping their conversation going.

"How did you get to me so quickly?" he asked.

"Um… when?"

"When I fell. I don't think I lost consciousness, but it seemed as though you were there really fast."

Crinkling her brow, she glanced to the side to see his expression wasn't smirking but instead held only curiosity. "I was out on the landing having my coffee. You had your back door open, and I could see a ladder in the kitchen. Then suddenly Daisy was barking. Not like her usual I'm-having-fun bark, but more of a my-owner-just-fell-off-a-ladder bark."

Laughter erupted, followed by a wince, and he lifted his hand to his forehead. "Ow. Damn, even laughing hurts."

"Then I guess it's good we don't usually laugh."

"Yeah…"

She once again felt his gaze on her while she stared out the windshield.

"Maybe we should laugh more often," he added.

At that statement, her head jerked around, searching his expression. "What do you mean?"

"It just seems a shame that we're neighbors yet don't talk and certainly don't laugh."

"And whose fault is that?" she snapped, then tightened her lips into a thin line of frustration. "Sorry. That was rude." Sighing heavily, she shook her head slowly. "I'm never this rude to people. I don't know what it is about you."

This time, a snort erupted from the passenger seat, and she shook her head again. "Damn, there I go again, saying something rude. Let me just say I'm very sorry, and I'll keep my mouth shut."

"No, don't do that. I like it when you talk."

They drove for several more minutes in complete silence. She wondered if he dozed off when he spoke again.

"If anyone owes someone an apology, it's me. I wanted to apologize for being obnoxious during our first meeting. I intended to go back to the island the next day but got called out early. By the time I made it there, you were already gone. Then I realized I needed to apologize again after I was an ass when you first moved in. But then we fell into avoiding each other, and I let it slide by. I have no idea why, Billie. That's not like me."

"What's not like you?" she asked, unable to hide her curiosity.

"All of it. Most people consider me to be very friendly, yet with you, I wasn't. And I was taught to apologize. I was wrong, yet I didn't apologize immediately. And I never want to put things off, yet with you again, I let the avoidance just keep happening."

A long sigh escaped his lips, and she could still feel his gaze boring into the side of her head, only this time, it didn't feel unnerving.

"You're not the only one who should apologize. I clung to my righteous indignation for longer than I should have."

"Well, there's a reason they call it righteous indignation," he replied. "Because you were *right*."

A smile slipped across her face. "Well, you were hardly the first person to have difficulty with my name. When I was a kid, I hated the name Wilhelmina because I was always made fun of. Now, I don't mind it because of the familial connection."

"You should never have to put up with someone making fun of you. And me? I'm really ashamed of myself. The only excuse I have is that I got sucker punched that morning. I was in a pissed-off mood and took it out on you. That was just fuckin' wrong."

"Sucker punched?" She glanced sharply toward him again, this time seeing a tinge of blush turn the tips of his ears red.

"Yeah, sucker punched by an old man."

"What the hell happened?" She turned onto his driveway, and he didn't have a chance to answer before she pulled up and parked next to his SUV. Hearing Daisy bark, she got out and hurried around, but Jared was already out of her car.

"I'll run Daisy out for you," she offered. He seemed steady on his feet, so she followed along as they moved to his front door. Afraid that the excited dog would jump all over its owner, she gently took the keys from his hand and unlocked the front door. Sliding in first, she bent and ruffled Daisy's coat, mumbling, "I know, I know, girl. You just want to see your dad, but let him get in and get settled."

Looking over her shoulder, she suggested, "Why don't you sit down, and I'll take her out." With some difficulty, she got Daisy to follow her with a promise of a treat and opened the back door so the dog could race out, do her business, then immediately run back inside.

Seeing a box of doggy treats on the kitchen counter, she snagged one and walked into the living room to see Daisy on the sofa, her head on Jared's knee, a loving gaze on the dog's face as she looked up at her owner. The sofa was in the center of the room and was still mostly covered with a drop cloth.

Jared had stripped off the hospital gown, and with no shirt on, his muscles were clearly defined. The full sleeve of tattoos up his arm once again captured and held her attention. She leaned against the doorframe and stared, realizing the expression on her face must match Daisy's. *Jesus, I'm ready to start panting like the dog!*

Uncertain of what to do or say, she blurted, "Would you like something to drink?" Glad to have an excuse to turn away and stop the drool fest, she walked into the kitchen. The overturned ladder remained in the middle of the dining area, and the floor was smeared with blood.

"You don't have to serve me," he grunted as he

walked into his laundry room. "I need to get a shirt first."

She quickly filled a glass of water, then looked over her shoulder to see him pull a shirt over his head. A little sigh slipped out at the loss of his gorgeous torso as it disappeared underneath the material. He winced slightly when he shifted his shoulder.

"Here," she said, handing him the glass and inclining her head toward the living room. "You should sit down." Leading the way, she glanced around, now understanding why the sofa was in the middle of the floor. The walls were freshly painted, and it appeared he'd also spent time on the trim work. He'd chosen a soft dove gray with a hint of blue and a slightly darker color on the wall behind the built-in bookcases that flanked the fireplace. She had to admit his work was beautiful, giving the room a homey feel. Glancing down, she admired the finished floors.

"They're original," he said, his voice breaking into her perusal. When she looked up, he continued. "The floors. They're original. One of the upstairs bedrooms had some water damage, but the floors down here were in good shape and just needed to be refinished. I got that done, but I probably did things out of order. I should have skimmed and painted the walls first. But I was really careful with my drop cloth and kept the plaster and paint off the floor." He shrugged, then winced at the movement of his shoulder. "Live and learn, I guess."

"It's beautiful." After his explanation, she took another look around the room, seeing the smooth walls and ceiling, and the beautiful detail work of the crown molding and bookcases. Walking to the fireplace, she trailed her fingers across the exposed brick. Looking over her shoulder, she smiled. "I love the idea of bringing an older home back to life. I can imagine the families who lived here through the years. You've done a really nice job."

Their gazes held for a long moment, the silence comfortable at first, and then she felt self-conscious under his intense perusal. Clearing her throat, she started into the kitchen. "While you rest, I'll go take care of the mess."

"No way, Billie. I'm not an invalid. Just a sore shoulder and a knock on the head. I'm not about to have you clean up after me." He stood and walked over, placing his hand on her arm. Warmth radiated from the touch of their skin, a blush rising along her neck to her cheeks.

"We can do it together, then," she compromised, feeling the heat move between them. She turned and hurried in front of him, not wanting to delve into why his touch sent electric shocks coursing through her body.

10

Jared watched Billie walk into his kitchen, his gaze sweeping from her silky blonde hair, haphazardly pulled back into a ponytail, down to her oversized comfy sweatshirt, then landing on her ass in stretchy black yoga pants as she knelt with a wad of paper towels in her hand. Immediately contrite, he choked back a sigh. *I'm objectifying the woman who ran over to help me, took me to the hospital, and is now wiping my blood off the floor.*

"Hey, hey, let me get that." He leaned over, then fought the dizziness that nearly dropped him to his knees.

He must not have been able to hide the woozy expression as she looked over her shoulder. Settling back on her heels, she pinned him with a pointed glare. "You're not being very smart. You have a concussion, and you really should be lying down or, at the very least, sitting down. Moving around, bending over, trying to be the I-can-do-anything man will only make it worse."

Knowing she was right, he still protested. "It doesn't feel right to be sitting while you're cleaning. On top of that, you're wiping up my blood. Shit, Billie, that's gross."

She rolled her eyes. "What would be gross was if I said, *'Oh, I don't want to clean this up,'* and just left it. That would be disgusting. But honestly, I'll have this cleaned up quickly, and then you can show me what you wanted to do with the ladder in the first place. I assume that ugly-ass fluorescent light was coming down?"

"Oh, hell no! I'm not having you change out a light fixture! It can wait until I can get someone over here who can help get the new light up."

Her eyes cut to the side where he had a new light fixture in the box. "I think little ol' me can handle installing a new light."

He opened his mouth and then snapped it shut again quickly. He'd only been around her a couple of times and had managed to piss her off each time until today. Nodding slowly, he said, "Um… okay. But let's do just one thing at a time."

It didn't take long to clean and disinfect the kitchen where blood had created a mess. She moved the old fluorescent fixture from where it had dropped to the side and then walked over to the new box.

Hoping to distract her, he threw out, "Maybe first we could eat something? I don't know about you, but I didn't eat breakfast, and here it is, the middle of the afternoon."

She blinked as though surprised by the time. "Sure. I'll fix us something, and then I can work on the light."

No matter what he suggested, she volunteered to jump in to take care of things. "Nope. I'm calling for pizza," he declared, deciding to take control. With his hand on her arm again, he gently pulled her away from the kitchen. "Please, just keep me company, and let's not worry about anything else right now."

Hesitation filled her face, and he stepped closer. "Come on, Billie. I hate to ask for another favor, considering how much you've done for me already today. But I really just want to sit down for a bit, and I can't do that if you're working here, fixing me dinner, and hanging a new light."

He looked around for his phone, then remembered it was still in the bag from the hospital, now lying on the counter. Sitting on one of the stools as he dialed, he asked, "What do you like on your pizza?"

"Anything except hot peppers."

"Can't take the heat?" he joked.

"Don't want to get burned," she fired back.

Laughing at her quick wit, he managed to order a meat lover's pizza while staring at the smile that had spread across Billie's face. His thumb disconnected the call, but his gaze never wavered from her. Beautiful, for sure. Smart. Funny. A curious mixture of confident and uncertain, bold and quiet. But the first time he'd met her, he'd had been pissed off that he'd forced down any attraction. Now, nothing stood in the way of his appreciation.

Silence surrounded them until she cleared her throat and looked around. "Why don't you tell me what all you've done to bring this old house back to life?"

He tilted his head to the side, considering her request. He loved this house, but other than his close friends who'd seen it as they occasionally assisted with projects too large for him to complete on his own, no one had expressed an interest in it. Remembering Stephanie's reaction, he scoffed. "I'm afraid there's not much to see."

Her head swung around and cocked to the side, and once again, he was ensnared by her icy blue eyes. "You wouldn't have bought it if there was nothing here to be excited about."

Not having a retort to her proclamation, he nodded. Clearing his throat, he waved his hand around. "Well, as I said earlier, the original floors survived, and I was able to sand and refinish them. Upstairs, a leak from a rotten window frame caused water damage on a small area of flooring, but after sanding and refinishing there, I was able to salvage all the floors up there as well."

"When was the house built?"

He watched as she walked about, her gaze slowly moving all around. "The early 1900s. This area boomed in population when a railroad was built, bringing goods and people from the north."

"And the kitchen? Did you take down a wall?"

Warming to his favorite subject, he continued. "Yeah. I wanted to make some changes in the way the space flowed. The wall between the kitchen and dining room made both spaces too confining, so I knocked it down once I determined it wasn't a supporting wall."

She looked up and grinned. "And that was where the old dining room light was hanging?"

He reached up to rub the back of his neck, still not believing that he'd fallen off a ladder. "Yeah. There was probably a beautiful light fixture originally, but one of the previous owners had gotten rid of it and replaced it with that god-awful fluorescent light you saw lying on the floor. I wanted it down and bought a light fixture that I thought would fit the space."

"Oh, I really like it!" she exclaimed, walking over to the box where the new light fixture still sat, waiting to be hung. Bending, she stared at the pictures on the box and then looked over her shoulder. "You found something that's modern yet maintains the integrity of this older home."

Pride swelled in his chest as well as surprise at how much her words meant to him. "That's exactly what I was trying to do."

"Have you restored a lot of houses?"

Chuckling, he shook his head. "No! This is my first and probably only attempt." Seeing the question in her eyes, he continued. "I really wanted to own a house, but there was no way I could afford something new or something very expensive. Housing is hard to come by around here, but when I saw this house, I could see the potential. I had it inspected carefully, and as soon as the inspector told me that the bones were good, and it just needed TLC, I snapped it up. Plus, the architecture would allow easy add-ons. I'm not in a hurry to get it finished. It gives me something to do on my days off."

As her lips curved slightly, her expression softened, and it punched him in the gut how very beautiful she was. *Wilhelmina.* As her unusual name passed through his mind, it struck him that it was as special and enigmatic as the woman in front of him. "I was a fucking asshole to make fun of your name," he blurted.

She startled, her head jerking slightly as her brows lowered. "What?"

"I never do that. I don't make fun of people or crack jokes at other people's expense. That's not how I was brought up. I can't believe I was such an asshole to you when we first met. I really hope you can forgive me."

Her tongue darted out to moisten her lips as she regarded him carefully, and he fought the urge to squirm under her intense scrutiny.

"I just remembered that you mentioned getting sucker punched earlier on that day we met. But we didn't have a chance to finish that conversation."

Sighing heavily, he nodded. "We were inspecting a man's boats. He rents them out knowing they're in shit shape, and we'd just pulled a group of people out of the water because of his negligence. It's fucking lucky one of them didn't drown. Anyway, he got pissed and took a swing at me. I wasn't expecting it, and he caught me on the jaw. He's a big guy, and while older, he can pack a punch. I was standing slightly out of his reach, so the hit was more of a glance and not full on, or it could have broken my jaw."

She gasped, eyes wide. "Oh my God! I can't believe that happened!"

"Yeah, well, his ass was arrested for hitting an officer, but that didn't improve my mood. The rest of the day was a shit storm, and I took it out on you." Stepping closer, his gaze not wavering from her, he repeated, "I really hope you can forgive me."

She nodded. "I'm afraid my reaction was rather curt as well. For reasons that aren't important, I'll also admit to being in a bad mood that day, and I'm sorry for making your job harder."

He waved away her apology. "It's not necessary." Uncertain of what else to say, he felt the loss as she stepped back and turned, still looking around the rooms.

"Keep showing me your house."

Relieved to have something to focus on other than the way her lips held his attention, they walked around the first floor. He explained the work he'd completed on the walls and ceiling. "Once I removed the wall, I opened the space and added the kitchen island last night with the help of some friends. I liked the cabinets, so I repainted them but had new countertops delivered and installed. I'll add a tile backsplash, but that's not pressing. I re-skimmed the walls, and with that last coat of paint in the living room, I'm ready to push the furniture in place and set up this room. The same thing happened in the now-open dining room. Through that door is a half bathroom and laundry room combination. I haven't done anything in there to update them yet."

She perused every wall, her nods and murmurs of approval causing his chest to squeeze. And if he was honest, her beauty was hitting his cock as well. A knock on the door reminded him their pizza had arrived, and he was starved. He paid and tipped, then turned to see she had pulled down some plates from a cabinet. He set the pizza box on the counter while she grabbed two water bottles for them.

The companionable silence they ate in felt strangely comfortable. He couldn't remember the last time he'd shared a meal with a woman who hadn't needed to fill the quiet with words, usually about themselves. While that thought struck him as sexist, it also struck him with the acknowledgment that the women's company he'd sought had been more for physical and not for conversation. A sigh escaped his lips.

"What are you thinking about so hard over there?"

Her soft voice cut through his thoughts. "Oh… just tired, I guess," he muttered, not willing to let her know what he had really been thinking.

After they ate their fill, he gave her a tour upstairs. She once again expressed interest and even delight at the work he'd accomplished in spite of how much still needed to be done. With only the larger bedroom and bathroom finished, he used the smaller one for storage.

"The bathroom is amazing," she gushed, then turned with a lifted brow. "A soaking tub plus a shower?"

"I didn't want to make it a glorified bachelor pad. I wanted it to be something that could grow with me." He wanted to explain more—tell her he wanted a wife and kids someday, but the words stayed buried. He forced his gaze to stay on her, breathing easier when her lips curved softly, and she simply nodded.

Once they were back downstairs, Daisy met them, prancing with her ball in her mouth. "Would you like me to run Daisy back outside?"

"No, I can do it."

"But shouldn't you rest? I've had you walk all over the house when I probably should have insisted you sit."

He smiled at her concern. "Nah, I'm good. No dizziness. No nausea. No blurred vision. I'm fine. I have tomorrow off work and won't need to drive anywhere. Looks like painting will be in my future."

She opened her mouth as though to speak, then snapped it shut, her gaze moving to the dining room. "Okay… well, I guess I'll go back over to my place. I'll check on you later."

Torn between wanting to spend more time with her and hating that she'd already given up a Saturday to tend to him, he simply nodded. "That'll be fine. But only if you have the time."

She turned and walked to the front door, and he followed. Just before she walked out, he reached over and touched her arm, drawing her attention back to him. "It seems like when I'm around you, I forget all my manners. I haven't even thanked you for everything you did for me today."

Her lips curved slightly, and she shrugged. "I'm just sorry you got hurt, but I'm glad we had a chance to talk."

"Yeah, me too."

He watched as she walked across the yard and bounded up the outside staircase. At the top, she bent to pick up a coffee cup, and he remembered she had abandoned it when he fell, and she came rushing over. Uncertain if he should be caught staring, he remained in place, and when she looked back toward him, he waved.

Her smile widened, and even from a distance, he felt sucker punched again. Only this time, it was by her smile, and the hit was much sweeter.

11

Billie stepped inside the garage apartment and looked around, almost in a daze. Everything was the same, yet it felt different. When she'd stepped out on the landing earlier that morning, her thoughts had been to enjoy the fresh cool air as she drank her coffee. Her biggest concern had been hoping that she could enjoy the quiet without feeling chased inside by Jared's presence.

But when she'd heard the crash and Daisy's frantic barking, her only thought was to get to him. Stunned to find him injured and bleeding, she launched into helping, giving no thought to their previous disregard for each other.

And now, after having spent most of the day with him, she had to admit the last couple of hours had been nice. She was impressed by the work he'd completed on his house, remembering the ugly comments his former girlfriend had thrown at him. Billie thought his purchase and vision were wonderful.

She wanted to check on him later but glanced down at her empty cereal bowl still on the counter, having not been washed yet. With her half-filled, now cold coffee in the cup in her hand, she walked over and dumped the contents down the sink before setting it next to the bowl and washing them both.

She made her bed, then walked into the bathroom to shower. Staring at her reflection in the mirror, she jerked slightly at the realization that her hair was still in a sloppy ponytail, and she hadn't even washed her face that morning. Her shirt was stained with a few drops of blood, and her worn leggings were for lounging at home and not for wearing out. She sighed, shaking her head. Not usually one for worrying what others thought of her, she winced at the idea that she looked unkempt when taking him to the hospital. *And at his house having pizza!*

While it didn't make sense to worry about her appearance before she went back over to his house, she still felt the need to clean up first.

After a shower, she hesitated while looking at her choice of clothing. "Grrrr," she groaned, finally pulling on an old pair of overalls with a long-sleeved blue T-shirt. Braiding her wet hair, she swiped on moisturizer, not worrying about makeup. *I'm checking on someone who's injured and helping hang a light. I hardly need to look like a model, even if that was possible!*

Going back down the outside stairs, she refused to delve into why she'd spent time worrying about what she looked like for Jared. *We may have apologized and buried the hatchet, but that hardly makes us compatible for anything other than neighbors.*

With that thought firmly planted, she walked to his front door, noting a few boards he needed to replace on his porch. He'd had to prioritize the work on his house, and she admired his ability to focus on one project at a time. Lifting her hand, she knocked gently, hoping he wasn't asleep.

The door opened, and even though it had only been a couple of hours since she had seen him, her breath caught in her throat. It appeared he'd showered as well, his hair still wet and finger-combed to the side. His short-sleeve T-shirt looked as though it barely contained his muscular frame, and the sleeve of tattoos stood out in stark relief of the white material. Neighborly thoughts flew from her mind, and her mouth seemed to take a vacation while overtaken with the desire to lick him like a lollipop.

"I feel bad that you had to check on me, but it's nice to see you again." He stepped back to give her a chance to move inside the living room.

Desperate to think of something to say, she finally mumbled, "Um." *Shit... get it together!* Opting for what she hoped sounded like a casual, unaffected air, she added, "I had nothing else going on today, but I figured since I was here, I'd get the light hung for you."

"Billie, I told you that you didn't have to—"

"I know, but I'm perfectly capable of installing a light fixture. You can spot me on the ladder if it makes you feel better."

A bark of laughter erupted. "I should've had you

come over this morning to spot *me,* and then we wouldn't have had to make a trip to the ER."

It was on the tip of her tongue to remind him that they hadn't been on speaking terms this morning, but she swallowed that quip. Whatever terms they were on now, she liked them. Instead, she simply spread out her arms. "Well, we can get this job marked off your list now."

With him carefully holding the stepladder, it didn't take long to connect the wires and screw in the ceiling plate for the new light. Once she hung it, he insisted she climb down as he walked to the wall and, with great exuberance, flipped the switch. The room was illuminated, and they both clapped at the same time, laughing.

She reached for the ladder, and they carried it to the side of the room together, propping it against the wall. Turning around, she realized how close they were and had to tilt her head back to keep her gaze on his.

He placed his hands on her shoulders and smiled. "Thank you, Billie. Sincerely, thank you for everything."

Licking her suddenly dry lips, she nodded. "Um… no problem." He stepped back, and she blurted, "In fact, I'd love to help work on your house if you want any help. Or don't mind the help."

No response came from him, and she winced, wishing she could pull the words back. "Or… um…"

"Really?" he asked.

Nodding, she replied, "I don't do anything other than work. I went to the American Legion meeting, but that's only once a month." Sounding pathetic to her ears, she could only imagine what he thought. He always had friends to rely on when he needed help. About to withdraw her offer of help to save him the embarrassment of having him turn her down, he grinned, and her mind emptied except for the way his smile lit the room more than the newly hung light.

"I'd love your input around here. You've got a good eye."

Her shoulders relaxed, and she blew out a breath. "I'm glad. I thought you were going to shoot me down."

His brows lifted, then he winced. "Damn. I took over-the-counter pain meds and forgot about the stitches."

"Why don't we sit down, and you can tell me more about your house projects? I noticed the front porch needed some work when I came in."

"Oh God, I hope you didn't look at it too closely. I mean, it's safe enough, but some of the boards and the railings need to be replaced. I probably should have put that higher on my list, but I really wanted the inside to feel more like home first."

He'd walked to the sofa, and she followed, sitting down next to him. "Hey," she said, placing her hand on his arm. "Stop. It's fine. You've got time to work on things, and as long as it's safe, you work on what you want to."

The crease in his brow eased as his smile returned. "Thanks."

She swallowed deeply, staring into his face, fascinated with each nuance. There was such a little boy quality to his expression. And a fully grown man as well. "Um..." She began, dragging her gaze away from him. "So... the house?"

He leaned back deeper in the cushions and glanced around, pride moving through his eyes. "My plan was to update the kitchen, primary bedroom, and upstairs bathroom first. I had some help from a few friends when I needed an extra pair of hands. I'm basically finished in here and can get my furniture in place. Next, I'm working on the dining room and downstairs bathroom." He rolled his eyes toward his injured shoulder. "I'll probably have to put aside some work until this is better."

"My offer to help is sincere," she said, shifting on the sofa to face him. "I don't have much to do outside my job and don't really hang out with anyone. I'm a hard worker, and... well, anyway, if you find yourself wanting an extra pair of hands and not just an opinion."

He stared at her for a long moment, not speaking. She tried not to squirm under his perusal. Her volunteering to help had probably come as a surprise, considering that before today, they hadn't really been on speaking terms. But his careful and probably doubtful consideration filled her with frustration. Suddenly, he smiled, and for a few seconds, the world fell away, leaving only the fluttering inside she felt at having his pleasure aimed toward her.

"I just might take you up on that offer," he said. "I have a lot of friends willing to help out, but I know they have their own schedules, and coming over here isn't always convenient. But I think I'll give it a day or two before I try anything strenuous."

Grinning, she nodded. "I think that's smart." She glanced at the clock on the microwave and stood. "How do you want to handle tonight?"

His eyes widened slightly, and he tilted his head to the side as his brows lifted. "Tonight?"

A snicker threatened to slip out at his stunned expression, and she quickly explained, "You need someone to check on you for twenty-four hours, and we've managed to make it through twelve of those, but I promised the doctor I'd keep an eye on you. I can set my alarm and come over in the middle of the night, but I don't want you to have to get out of bed to let me in."

He opened his mouth, and she could tell he was about to protest. Lifting her hand, she wagged her finger in front of his face. "Oh no, you're not getting out of this. Look, it's not every couple of hours. It's just once in the middle of the night and first thing in the morning."

He sighed but nodded. "You're right. I'll give you a key, and you can let yourself in." They stood, and he walked over to a hook next to the back door and pulled off an extra set of keys. "Here, take these."

Their fingers touched as the keys slid from his hand to hers. Once again, she felt the warmth pass between them. Her breath caught, then she dropped her gaze, staring at the keys. "I'll wake you up when I come a little after midnight just to check to make sure you're okay. Then I'll come back early in the morning to do the same."

He walked her to the front door, but before she could leave, he reached out and gently placed his hand on her shoulder. She turned to look at him, waiting for him to speak.

"I want to thank you again, Billie. For accepting my apology, for rushing to help me today, and volunteering to help with the house. I'm really glad we've had a chance to start fresh."

The warmth she felt from his touch now moved through her again, and she smiled. "I'll see you in a few hours." Hurrying across the yard and up into her apartment, she slipped inside.

Getting ready for bed, she thought about what she'd told him. *I don't have much to do outside my job and don't really hang out with anyone.* She scrubbed her hand over her face to the back of her head, and when her fingers tangled in her braid, she jerked in frustration. The words were true but hearing them back in her head gave proof of her rather sad, lonely existence.

Other than the necessities, she hadn't personalized the apartment at all. It was only temporary and not really hers. Thinking back on the last few places she lived, she realized the same could be said for them as well.

Pushing those thoughts to the side, she got ready for bed but left a pair of jeans within easy reach in case Jared needed her. Walking toward the bed, she stopped and dropped to a squat, dragging out a plastic tub from underneath the bed frame. Popping open the top, she rummaged until she found what she was looking for.

A sad smile curved her lips as she stared at the photograph from her childhood. Her fingers hovered over the picture, the smiling faces staring back at her memorized. But with a heavy sigh, she looked around the room before putting the lid back on the box and pushing it under the bed again. The small dresser that was next to the bed held a small lamp. Propping the picture against the base of the lamp, she gave it one last look before setting her alarm, turning off the light, and crawling into bed.

12

Jared stood on his back patio the following evening, breathing the fresh air, and looked up toward the garage, indecision scoring through him. Daisy had been racing around the backyard with the continuous company they'd had and was now lying on her side, sleeping in the setting sun.

True to her word, Billie had woken him gently in the middle of the night, checked to make sure his vision and memory were unaffected, then slipped back out. She'd been so stealthy that when he'd woken the next morning, he wondered if he'd dreamed of her visit. He'd barely been awake when she'd returned wearing a smile on her face when he sat up in bed and could see how many fingers she held up and proved he knew the date, his address, and the president's name.

Laughing, she'd proclaimed, "I think you're good to go. I guess my final warning would be to not climb any more ladders for a while without a spotter."

He liked the new truce they'd established. *Hell, it's a*

lot more than a truce. He wanted to know more about her and spend more time with her.

When he'd climbed from bed wearing drawstring sweatpants, he'd caught her staring at his naked torso, her gaze roving over the muscles and seeming to center on his tats. He couldn't help but preen a little, seeing the appreciation in her eyes and knowing he wasn't the only one affected. She was gorgeous, and he was pleased that she also appeared to like what she was viewing.

She'd fixed breakfast, and their easy conversation made the simple eggs, bacon, and toast a much more pleasurable meal than oatmeal by himself. He'd hoped they would spend most of the day together and was just asking her to stay when a call from Callan interrupted their time.

Callan had wanted to check on their work schedule for the next week, but as soon as he'd found out that Jared had been to the ER the previous day, suddenly, it seemed as though everyone he knew was calling or dropping by. Some offered to help, some brought food, and others just came to hang out and give him shit for falling off a ladder.

Ryan had called to let him know that his wife, Judith, who was also a doctor in town, would need to give him the okay to return to duty. Not wanting to miss more work than necessary, he told his chief he'd go to the clinic on Monday morning.

All the visits and calls had made him appreciate his friends, but they'd served to keep Billie away for the rest of the day. She'd startled when the sound of trucks and SUVs coming down his drive and parking in the front interrupted their conversation as they finished washing the dishes. She'd excused herself, mumbled something about letting him have time with his friends, and slipped out the kitchen door when Andy and Jose showed up. Callan and Sophie followed closely. Disappointment filled him as he stared longingly as Billie quickly disappeared inside her apartment. He'd hoped she would stay and hang out with his friends.

By that evening, it was quiet at his house, and from all indications, it was equally quiet at her apartment as well. *I could go over and see her.* Indecision rocked through him, an emotion he rarely experienced. He hated to disturb her in case she was resting. *She was with me all day yesterday and then came over in the middle of the night and this morning.*

Deciding to wait until tomorrow, he walked back inside and got ready for bed. But sleep slowly came as he rolled to his side and stared out the window toward her apartment.

By the time he'd let Daisy out the following morning, Billie had already left for work. Frustrated, he hoped she wouldn't start avoiding him again. But with no choice to do anything about it now, he got ready for work and drove into town. Walking into the clinic, he grinned as Judith welcomed him back to an exam room.

"Sounds like you had an interesting weekend," she said, patting the exam table.

He sat down and nodded. "I feel like an idiot."

Chuckling, she said, "Most home accidents tend to make people feel that way. I'm curious, though. With all the work you've been doing on the house, how did you tip the ladder over?"

"I was lazy," he groused. "I had to lean too far to reach for something when I should have just gotten down and moved the ladder. The next thing I knew, the light fixture gave way, it crashed to the floor, the ladder tipped over, and I went down, too."

She manipulated his shoulder for range of motion and then checked his sutures as well as asked him the same questions Billie had asked. "I heard your pretty neighbor took you to the ER?"

"How the hell did you…? Oh, Callan told Ryan."

"You know how the men gossip worse than the women around here." She laughed. "Is she as nice as she is pretty and efficient?"

Unable to keep a smile off his face, he nodded. "Yeah, she is."

"Well, good. You deserve someone nice."

Wanting to move the conversation along, he cleared his throat. "Can I go back on duty?"

"Nice try to shift me off the subject of your neighbor," she said, rolling her eyes. "But the answer is yes, with limitations. Restricted duty for five days. Come back on Friday, and I'll evaluate you for full active duty at that time."

"Seriously? I have to stay in the office and not go out on the water?" He sounded like a petulant child but hated to face a week of paperwork.

"You know the drill, Jared. If you aren't one hundred percent, you could end up harming yourself or others. You'll have to stay in the station this week and come back so we can make sure you're ready."

He thanked her in the least-grumbling voice he could manage and headed straight to the station. Giving his paperwork to the administrative manager, he walked to Ryan's door. Knocking, he entered. Explaining what Judith had said, he noticed Ryan's grin. "Glad you find my grounding to be amusing."

Ryan chuckled. "This means you can do reports this week, and I get more time out on the water."

"Don't rub it in," he mumbled.

For the rest of the day, he worked on requisition reports, arrest reports, and forms that had to be sent to the county as well as the state.

He listened to the dispatcher with each call out, and every time one of their boats docked, he made his way out to check on the crews. He thought of all the times Ryan wasn't on a boat with them, yet he often met them at the dock. Jared now understood why their chief did that. There was something about being connected to your fellow officers, seeing for yourself that they were safe, and wanting to hear in their own words how everything was going.

By lunchtime, he was even more antsy when they came in and was willing to put up with their jokes just to have the camaraderie.

"I saw the pretty water analyzer out today," Andy said, wiggling his eyebrows, immediately drawing Jared's attention.

"Billie?"

"I sure as hell don't mean that other guy who'd been

here before her!" Andy laughed. "Sure made patrols this morning better."

"Don't rub it in," he groused.

"Hell, she's your neighbor! You get to see her all the time."

"Hardly! With everyone who came by yesterday to check on me, you saw how she disappeared back into her apartment, and I didn't see her again for the rest of the day."

"You were awfully lucky that she was around when you fell," Jose pointed out.

"Don't I know it!"

"Well, I'd hate like hell for you to have to fall again to get her attention back," Callan added, nodding toward Shiloh as their food was delivered to the table.

"What are you waiting on?" Bryce asked. "She's your renter, living on your property. Go knock on her door!"

"I figured she needed the rest. She was with me all day on Saturday and came over in the middle of the night and first thing yesterday morning to check on me."

"Well, maybe you'll get lucky and see her when you get home tonight," Andy suggested.

He nodded but remained quiet. The truth was he really did want to see her again and would consider himself lucky if he did. But the last thing he wanted to do was push her if she wanted space. Scrubbing his hand over his face, he winced when his fingertips brushed against his stitches.

They finished lunch, and the others were back on

the water while he went into the office, chained miserably to the desk.

The air turned cooler and the breeze whipped by as Billie steered her boat back through the inlet she'd been in the other day. Wrapping her jacket tighter around her body, she moved to the side and pulled out her phone.

"Rita? Hey, it's Billie."

"I wondered if you were going to call after getting your message last week. So things are the same?"

"Yes. My findings are exactly the same each time. Chlorpyrifos. Besides the water testing, which is conclusive, I'm going to start taking fish samples." She shivered as another chilly breeze blew over her. "If I wasn't starting from scratch, this would be easier," she complained. As Rita read off some of the tests she could use, Billie looked up to see a tall, thin man in overalls with a ball cap covering his head walk to the edge of the water on the opposite side from the Harper farm, his gaze pinned on her. Sighing, she interrupted her boss and said, "Sorry, Rita, but I have another possible landowner to talk to. Looks like he's curious, and I don't want any trouble."

"Okay. Stay safe, and let me know what you find."

"I'll send the results when I get them written up this evening." She grimaced and rubbed her forehead. "Or it may be tomorrow. I have a killer headache coming on and really just want to get home."

With goodbyes said, she maneuvered her boat over to where the man stood. "Hello," she greeted.

"I heard from the Harpers that someone was around here looking into our farms," he said, using his forefinger to tip the brim of his hat back a little.

"I'm not looking into the farms, sir. I'm with the Chesapeake Bay Foundation, and I'm testing the water along the bay."

He snorted. "Uh-huh. And what you find can lead right back to us. That's what's wrong with all you government types. Trying to stick it to those of us just making a living. It's hard enough without you people buttin' in."

She sighed and rolled her shoulders, fatigue beginning to pull at her patience. Knowing nothing she could say would appease the farmer, either about her job or that she would have nothing to do with any possible investigation into his insecticide usage. "Have a nice day, sir," she said, turning away from him and restarting her engine.

"Name's Nevins. Porter Nevins," he called out. "I reckon I'll see you around."

Not sure if it was a friendly statement or a threatening one, she tossed a small wave his way and then faced forward as she guided her boat back into the bay. A shiver shook her body again as the headache bloomed into a blinding pain, and she knew it was time to head home.

As she made it to the marina on the north side of Baytown, she docked and hefted her cases with testing equipment protected inside. *Ugh... why does everything feel heavier and harder?* Hauling her body onto the dock, she sighed heavily as she stood and gathered her belongings. Once inside her car, she cranked up the heat and drove home. Pulling up next to the garage, she looked over but didn't see Jared's truck.

When she'd run into some of the other marine police officers earlier in the day, they'd thanked her for helping him. She'd waved off their gratitude but secretly grinned at the memory of their shared Saturday, even if it began at the ER. The one who introduced himself as Andy mentioned that Jared was stuck in the office for the rest of the week. From the amused looks passing between the men on the VMP boat, that seemed to be a task that Jared would hate.

Climbing from her car, she shivered once again before reaching into the back seat and gathering her equipment. Walking up the wooden steps by the side of the garage to her landing, she fumbled with the keys. Once inside, she dropped her cases, kicked the door closed, and bent to pull off her boots. Her head felt heavy, and she staggered slightly on her way into the bathroom. The shower warmed her, but instead of invigorating, it was far too short before her body's fatigue threatened to suck every last ounce of energy from her.

Too tired to eat, she crawled into bed, sniffling as she grabbed a handful of tissues. Shivering again, she pulled the covers up and closed her eyes, willing the darkness to overtake her.

13

As soon as Jared drove down his driveway, he spied Billie's car near the bottom of the stairs, not in its usual place on the far side of the garage. Parking in front of his house, he could hear Daisy barking. He hustled inside and knelt to run his hands over her, laughing as she rolled onto her back so he could rub her belly. "Come on, girl, let's get you outside."

Throwing open the back door, he watched as she raced through the yard during her evening ritual. His gaze continually moved to the garage, wishing he would find Billie watching and she would decide to join him. Glancing down where she'd haphazardly parked her car, he wondered if she'd shopped at the grocery store, then stopped closer to the stairs to make it easier to bring bags into her apartment.

He wanted to head over to see her. *But if she wanted to see me, she would have come over. I think. Or maybe she thought she'd bother me. Or maybe...* Hesitation filled him. *Fuck it!* He pushed off the doorframe he'd been leaning against and called for Daisy to come inside. Once she was secured, he walked outside and through the gate leading to the garage.

Climbing the stairs, he stopped just outside her door. It was quiet inside the efficiency. Knocking softly, he wondered if she was taking a shower when she didn't answer his knock. He rapped his knuckles against the wooden door again, this time a little louder. A grimace crossed his face as it hit him that there was no security view in the door for her to see who was outside. *Why haven't I thought of that before?*

"Who is it?" a raspy voice asked from inside.

He jerked slightly at the unfamiliar sound, and his hand stayed fisted against the door. "Billie? It's Jared."

The sound of the deadbolt flipping met his ears before the door was opened. Billie stood in front of him, her face pale and eyes slightly red. Her hair was limp, hanging about her shoulders. "Ja… Jared?" She cleared her throat, then asked, "Are you okay? Do you need something?"

"No, I just… well, I hadn't seen you… I thought I'd come by to say hi," he finally managed to say, filled with uncertainty as his gaze raked over her.

"I didn't check on you yesterday because you had a lot of visitors, and I was afraid you might be tired. Then I had to work."

Her voice sounded rough, so he asked, "Are you okay?"

"Yeah. I developed a headache this afternoon, but I'm fine. I figured I'd call it an early night."

He didn't want to lose her company but didn't want

to be a bother if she didn't feel well. "I'm sorry, Billie. I'll go, but promise you'll let me know if you need anything."

His offer brought a little smile to her face, and he could swear his heart skipped a beat. Hating to leave but not having a good excuse to stay, he said, "I'll check on you tomorrow."

As he stepped back onto the landing, she chuckled. "I think I'm supposed to be the one checking on you."

Waving his hand in dismissal, he shook his head. "Nah, I'm all good."

"As soon as my headache meds work and I get a good night's sleep, I'll be better tomorrow."

"I got cleared by the doctor for light duty, so I'll be back at work tomorrow, also. But if you don't feel good, you should take a day off."

Now it was her turn to wave her hand in dismissal. "I'll be fine."

"Seems like we keep assuring each other that we're fine." With his hand on the doorknob, he hesitated before offering a chin lift. "Well, um… goodbye." Reluctantly turning, he walked out onto the landing, his gut strangely empty as he left her side.

She offered a goodbye as well before closing the door. He jogged down the stairs, and once back inside his house, he met Daisy in the kitchen. She whimpered while pacing around. "Looks like it's just you and me, girl."

He hated that Billie didn't feel well, but relief spread through him that she wasn't avoiding him. He wanted to believe that they had moved past the initial confusion, assumptions, and irritations.

By the time he ate dinner, he'd looked toward the garage dozens of times, but the lights had remained out. It dawned on him that she probably hadn't eaten. The lasagna that he'd bought pre-made at the grocery store wasn't special, but it would still be easy for him to take. Wrapping up a plate, he retraced his steps and headed to the garage.

At the top of the stairs, he started to knock again when he noticed the window near the kitchen was open slightly at the bottom, and the odor of something having burned wafted past. He lifted his hand to knock when her voice came through the kitchen window.

"I burned a piece of toast," she said, sounding more croaky than earlier. "I know, James. I'll be more careful."

Jared halted his hand, not wanting to interrupt but not wanting to eavesdrop. Unfortunately, staying still meant he could hear her words.

"I miss you, too. I'll try to get to you soon, but the last thing I want is for you to get sick. I'll cancel this weekend's visit."

Jared's breathing slowed as he wondered who James was. It never dawned on him that she had a boyfriend. She'd told him that she didn't have anyone to hang out with, so he must not be local. *That's probably why she needed a cheap, short-term place to live.*

"I love you, too, James. I'll talk to you in a couple of days."

A strange sense of emptiness filled him, and without thinking it through, he turned and hastened down the stairs as quietly as possible. Once he was back inside his house, he stared at the plate of lasagna in his hands and groaned. *I could have given it to her. I should have given it to her.*

Shoving it inside his refrigerator, he headed upstairs, not interested in watching TV. Lying in his bed with Daisy snoring at his feet, he stared out the window toward the now-dark garage, disappointment swirling throughout him. Frustrated, he rolled over, dislodging Daisy, who grunted, then settled again. It shouldn't matter that Billie had a boyfriend. They had just started talking. Just started a casual friendship that he'd hoped would grow. Just started... *yeah, I was just starting to get feelings.* Closing his eyes, he tamped down his gut-clenching disappointment.

By the following morning, he saw no movement at Billie's apartment, and her car was still parked in the same place. All day at work, he wondered how she was, barely able to focus on the reports he was finishing. Sighing heavily, he thought of the tingle he'd felt whenever their hands touched. Even knowing she had a boyfriend didn't keep her from his mind. The minutes crawled by, and he left as quickly as he could, not staying to chat with any of his coworkers.

As soon as he pulled into his driveway, he could see that her car had not moved all day. He jumped out, Daisy barking her greeting to him. An inner battle ensued, uncertain which direction to head first. Making his decision, he pounded up the stairs to the apartment. Hesitating for only a few seconds, he rapped briskly on the door, calling out, "Billie? It's Jared." It took several more knocks before he could hear the locks on the door unlatching.

He almost didn't recognize the woman standing in front of him. Her hair was pulled back in a braid, but the strands around her face stuck to her sweat-slicked forehead. Pale with dark circles under her eyes and a red nose that almost matched her red-rimmed eyes. She blinked as she looked up at him, seeming confused. "Jared?"

He reached out and placed his hand on her belly, gently pushing her backward and stepping inside. The curtains were closed, keeping the room dark. The heat was turned up, and as she shivered, he realized she'd tried to find warmth.

Concern flooded him, and he gently took her by the arm and led her over to the sofa, pulling her down next to him. "Billie, this isn't just a headache. What's going on?"

She shrugged, sniffed, and shivered again. "I don't know. I feel like I was run over by a truck. A lot of people in the ER had sounded like they had the flu, and I'm afraid I might have gotten something from them."

"Oh shit," he groaned. "It's my fault that you were exposed to that environment." He reached out and touched her forehead, his hand meeting the heat pouring off her. "You've got a fever."

"You think?" she quipped before turning away to cough, one hand covering her mouth and the other arm wrapped around her waist.

"I'm calling Judith."

"Who's Judith?" she rasped.

"It's my boss's wife. Judith Coates. She's a doctor in town, and the one who checked me over for the clearance to go back on light duty." He pulled out his phone, but Billie shook her head.

"That doesn't make any sense to call her, Jared. I have the flu or something like it. There's not much she can do for me."

"Well, I'd still like to find out anyway." He called the clinic but was told Judith had already gone home. Next, he called Ryan. "Hey, boss. Is Judith at home? My neighbor may have the flu, and I just wanted to see what I could do for her."

"Yeah, sure, let me get her."

He could hear words spoken before Judith came on the line.

"Hey, Jared. When Ryan said it was you, I thought maybe you were having more symptoms, but he said you're calling about your neighbor?"

"Yeah, I'm feeling fine, but my neighbor, who took me to the ER the other day, may have picked up the flu from the waiting room. She's got a fever, chills, headache, coughing, and congestion."

"Oh, I am sorry," Judith sympathized. "The best thing you can do for her this evening is to give her over-the-counter pain relievers and fever reducers. She needs to drink plenty of water and clear liquids to avoid dehydration. And the most important thing she needs to do is stay home and rest. Obviously, if she takes a turn for the worse or things don't get better, she needs to come in and see me."

"Got it, Judith. Thanks a lot." Disconnecting, he

turned toward her, guilt spearing through him at how sick she appeared. “Okay, the doc says rest, lots of fluids, and over-the-counter pain meds and fever reducer.”

Even sick, she managed to offer him an incredulous expression, complete with a cocked eyebrow and tilted head. “You really didn’t have to call the doctor for that information, Jared. I’m pretty sure an internet search would produce the same thing.”

“Hmph,” he muttered. “I think it’s always better to get medical advice from a professional instead of the internet anyway.”

The fatigue in her face relaxed slightly as her lips curved, and she nodded. “Actually, you’re probably right. Anyway, it was really nice of you to check.”

“Is your throat sore? Because you sound like a frog.”

“Oh, so you don’t think this is a deep, sexy voice?”

Jerking his head back, he bit down the response that he found everything about her sexy. “Is…” He cleared his throat. “Is that what you were going for? Sexy?”

She snorted and shook her head. “Actually, no. I think sexy is about the last thing I feel or look like right now. But to answer your question, yes, my throat is sore.”

“Did you work outside all day yesterday?”

“Yeah, but in my defense, I didn’t feel bad in the morning. A little bit of a headache, but that was all. I started feeling worse as the day went on. And after I finished my last test and was already getting nasty comments from one of the farmers, I decided it was time to come home. Today, I haven’t left the apartment.”

Jared was in the process of walking over to her kitchenette to see what she had and what she might need when her last statement caught his attention, and he looked over his shoulder. He started to ask about the nasty comment and farmers, but she looked exhausted, and he hesitated.

Bending, he opened the mini fridge, sighing as it dawned on him how small it was. It hadn't bothered him when he first bought the property and started the renovations, living where she lived now. He certainly hadn't given it any thought when he put the efficiency up for rent. But now, the idea that she had very little room for cold items struck him. There were only small containers of milk, orange juice, lunch meat, a half carton of eggs, and a wedge of cheese.

"Do you have any water, Billie?"

She laughed, then fell into a coughing fit. "Yeah, just grab a glass from the cabinet above and fill it from the sink."

Pressing his lips together, he opened the cabinet door. One mug. One glass. One plate. One bowl. The singleness of her belongings struck him. Even when he'd stayed here, he'd kept a few things around for the friends who dropped over. Billie had only been renting from him for a few weeks, but it struck him that he'd never seen anyone over here but her. *Why the fuck isn't her boyfriend coming around?*

Another round of coughing jerked him out of his musings. He reached up to grab the glass and fill it with water from the sink. Walking back to the sofa, he handed it to her, pleased when she downed the entire contents. "Do you have any medicine here?"

She nodded, wincing as though the act of moving was painful. "Um… I have ibuprofen. That should help with the fever and aches."

"Can I go into your bathroom and get something?"

"Yeah, thanks."

He walked into the small bathroom and opened the old-fashioned medicine cabinet over the sink, easily finding the bottle. A quick glance exposed how sparse she lived compared to some of the women he'd known. The only makeup he saw was a powder compact, mascara, and a tube of cherry lip balm. Suddenly, the idea of discovering if her lips tasted like cherries hit him.

"Did you find it?" she asked, the raspiness of her voice making it difficult to understand.

Jolting back to the business at hand, he hustled over, shaking two pain reliever pills into his palm. Handing them to her, he grabbed the glass and refilled it from the sink. She managed to swallow the pills and the entire glass of water. As she handed the empty glass to him, she shivered again. Reaching out, he gently pushed a damp tendril away from her face, the touch pulling at his heart.

"You need to get back into bed," he said, glancing over his shoulder toward the bed in the corner. It was the one area of the room that added a touch of personality. The sheets were pale blue, and the comforter was navy. Spread over the top was a blanket with color swirls of blues, pinks, greens, and yellows. Somehow, the riot of hues seemed incongruent with the rest of the decor, yet now that he stared at the faded but beautiful bedcover, he instinctively knew it held meaning to her.

She stood, and his attention whipped back to her. With her arms crossed protectively over her body, she offered a little smile before dropping her robe and crawling into bed. He tried to ignore his body's response to her breasts in the thin T-shirt and the way her exposed legs drew his gaze to her ass showcased in her striped sleep shorts. Blowing out a breath, he swallowed deeply.

"I'm so tired," she whispered, her eyelids fluttering.

"Shit, Billie, I didn't get you to eat anything."

She yawned and shook her head. "I had some soup earlier. I'm okay. You can go. Thanks for checking on me."

He watched as her eyes closed and her breathing eased. He started to turn away when she whispered, "I haven't had that in a while."

He wanted to ask what she meant. *Haven't had soup in a while, or haven't had someone checking on her in a while? And where the fuck is James?*

She was an enigma. It hit him that while she'd taken care of him, she'd asked the questions, and he'd done all the talking. *But she's still a mystery... a puzzle.* One he wanted to figure out. A photograph lay on the dresser, and he looked at the picture of a man with his arm around a pretty blonde woman and a white-blonde-haired little girl in front of them, smiles on everyone's faces. Pressing his lips together, he wondered why the only picture she had in the apartment was one from many years ago.

Torn, he wanted to stay in case she woke but didn't want to seem like a creeper staring at her while she slept. He sat on the sofa for a little while, just in case she needed him, but her sleep appeared steady. Tiptoeing to the door, he let himself out after looking over his shoulder at her one more time.

14

Billie wondered if a boa constrictor had wrapped itself around her head and body during the night. The effort to drag oxygen into her lungs made her whole body feel tight. She lay in bed, uncertain if she could even make it to the bathroom to pee, but feeling like a human torch, she finally managed to shove off the covers. Crawling into the bathroom, she was hit with chills again when the cool air only felt refreshing for a moment.

She managed to use the toilet, wash her hands, and stare at her horrendous reflection in the mirror before she began coughing again. Her brow scrunched as she looked at the bottle of pain reliever sitting on her sink. *Jared. Was he really here last night?*

With two ibuprofen in her hand, she swallowed them with water, wincing at the pain that felt like glass shards going down her throat. *And if he was, why?*

In the kitchen, she noted her glass sitting in the sink and remembered that he had been here the previous evening. *God, I must have looked like shit.* That she cared about him seeing her that way bothered her. It seemed they were becoming friends, but deep down, she wished for more.

Fixing a cup of tea, she liberally laced it with honey while wishing she had some whiskey. Shuffling over, she stood looking down at the messy bed linens. She was exhausted, but the bed no longer held appeal. Grabbing the blanket she loved, she made it to the sofa and wrapped the comforting material around her.

Sipping the hot tea, she willed the pain and fever reliever to work. While it offered minimal comfort, her eyelids drooped, and she slid down on the sofa, praying for blissful oblivion.

Her weird, crazy dreams were disturbed by the rhythmic sound of bongo drums. The banging didn't last long before her body began to shake. Peeling open her eyes was difficult, considering someone had super glued them closed while she slept.

"Hold on."

She had no idea why the voice in her dream told her to hold on, but she struggled to sit up, barely able to crack her eyes open. Disoriented, she was startled when a warm, wet cloth was placed over her eyes.

"Jesus, Billie. Why the fuck didn't you call me?"

"James?" she rasped.

"No, it's Jared."

Unable to see with the crud in her eyes, she focused on the hard voice clipping the words. "Jared?"

"How out of it are you, Billie?"

Her mind functioned several steps behind what was happening around her, and she decided to focus on the comforting feel of the soft, warm, moist cloth gently dabbing at her eyes. When it pulled away, she was able to blink her eyes open, seeing Jared's face. "How did you get in?"

"I used my key. As the landlord, I kept one in case I ever needed to get in during an emergency. I knocked and knocked, but you never came to the door. I was afraid you might be passed out on the floor, so I let myself in."

"Oh."

She pulled the blanket tighter around her as his hand pressed against her forehead.

"You've still got a fever. I didn't see a thermometer when I was here yesterday, so I stopped by the drugstore."

"What time is it?" she mumbled.

"It's about two o'clock in the afternoon. I took a late lunch, ran by the pharmacy, and then came to check on you, but when you wouldn't answer the door, I called my boss and told him that I was going to be off this afternoon."

Coughing again, she started to shake her head but felt dizzy as soon as her head moved back and forth. Giving up on the motion, she sighed. "You don't have to do that."

"I know there's probably not much we can do except treat the symptoms, but I have to tell you, Billie, you seem really sick. I wanna get the fever down, get some food and liquids in you, and make sure you'll be all right."

"You don't have to do that," she mumbled in

repetition.

"I didn't say I have to do it. I want to do it. Someone needs to take care of you, and it sure as hell isn't your boyfriend." He straightened and glanced around before looking back at her, then held out his hand. "First things first. When was the last time you took your ibuprofen?"

Her face scrunched as she attempted to make sense of the boyfriend comment, but then she tumbled to his next question and tried to answer. "Sometime this morning."

"Early?"

"Yeah. I remember the time on the microwave. It was a little after eight o'clock."

"Okay, let's get more liquids and meds in you."

She watched as he walked the few steps to her kitchen counter, filling the glass before moving into the bathroom to grab the pills. Shaking out several, he handed them to her, and she drank, grateful for the cool water gliding down her parched throat. With a less croaky voice, she asked, "What's next, captain?"

"Captain?" His voice held mirth, and her gaze fixated on the smile gracing his lips. *His lips are gorgeous. So are his eyes. So are his arms. So is his—*

"You with me, Billie?"

She blinked in slow motion, struggling to discern what *with me* entailed. "Uh..."

"Come on. Let's get you into the shower. It'll cool you down, make you feel better, and then I'll fix more soup."

"I don't think I have any more soup."

"Don't worry about it. I took care of it. Now, up."

Heat infused her cheeks, but she couldn't decide if it was from the fever or embarrassment. She waved her hand dismissively. "I'll take care of everything, Jared. You can leave me to my misery."

"No can do, sweetheart." He reached down and gently lifted her to her feet.

The endearment fell from his lips, piercing deep inside, but she knew it was a throwaway. Even so, the word tugged her back to the past where memories lay buried.

While she was still hanging on to the way *sweetheart* left his lips, he wrapped his arm around her shoulders and guided her slowly to the small bathroom. It was definitely built for one person, and even sick and feverish, she realized how intimately they were pressed together in the tiny room. He leaned around her and turned on the water, testing it with his hand.

"It's only lukewarm, but that should feel good to you. I'll step out and let you take care of what you need to."

He walked out, leaving the door cracked slightly, but even through bleary eyes, she could see that he'd stepped far enough toward the kitchen that he couldn't see in. Needing to pee more than she cared about her dignity, she quickly used the toilet. Standing, she weaved and grabbed hold of the sink. Afraid to let go, she glanced behind her at the shower, now concerned about the possibility of fainting.

"Do you need help?" His voice came through the crack in the door.

"I don't think this is going to work," she mumbled.

Suddenly, he was right beside her with his hand around her waist, providing steady support.

"Are you wearing anything under this T-shirt?"

"Huh?" Her groggy reply sounded strange even to her ears.

"Oh, fuck it," he grunted. "Lift your arms."

She immediately obeyed, then gasped as the cool air hit her heated skin when he gently pulled her T-shirt over her head and tossed it to the floor. She instinctively wrapped her arm across her breasts, but he'd already knelt and was pulling her sleep shorts and panties to the floor. An indignant exclamation was swallowed by more coughing. Barely aware of his hand on her upper arm, he guided her under the spray of the shower, then jerked the small curtains closed. He was now hidden with only his hand still visible, holding her arm. The feel of the water hitting her body helped her brain kick in gear.

"I'm going to keep you upright, Billie, but I need you to wash off yourself unless you want me to do it."

A snort managed to erupt at the ridiculousness of the situation. She should've been mortified, at the very least, and pissed off at his high-handedness. But at the moment, all she felt was the wonderful tepid water sluicing over her hot skin, helping to wash away the sweat and stink from the fever. Her body jiggled slightly as he shook her arm.

"Billie? You need to wash off," he repeated.

With his arm holding securely, she was no longer afraid of falling and reached out to grab her shower gel. With great effort, she managed to squeeze a liberal amount into her hand and lathered it over her body, aware of how close he was to her nudity on the other side of the curtain. Pushing that thought down, she reveled in the familiar floral scent of the sweet pea suds giving comfort and making her feel less gross.

She wanted to shampoo and condition her hair but doubted she had the energy, so she gave into the shortcut and simply scrubbed her hair with her sweet pea body wash. By the time she finished, her legs could barely keep her standing, and she knew she would have crumpled to the floor without his help holding her in place.

Jared's other hand snuck in and turned off the water while he managed to keep his face behind the curtain.

"I'm going to hand you a towel, okay?"

A giggle slipped out before it turned into another wracking cough, and she doubled over at the waist, trying to catch her breath.

"Oh, fuck it," he said again. The shower curtain jerked back, and a towel was wrapped around her almost instantly before his strong hold guided her onto the bathmat.

"Sit here." He turned and grabbed another towel for her hair.

She plopped down on the closed toilet lid while he continued to rub her hair dry. He leaned over toward the sink, and his torso was almost pressed against her face. She could smell the masculine soap he'd used, and her fingers itched to slip under his shirt to discover the delicious skin underneath. Before she could act on her feverish ideas, he turned and stepped to the side again, dragging her comb through her hair. All thoughts of his torso flew from her mind at the tingling feel of her clean hair being combed. "Mmm. You're good at this," she mumbled, leaning back against his body. "You could make a living helping women take showers."

"Well, it's the first time I've helped a woman take a shower without actually being in the shower with her."

Her eyes widened as she looked up at him, "Do you take a lot of showers with women?"

His head jerked back slightly. "I… well, I wouldn't say a lot. Why do you ask?"

"I've never taken a shower with a man before."

His head jerked again. "Uh… "

Her chest still felt like a boa constrictor was wrapped around her, her throat was still raw, and a fever still raged inside. But the shower had revived her enough to make her glad she wasn't alone. Shrugging, she said, "Not that I'm a prude. It's just that I've never been with anyone I cared enough about to shower with. A shower seems so intimate."

Her back was to him, but she could tell he jerked once more when the comb seemed to get stuck in a tangle, and he pulled lightly on her hair.

He cleared his throat. "Well, to be honest, I haven't taken a shower with anybody in a long time. You're right, though. I guess the last time was with a girlfriend, and that's been a while."

"I can't believe you don't have a girlfriend now. You're nice. And you're pretty."

He turned to hang the towel he used on her hair

over the shower bar and chuckled. "I'm pretty? I don't think I've ever been called pretty before."

Standing, she barely hung on to the towel wrapped around her body. "Well, someone should let you know you're pretty." She took a step toward the open door and then swayed backward before hitting something hard.

His front was plastered to her back as one of his arms banded around her middle. "Jesus, Billie. You're so weak you can't stand."

"I'm sorry," she mumbled, dropping her head back against his shoulder.

"Well, at least I've had some experience with drunk dates. Let's get some clothes on you, and then you need to climb back into bed while I make the soup."

"Clothes are hot," she grumbled, fatigue now pulling at her again, her body jerking as she coughed more. "I bet with drunk dates, you want them out of their clothes."

"Nope. When I'm with someone, I don't mind if they've had a couple of drinks, but I won't sleep with someone who's drunk."

"Aw, that's sweet, Jared." She slumped deeper into his embrace as her eyes drooped.

Scoffing, he frog-walked her into the room and gently helped her sit on the side of the bed. The towel was slipping, and he grabbed the top. "Hold on, babe, or I'm going to get more of a view than I already have." The dresser was next to him, and he opened several drawers, pulling out items. "Hopefully, your fever will go down soon, and you'll be less delirious."

"Oh God, you have my panties in your hand," she groaned, her hands covering her face.

"I've already seen your panties." He knelt and slid her feet through the leg holes, then dragged them upward. "I'll close my eyes, and you lift your hips."

She managed to do as he instructed but sucked in a breath as his fingertips grazed her thighs and ass. Next, he slid a T-shirt over her head and assisted her arms through the sleeves, letting the material drop before gently pulling the towel away.

Billie looked up, too tired to be embarrassed, and a part of her wondered if this entire experience was all a dream. She scooted against the headboard where he'd fluffed the pillows and watched as he moved into the kitchen again. This time, he bent to take out a plastic container from a bag she hadn't noticed before.

He popped it into the microwave before pouring a glass of ginger ale for her. Once heated, he placed the contents into a bowl, added some crackers, and brought it over to her. "Chicken noodle soup from the diner."

The scent of the warm soup surrounded her like an embrace, and her face crumpled as tears streamed down her cheeks.

15

Jared wasn't sure how much more he could take. When he'd come over, he hoped to find her health improved but found her dead to the world on the sofa in a feverish state. He hated that he hadn't checked on her before going to work but was grateful he'd decided to come home early.

She'd called out James, but if her boyfriend was around or expected, the fucker never came. Not willing to let her go through this alone, he wanted to get her temperature down and was hopeful the lukewarm shower would help. But when he'd made the suggestion, he thought she'd be able to handle it on her own. Seeing how weak she was, the risk of possible injury let him know he'd need to take control of the situation. The problem became having to take control of his own physical reaction while having to strip her and trying not to stare at her beautiful body.

Having gotten her into the shower, he'd thought he could take a breather until he realized she still needed help. Desperate to maintain her dignity and a semblance of not seeming like a perv, he'd tried to stay on one side of the shower curtain. But with her slippery body, there was no way his fingers didn't occasionally brush up against her curves. And, oh yeah… his cock took notice.

With her fever high, she'd talked, but it was more from the delirium. *Pretty.* He couldn't help but chuckle again. *She called me pretty. That's a first.* Yet because it was said from an unfiltered, honest place, and not to impress him, or try to sleep with him, or try to flirt with him, it was real. And now that he thought about it, it was fuckin' adorable. Just like her. Adorable. Smart. Independent. Beautiful. *Yeah, and fuckin' adorable.*

Now, filling her bowl with warm soup, he turned to face her only to watch as silent tears fell from her eyes. Setting the bowl on the counter, he rushed over to sit next to her and pulled her into his arms. Rocking her back and forth gently, he smoothed his hand over her back.

"Billie, what's wrong? What can I do?"

She didn't speak for a moment, and he continued to hold her while she cried. Leaning to the side, he grabbed several tissues from the box sitting on the dresser and handed them to her. He waited until she wiped her eyes and blew her nose, then turned her face up to his.

"Oh God, I'm such a mess. I'm sorry, Jared. I'm never a mess like this."

Even though she wiped her tears with a tissue, he moved his thumb over her cheeks, wanting to feel the soft skin. "You're entitled to fall apart, you know. You've got the flu. You feel like shit. And I have a feeling you're so independent that accepting help from someone is difficult."

"Am I that easy to read?"

He snorted, rolling his eyes. "Quite the contrary. I think I've been trying to figure you out since I first met you."

Her lips curved softly. "Of all the things you did for me—the medicine, the fluids, helping with my shower, even drying and combing my hair, it was the smell of the chicken noodle soup that took me back to a time when I didn't have to try to do everything on my own."

"Everyone loves chicken noodle soup," he said, wanting to see her lips curve into another smile. "Let me get it for you. You can eat, and then we'll check and see if your fever has come down."

A few minutes later, her spoon scraped the bottom of the bowl. A contented expression filled her face as her breathing seemed easier and her coughing fits had lessened. After he washed the bowl and placed it back into the cabinet, he walked to the sofa and picked up the well-loved blanket to bring it over to where she sat in bed. Draping it across her lap, he sat on the edge of the mattress. He thought she might be ready for another nap, but her gaze held his. Sucking in a deep breath, he plunged ahead, deciding to see how much of herself she would give him. "Do you want to tell me about the memories that the soup brought back?"

She looked down at her fingers splayed out over the blanket. "My mom made this blanket for me when I was a little girl. She used pieces of cloth that came from dress material from both of my grandmothers, my baby blanket, and even a tablecloth that she said came from my great-grandmother. She called it the family blanket. In many ways, it's all I have left."

Like a punch to the gut, her words jolted through him. He wanted to ask questions but remained quiet, giving her a chance to simply talk.

"My daddy was a fisherman, and I was raised in Maryland along the Chesapeake Bay. I grew up loving the boats, the beach, digging for clams, or catching crabs for dinner. I was an only child, but not for lack of desire or trying. My parents had several miscarriages before they had me and used to call me their miracle baby. She had a few more miscarriages afterward, but they never made me feel like I wasn't enough. Daddy always called Mom his sweetheart, and I was his little sweetheart. It was the three of us, and it was a good life."

She leaned back against the pillows, a soft sigh escaping her lips. "But fishing is also a hard life, and my parents were older by the time they had me. When I was nine, my dad had a heart attack and died. It broke my mom's heart, and I felt as though I'd lost half my world. Things got really tight, but we were surrounded by good people who stepped in to help. One of them was another fisherman that we'd known for years, and when I was eleven, he and my mom married. He was such a good man and such a good stepfather. He never made me feel like I was extra baggage but always treated me like I was his own. They never had any children, and James used to say that I was his bonus daughter, the one he never thought he'd have."

James. Her stepfather is James... Not a boyfriend. How many times can I make an ass of myself in front of her? Not wanting to know the answer to that question, he hoped, in some small way, he was making it up to her.

Another tear slid down her cheek, this time caught by Jared's fingertip as he brushed it away. She coughed, the sound so hoarse that he almost told her she shouldn't speak more, but whatever was on her mind needed to be said. And the desire to know all about her ran deep, and he remained quiet, waiting as she unburdened herself.

"I wasn't sure what I wanted to do when I graduated from high school, so I joined the Coast Guard and worked as a marine science technician. I was stationed in Miami, did training in California, and was thrilled when I ended up at the base in Chesapeake. The honest truth was that I missed home. I missed Mom and James. I don't make friends easily and always feel alone in a crowd, even in the service. I started volunteering for the Chesapeake Bay Foundation and spent time with NOAA. When I was twenty-six, my mom was diagnosed with cancer, and I left the Guard. I used to make chicken soup for her when she couldn't keep anything else down." Her shoulders hefted, and she gave a slight shrug as her fingers gripped the blanket. "For a year, James and I took care of her as she weakened. When she died, we were both despondent."

"Oh, sweetheart, I'm sorry." He reached over to hold her hands resting on the blanket.

"It was just James and me. I got a job with the NOAA but didn't want to leave the bay, so I now contract with the foundation. It lets me do the job I love and keeps me close enough to my stepfather that I can see him when I want."

"Jesus, Billie, I'm so sorry."

Another little shrug lifted her shoulders. "I was incredibly lucky."

He couldn't imagine what she meant by lucky, considering she'd lost both parents. Other than her stepdad, who sounded like a great guy, she was alone in the world. Reaching down, he placed his hand over hers as it lay on the blanket that he now knew held the history of her family. "Lucky?"

"Yeah," she said, her eyelids blinking as though growing heavy. "A lot of people don't have what I had. Wonderful parents and then a phenomenal stepdad. I know what's important, and I guess that's why I rely so much on myself. I know how quickly things can be taken away."

He wanted to know more, but she yawned and then fell into another coughing fit. He hated to see her small body shaking with the wracking movements. He stalked over to the kitchen and filled her glass with water. Handing it to her, he watched her drain it before handing it back to him with a little smile.

"I can't believe you're really here, Jared."

"Hey, you took care of me last weekend. And it was because of me that you were around all those sick people and got the flu."

"I don't want you to feel obligated."

"No," he rushed. "That's not why I'm doing this. I really want to help." Her eyelids drooped even more, and he said, "Try to sleep. I'm going to run over to my place and let Daisy out, but I'll come back and make sure you're okay." Glad when she didn't argue, he watched as she slid down under the covers, closed her eyes, and fell asleep almost instantly. He gently touched her forehead, relieved it felt cooler, but knew she wasn't over the illness yet.

Standing, he looked down. Her face finally relaxed, and something shifted deep inside his chest. He had no idea what emotion was hitting him, but he wasn't about to deny its existence. There was a helluva lot more to Wilhelmina Schmidt than he'd originally thought, and he wanted to explore everything about her, praying that she'd let him. Bending, he kissed her forehead and slipped back out the door.

Daisy greeted him with enthusiasm, sniffing and seeming to dance when she caught a whiff of Billie's scent on his clothes. "I know, girl," he said, letting her outside. "I kind of feel the same way."

He fixed her dinner when she trotted back into the kitchen. While she ate, he grabbed the sandwich he'd bought from the diner when he bought Billie's soup. Sitting at the counter for his own meal, he glanced around at his house. He wished he could bring Billie to his place to recuperate. *It'd be easier to keep an eye on her.* But his place still needed a lot of work. He'd just gotten the living room set up, although the TV wasn't hung on the wall yet. Looking out the window toward the garage, he then shifted his gaze to Daisy's brown eyes, staring expectantly up at him.

"You want to go, girl?"

Her tail immediately thumped on the floor, and he grinned. "Well, all right, then." He cleaned the kitchen, grabbed a grocery bag with a few items, and secured his house. With Daisy following, he went back up the steps to Billie's apartment. After knocking gently, he let himself in after telling Daisy to stay quiet. Billie was still sleeping, and he walked over to make sure her fever wasn't raging. She was warm to the touch but not as much as she had been earlier.

Taking Daisy's bowl out of the bag, he filled it with fresh water and set it next to the sink. The sun was setting, but it was still early. Settling on the small couch, he leaned back and pulled out his phone, finding the latest book he'd been reading.

At some point, Daisy curled up on the floor next to the bed, her little grunts and snores joining Billie's. The emotion that had moved through his chest earlier shifted deep inside once again. Closing his eyes, he drifted off to sleep with the two girls in his life close by. Hours later, he jerked awake, hearing both Daisy's toenails on the wooden floor and a soft, raspy voice.

Shifting around, he watched Billie sitting in bed, chatting with Daisy. "Oh my, Daisy, I didn't realize I had company. But aren't you such a pretty girl? I'm lucky to have such a sweet Daisy come to see me."

He grinned and sat up, his smile widening when her gaze jerked over to him. Standing, he walked toward the bed, excited to see that she looked less feverish. "You look better, Billie. How do you feel?"

"I ache like I was hit by a truck, but I feel better than yesterday, so that's an improvement." Her eyes moved from his face to the sofa behind him. "Did you sleep there last night?"

Hoping she wasn't angry with his presumptuous decision to stay, he nodded. "I just really didn't want you to be by yourself in case you needed me. You were really out of it yesterday."

"Oh," she mumbled, blushing. "I'm not upset. I just feel really bad that you had to sleep on that sofa. I can't imagine it was very comfortable for you."

He shrugged, then sat on the edge of the bed, one hand rubbing Daisy's head while the other reached out to hold hers. "To be honest, I've slept on worse." Thinking back to her camping out the first night they met each other, he winced. "I'm sure you have, too."

"Oh yeah." She coughed several times but didn't fall into a spasm where she could barely catch her breath. "Are you going to work today?" Before he had a chance to answer, she rolled her eyes and shook her head. "That was a stupid question. Of course, you are."

"Well, I was prepared to call in for a personal day if you weren't any better, and I was going to take you to the doctor. But it seems like your fever has broken."

"I woke up sometime during the night and was sweating like crazy. I kicked off the covers to stay cool. I have body aches, and I still feel like a weight sits on my chest when I breathe, but I feel a lot more human today."

"I'd rather stay here with you," he confessed. Seeing her raised eyebrows, he kept going with his admission. "That's the truth, Billie. Since I started getting to know you last weekend, I'd like to get to know you more. And it also makes me kick myself for the stupid assumptions I've made—"

"I told you that I forgave you for how we met."

"Well, when I came over yesterday, I made a shit comment to you about why your boyfriend wasn't here to take care of you."

Her brow scrunched, and she shook her head. "I don't remember that."

"I think you were delirious before we got your fever down yesterday. But nonetheless, even if you don't remember, I'm sorry I made that comment."

"But I don't have a boyfriend."

"Yeah, I figured that out. I overheard you on the phone with someone named James, and you said you loved him. Then you called me James when I came over yesterday." He sighed heavily while holding her hand and hoping she wouldn't pull away. "And yes, I made a stupid assumption that your boyfriend should be here taking care of you."

"James is my stepfather..." Her nose crinkled, then she added, "Did I tell you that last night?" Her eyes widened suddenly. "I did! Now I remember rambling about my family."

"It wasn't rambling, I promise. I loved hearing everything about your family, but I'm just sorry that you were talking when you probably don't remember anything. Honestly, you didn't say anything bad. You just told me about your parents and James. And you also told me how you went from the Coast Guard to the CBF."

Jerking slightly, she shook her head. "Damn, I must've really been on a roll to talk that much. I never tell people about myself."

"Well, I'm sorry your illness is the reason you did, but I'm really glad to know you better." They were silent for a moment, and the only sound was Daisy's panting. "I guess I need to get ready to go to work."

"I need to let my boss know that it'll be a couple more days of recuperation before I can go out on the water." She squeezed his hand, and his attention shot to where they were connected. "Can Daisy stay with me?"

"I have a better idea. How about you stay at my place today? You can move around on one floor, let her out into the fenced yard, and have a better kitchen."

"Oh… I don't know, Jared. I shouldn't—"

"Yes, you should." Seeing her red-rimmed eyes, red nose, limp hair, and pale complexion, he still thought she was the most beautiful woman he'd ever seen. It was all he could do to keep from pulling her into his arms. The only reason he didn't was that he had a feeling she'd pull back. *With her, I need to go slow and steady.* "Look, you're sick because of me… indirectly, but because of me. But I'm not offering this out of obligation. I'd love to have you there. You can snooze on the sofa. There's a bathroom downstairs. And I have more food in my kitchen."

She pressed her lips together, and her face scrunched in thought. Finally, she shrugged and nodded. "Okay, but I'll shower here and then come over.

I'll bring some work, and I can type up a couple of reports between naps."

"Sounds good but don't get too adventurous. You feel better now because you slept and your fever broke. But you're still in bed and will be shocked at the body aches when you move around." He glanced toward the bathroom door. "Um… should I…?"

"No! I can handle my shower this time." A deep blush filled her cheeks. "I should be mortified that you had to see me at my worst. Sweaty. Stinky. Totally yucky—"

"Beautiful," he interrupted. She blinked but snapped her mouth closed, so he continued. "Even sick, you're beautiful."

She blinked again, but he just squeezed her hand this time and stood. "Come on, Daisy. Let's leave her to shower." He walked to the door and said, "I'll shower at my place and then come back to take you over. I don't want you to fall on the stairs."

Another blush crossed her cheeks, and she nodded. Grinning, he opened the door and let Daisy bound down the stairs, excited for what she could tell must be a new adventure.

If he had his way, his dog wasn't the only one excited about a new adventure.

16

"She's at your place?" Callan asked while checking the equipment on the vessel.

"Yeah. I got her settled before I left." Jared still had more time left on his light-duty restrictions but felt good and was assisting with the restocking.

"Why? I mean, she just lives over your garage, so why have her in your house?" Andy asked, his incredulity apparent. "If she's that sick, you don't want her spreading germs everywhere." He was hosing down the deck and turned to look over his shoulder. "I guess she could clean for you since you'll have to disinfect the house when she leaves."

Hands on his hips, Jared caught Callan's smirk before he turned his full attention toward Andy, who'd never met a woman he wanted to spend more than one night with. He didn't know a lot about his friend's background, considering Andy tended to keep conversations light. All he knew was that his mom had left when he was a kid, leaving Andy's dad to raise him and his brother. Jared wasn't into psychoanalyzing his friends and coworkers, but he had a feeling Andy's non-trust of women stemmed from *mommy* issues.

"Look, man, I'm not making her scrub my house. She got sick because she was stuck in the ER after being a good person and taking care of me. I was an asshole to her on more than one occasion, and she didn't deserve that. While I'm at work for the next couple of days, she can recuperate at my house, keep Daisy company, and with a full-sized stove and refrigerator, she'll have more than what she has in the efficiency."

Ryan had walked out onto the deck, bringing another box of supplies with him, hearing the last of their conversation. "Makes sense to me, but I'm curious. You make it sound like there's something wrong with the efficiency, yet you stayed there when you first bought the place. And you've been renting it to her."

He worked to keep the grimace from his face. "No, there's nothing wrong with it, per se. It's exactly as advertised—an efficiency. Plus, the real estate agent went over everything with her when she rented, so she knew there was just a mini fridge, a hot plate, and a small microwave. And when I was over there checking on her the last couple of days, she's a perfect renter. Neat and clean. But it's also really… well, closed in and small for someone who's sick."

"I don't know a woman that doesn't spread their shit out everywhere!" Andy said, shaking his head. "Hell, that's why I don't take anybody back to my house. The last time I had a bar pickup at my house, I woke up the next morning, and they had all their makeup on my counters, travel bottles of shampoo in my shower, and they were digging through my refrigerator! Nope, not for me!"

Torn between wanting to slap Andy on the back of the head and rolling his eyes, Jared decided that ignoring his friend for the moment was the best course of action. Looking over at Callan and Ryan, he continued. "Her mini fridge is fine for keeping a few items in, which is all I was doing. But there's not a lot of room to keep any kind of supplies, considering she doesn't feel like going out shopping. I have plenty of stuff at my place, so it just made sense to let her hang there."

"Just be careful," Andy said, shaking his head. "Women can get really used to stuff. When she gets better, she won't want to go back to her place."

"I don't think that's going to be a problem." He laughed at the thought of her not wanting her own space. "She's too independent to want to rely on anyone else. It's been like pulling teeth just to get her to let me help take care of her."

Conversations rolled around to other topics, but Jared found his mind wandering. Standing on the docked vessel, he couldn't wait to get back out on the water. He also thought of several of the projects he wanted to start next on his house and wondered if Billie was serious about helping. She'd certainly hung the new light fixture perfectly.

Callan's radio sounded with a call out from their dispatcher, startling Jared from his thoughts. Hopping off the vessel, he threw his hand up in a wave, hating that his fellow officers had to leave him behind.

Ryan clapped him on the back. "Won't be long. As soon as Judith clears you, then you'll be back out there."

Nodding, he said, "I'm going tomorrow to see her again. Hopefully, I can get cleared so that I can be back out on Friday and not have to wait until Monday."

"Don't rush it. Some things need to take time."

He watched as Ryan headed back inside, then turned to stare out over the harbor, Billie on his mind. "True words," he mumbled to himself, then smiled at the thought of the time he'd willingly spend to get to know her more.

"No, Rita, I swear, I'm getting better."

"Well, you sound like shit, Billie. I don't want you back on the water until you're sure you're better. In fact, you need to see a doctor. What if you end up with pneumonia? Or bronchitis? Or..."

"Okay, I get it. Not getting back to work on the water for a few more days. But I can do a little more research. At least you'll be able to send the results to the EPA. It'd be nice if all the farmers would work together to reduce the chemicals, but I've already run into a few that aren't happy to see me. One even had a rifle prominently displayed in his hands!"

"Oh lordy," Rita exclaimed. "Just be careful."

"You know me... I do my job and stay out of other people's business. I'll send you the latest reports once I get them updated."

With goodbyes said, she disconnected her phone and

walked to the back door to see Daisy lounging on the sunny patio. Opening the door, she decided that the sweet dog had the right idea. Grabbing her jacket to keep off any possible chill, she settled into a lounger and closed her eyes, one hand resting on Daisy's head.

"Hey," a soft voice said from close by as a gentle touch shook her shoulder.

Sitting up quickly, she snapped her eyes open to see Jared standing next to her with Daisy trotting around with her ball. "Oh! I must have fallen asleep!"

"You think?" he asked, mirth dancing in his eyes.

Mesmerized by the blue eyes that were staring straight at her, sending swirls of ache through her that had nothing to do with the flu, she hoped she wasn't drooling. Wiping her mouth, she mumbled, "What time is it?"

"It's five o'clock. I got off shift and ran by the pub to get some turkey club sandwiches. I wasn't sure if you'd feel like eating, but I thought they would be a little more substantial than just soup."

Her brain was stuck back on the time. "I can't believe I slept so long! Oh God, my back is stiff!" Before she had a chance to push herself up farther, his face was close to hers as his hands moved under her armpits, and with little effort, he lifted her to her feet, sliding his hands down to her waist to steady her.

"I'm not surprised you slept. You're still recuperating. And I'm glad you rested because that's the best thing for you right now."

She stretched, working out the kinks while trying to ignore the fact that his hands were still spanning her waist. “Well, I meant to get a few more reports complete. I did a little work this morning and talked to my boss, then came out here, and well, I guess that’s the last thing that happened before I fell asleep.”

“Do you feel like you can eat?”

Grinning, she nodded. “Oh yeah. For the first time in several days, I’m really hungry.”

“Good! That’s another sign that you're healing.”

He let go of her waist slowly as though reluctant. As soon as his fingers left, she felt the loss, but then he threw an arm casually around her shoulders and guided her back inside.

With Daisy trotting along, Billie couldn’t help but feel the brand his touch created on her skin through her sweater. They sat at the counter as he pulled out the toasted sandwiches, and while he had a beer, she drank water and ate half of her large meal. “I can save the other half and eat it tomorrow.”

He nodded while still chewing.

“And I can stay at my place tomorrow. It was nice to sit outside since the weather was so comfortable, but I’ll be fine at my place tomorrow.”

“There’s no reason for you not to stay over here during the day, Billie. Seriously, I know Daisy loves having you around. And as you said, you can enjoy the backyard more from here. Plus, I have to admit that when I lived there, it never dawned on me how few windows the apartment had, making it pretty dark.”

“But it’s my home, Jared.”

He shifted around on his counter stool and held her gaze. She battled the desire to shift on the stool as he stared, seeming to want to see deeper inside. Feeling the need to explain her last comment, she added, "I mean, it's not my forever home. And, of course, it's just a rental, but it's mine for now."

He wiped his mouth with a paper towel before wadding it and tossing it onto his empty plate. Nodding slowly, he continued to hold her gaze. "I get that. And even though there's not a lot of your personal stuff around, I don't mind if you decorate it to make it seem more like your space. And I'm not trying to take away your independence, but it doesn't make sense to stay closed up there during the day when you could be here."

He chuckled, and she noticed the tips of his ears pinkened as he continued. "It's just that I like the idea of you having more space, more light, more of an outdoor area, and a bigger kitchen for these days when you're stuck at home and can't go to work. And I know that Daisy loves having company. While I can't insist, I do hope you'll keep coming over."

She'd given him every reason to take back his invitation, but he turned her down, his sincerity palpable. Smiling her thanks, she nodded. "Well, my boss told me she didn't want me back out on the water until after this weekend, anyway, so I do have several more days where I could certainly help keep an eye on Daisy."

He clapped his hands and then rubbed them together while grinning. "Good, that's settled! Now, since you've been resting, eating your first full meal, your fever is gone, and your coughing spasms are fewer than they were, how about helping me figure out my next household project?"

She couldn't keep the smile from her face at the idea of planning another project. When she turned back, her breath halted in her lungs at the sight of his smile aimed at her, filling the empty spaces inside. "Yeah. I'd love to."

"Come on." He reached out to take her hand and gently pulled her from her seat.

She followed eagerly, assuming he'd drop her hand, but when he didn't, she tried not to read anything into the gesture. He made it to the bottom of the stairs and turned, his brow furrowed. Halting, she waited to see what brought about the concerned expression.

"Are you gonna be okay? Going up the stairs?"

"I better be! I'm in trouble if I don't have the energy or the lung capacity to climb stairs!"

"Whenever you start feeling better after being sick, you always think you can do so much. And then, when you actually start doing it, you realize how much more healing you have to do."

Still holding her hand, he started up the stairs slowly, then pointed at the railing. "The railing is secure, but someone redid it years ago, and it's not very well done. I want to replace it, but only when I can get spindles that look like they might be closer to the originals."

"They were originally square in this type of house, weren't they? Less ornamental?"

He whipped his head around, his hand holding hers, jerking slightly. "Yeah. How did you know that?"

She reached out with her free hand and ran it gently over the railing. "When my mom was sick, we'd watch TV together. James and I agreed that I wouldn't go back to work for a while and take care of her. We both loved the home TV shows. I fell in love with the idea of taking something old and bringing it back to life. You're living my dream," she admitted with a little shrug.

He said nothing, so she looked up in embarrassment only to find his warm gaze moving over her. Neither spoke as the warmth settled around them, as comfortable as her old blanket.

Finally, he whispered, "Come on."

She nodded, and they continued up the stairs slowly. She had to admit that by the top landing, she was breathing heavily. He'd been right in his assessment that she still had more recuperation even though she was much better. The idea of trying to get out on the water and do anything physically demanding was out of the question right now.

"I know I showed you this the other day, but we can take a more thorough look now. Up here, I redid the floors and painted my bedroom because I wanted to be comfortable here. I also upgraded the bathroom."

She took a long look at his bedroom, not surprised at its neatness. She noticed that other than some of the work materials downstairs, his space was clean, and everything was put away. The room was not huge but managed to hold a king-size bed, a chest of drawers, and a comfortable chair with a floor lamp in the corner. The walls were soft gray, with the one behind the headboard painted a darker bluish-gray, similar to the color scheme he'd used in the living room. With a navy comforter, the room gave off a masculine vibe.

The top of the chest of drawers held a tray, where he placed his keys and wallet. Two framed photos grabbed her attention. One of them showed him in a Coast Guard uniform with several uniformed men and women surrounding him.

"Those were my best buddies from the Guard. That was taken not too long before I got out."

She nodded silently as her gaze moved to the next photo, obviously his family from their similar looks. An older man with the same build and hair color and piercing blue eyes had his arm around a beautiful woman, also with blue eyes. She easily recognized a teenaged Jared, grinning widely at the camera while his arm rested around the shoulders of a girl who appeared several years younger than him but had the same fine-boned face and blue eyes as the mother.

"That's my dad, mom, and little sister."

"Genetics are strong in your family. You look just like your dad, and your sister looks just like your mom. But considering they both have dark brown hair and blue eyes, it makes all of you look alike." She continued to allow her gaze to soak in his family, then glanced to the side. "Everyone looks happy."

"Dad probably ordered us to smile, so we all did," he admitted. Shrugging, he added, "My parents were good people, but my dad was authoritarian in his job as a Naval officer, and those traits carried over into the family."

"Oh," she said, chewing on her bottom lip, unsure what else to say.

"My dad and I butted heads a lot when I was growing up, especially when I hit my teens until… well, for quite a few years. He wanted me to attend a military academy, and I just wanted to get on with life, so I joined the Coast Guard right out of high school." Sighing, he shook his head. "He was pissed. Said a lot of shit about me giving up, not living up to my potential, being defiant... you name it, he said it." Shrugging, he added, "But things are better now."

She couldn't imagine having that kind of pressure when she was growing up and wondered if his dad ever accepted the wonderful man Jared had become. She stared at him, trying to figure out if he was truthful when he said things were better now. "And your mom?"

He hesitated, wincing slightly. "She... um... this feels insensitive."

Cocking her head to the side, she waited.

"Oh hell, Billie. Mom had a cancer scare about seven years ago, but she's fine now."

She could feel how uncomfortable he was discussing cancer, and she rushed, "Jared, I'm sorry for your family but thrilled that your mom is well. I would never be upset that someone else's mom got better!"

"I know that, Billie. You're just that caring."

His gaze bore straight into her, and for a moment, neither spoke as emotions swirled around the room, embracing them. Finally, she broke the silence. ""Where are they? Your parents?"

"They live in Florida. They've got a great place with a pool and a view of the gulf. My sister went to college and then decided to become a pilot. She flies commercial jets all over the country for a major airline."

"I'm impressed," she said, smiling at the obvious pride he had with his family.

"I think Mom's illness finally shook something loose in my dad. He'd just retired from the Navy, and the idea of not having her around for the things they'd planned on doing scared him into realizing what was important. He became… easier to talk to. Less judgmental." Snorting, he added, "He actually said he was proud of me the last time I visited."

Once again, she spied the little boy hiding deep inside the body of a man and smiled. "I'm glad."

His lips curved, and he took her hand again, leading her from his bedroom and into the bathroom. She looked around appreciatively. "This truly is a dream room!" The white tile with swirls of gray covered the floor and walls around the large soaker tub with a navy shower curtain pulled to the side. The walls were pale blue, and the bottom panes of the window were frosted to let in light but keep anyone from seeing in.

He opened the door to the other bedroom but winced when he stepped inside. "You saw my mess the other day, but I don't know if you got a chance to see the walls."

The room held hideous floral wallpaper, some of it peeling from around the window, which was new.

"The room is a good size," she said, looking around, already imagining it being as nice as the primary bedroom and making a perfect guest room.

Once downstairs again, he talked about his plans for the downstairs bathroom and laundry room. "One day, I'd like to enlarge the house by adding on to the back."

Turning around, she smiled. "I think the work you've done is fabulous, Jared. You were smart to buy a home that had good bones yet gives you the opportunity to make your own."

"What do you think I ought to do next? The guest room or finish the work downstairs?"

"Do you really wanna know what I think?" Shrugging, she added, "I've never been a homeowner before. Renting or even camping out always worked for me."

His head jerked slightly at her response.

"Oh." She waved her hand dismissively. "I don't mean to make it sound so dire. I went from living at home to the CG, where housing was provided. Then I was back at home. Since being on my own, I've mostly just rented. And I've certainly camped when I had some work to do on the bay that kept me from going home each night. Before renting your place, I thought about buying a small camper to make things easier."

"God, I'm glad you didn't!" he blurted.

She opened her mouth to agree but snapped it closed again, uncertain about reading too much into what he was saying. *Maybe he's just glad to have the rental money.* She looked away, his gaze too penetrating for her to hold.

"I'd really like to know what you think," Jared said, stepping closer, and reaching down to take her hand again.

Uncertain about the closeness, she couldn't deny how nice it felt. But just walking up and down the stairs had made her tired, and she knew it wouldn't be long before sleep claimed her again. "I guess my simple answer would be, what do you need the soonest? If you think your parents or sister will come visit, then you might want to work on the upstairs guest room. Of course, if you weren't renting to me, you'd have a guest room over the garage."

"I don't think they're going to come anytime soon. They visited a couple of months ago, so it'll probably be the holidays before I see them again."

"Then I'd say paint the dining room, furnish it, and decide what you want to do about the laundry room and bathroom. Right now, that's one big space, but I actually like the idea of a smaller powder room that opens onto this hall and then a separate laundry room."

A smile curved his lips as he nodded. "That was exactly what I was thinking, so it's nice to hear you're in agreement."

Throwing her head back to laugh, she ended up coughing again. Once she gained control, she mumbled, "Sorry."

"Don't be sorry for something you can't help." He reached out to tuck a strand of hair behind her ear. "You look much better than you did, and I almost forgot that you're still sick. I'll walk you back to your place."

Waiting for their evening to end, she knew it was best. With Daisy running around the yard, he escorted her back to her front door, checking to make sure she had everything she needed.

Turning to say goodbye, she hesitated. "I was serious when I said I'd like to help with your house. I totally understand if that's not something you want. But if you ever need an extra pair of hands, let me know."

He stepped closer, ducking slightly to hold her gaze. "Oh, I plan on holding you to that promise." Before she had a chance to react, he leaned forward and kissed her forehead, holding his lips on her skin for a moment, then leaned back and whispered, "Lock up after me."

She stood in the middle of her apartment, mouth open, eyes wide, staring at the now-closed front door, listening to his steps going down the stairs. Feeling as though she had fallen asleep and woken up in an alternate universe, she shook her head before getting ready for bed. Having no idea what universe she might wake up to the following morning, she hoped it was as nice as the one she had just been in.

17

"Hey!" Jared called out, turning around to see a grinning Billie with paint swipes on her cheeks, arms, and pants. "Are you getting any on the walls?"

"Take a look," she demanded, cocking her hip as she waved her arms.

He was looking, but it wasn't at the wall. His gaze filled with the glow on her skin, the bright twinkle in her eyes, how she'd pulled her light-blonde hair into a messy bun with tendrils framing her face, and the way the old T-shirt stretched over her figure, including a gray paint smudge just over her left breast. His mouth went dry, and he had to clear his throat to be able to speak. Dragging his gaze to the wall next to her, he could see that she had indeed painted more than just herself. The wall looked perfect. *And so does she.*

He wrapped his arms around her and hugged her back and forth, eliciting a giggle that he'd fallen in love with hearing. Tamping down the idea that there were other things he loved about her, he said, "Looks great!"

With a few more days of rest and sleep-filled nights of recuperation, Billie had started helping him with the house project they'd agreed upon—putting up a wall to divide the downstairs half bathroom and laundry room. The division of the space made sense when he thought of giving house guests more privacy. Plus, it allowed the laundry room to be used as storage and a pantry. Since they built the wall between the two spaces, he wouldn't need new plumbing or electrical work, which was a huge savings for him.

They'd worked on the project together, filling their time with conversations about work, families, favorite shows, and movies. And every minute he spent with her only served to make him interested in spending more minutes in her presence. He'd often reach out to touch her shoulder, link fingers with her, and tuck a strand of hair behind her ear. Always cautiously, never wanting to touch her without her willingness. But so far, each time, she'd offered a small smile as though surprised. How someone as beautiful and special as Billie should be surprised that any man wanted to be with her, he had no idea. But each day, she not only filled space in his house but also in his heart.

Still in his arms, she lifted and leaned back to hold his gaze. "Thank you."

"For what?"

"For letting me be a part of this. A part of what you're creating here. For letting me hang out with you. For keeping me from just staying in my apartment alone."

"You don't have to thank me for anything. I love having you help."

Her breath hitched slightly as her gaze dropped to his lips. His arms flexed, tightening around her. Lowering his head slowly, he waited to check her response, wanting her acquiescence yet willing to stop if she needed that. She lifted on her toes again, meeting him halfway. Their lips sealed, and he felt her weight as she leaned farther into him. He wanted to take the kiss further… deeper. Calling upon every ounce of self-control he could muster to keep from plundering her mouth, he angled his head and touched his tongue to her lips, sweeping inside when she opened for him. She tasted of chocolate, courtesy of the cake he'd brought home when he'd stopped by the Seafood Shack for wings. Her mouth was velvet as her tongue glided over his, and his cock leaped to attention, a common state ever since she'd been around.

Pulling back regretfully, he smiled at her hooded eyes, kiss-swollen lips, and sweet breath puffing over his face as she breathed heavily. Seeing her as affected as he was sent a thrill through him.

"Wow," she breathed, blinking as though awakening from a dream.

"Yeah, wow," he agreed. No doubt a lightning bolt of lust had struck him, but unlike any woman before, he wanted more. Not just sex. Not just one night. He wanted to carry her upstairs to his bed. Lay her out across the mattress. Let her hair flow over his pillow. And take all night to discover the pleasures of her body and give as much as he received. Swallowing deeply, he loosened his hold. *Not tonight. Not until she's sure 'cause there's no way I want just a one-and-done with her.*

The sound of tires on his oyster-shell driveway met his ears, and from her jerking in his arms, she'd heard it, too. He looked out the kitchen window and spied several SUVs and pickup trucks pulling up to his house. Recognizing several of them, he sighed. He looked down to catch Billie's surprise. "I'm sorry," he said. "Looks like some friends are coming by."

"Oh… um…okay. I'll just head up to my place."

"Hell, no, Billie. I want you here. Most of them you'll meet at the AL activities, and from the looks of it, some women came also. If I had to guess, they want to meet you." She started to pull away, but he held tight as she looked out the window, the tension in her jaw. "And Billie?"

She looked back toward him.

"I'm always glad to see friends, but this time, their timing sucks. I'd like to finish what we started." He held his breath, waiting to see her response. She didn't disappoint.

A wide smile curved her lips. "Me too," she whispered, lifting on her toes to place a chaste kiss on the corner of his mouth.

The air rushed from his lungs, and he considered the possibility of heading outside to tell his friends to get lost. But before he could ponder the validity of that idea, Billie tugged on his hand, and he gave in, following her onto the patio.

Several hours later, he looked at a group of women sitting on the patio. Ginny, one of the women Billie met at the AL meeting, had come with her husband, Brogan MacFarlane, one of the pub's owners. When Jared had picked up their food, he'd mentioned to Brogan that Billie was his renter and had been sick, so he was getting extra food. His brother, Aiden MacFarlane, was nearby and gossiped as much as any of the women. He'd wrangled the rest of the MacFarlanes—his wife, Lia, his sister Katelyn and her husband, Gareth. Callan brought his wife, Sophie. Several of their kids ran around with Daisy, and they soon had an impromptu meal with the food the others brought.

At first, he'd been terrified that Billie would back away, but he should have known that the women of Baytown had a history of welcoming newcomers. Callan and Billie discussed where they'd been stationed in the Coast Guard. Sophie was an interior designer, and she'd walked around with Billie as they talked about a few ideas for the house, which thrilled Jared. It wasn't lost on him that with any other woman, he'd be pissed if they'd offered decorating ideas. But with her, he knew she wasn't taking over but sincerely enjoyed the idea of a house with history.

"Looks good on you."

He turned to look at Callan approaching with a beer in his hand. Taking it, he cocked his head to the side.

Callan chuckled. "A relationship with a woman who's deserving of you."

His gaze moved from his friend over to where Billie had thrown her head back in a laugh, and he swallowed past the lump that had formed in his throat. He simply nodded while gathering himself and finally managed to say, "It feels good to have met someone who fits. Who makes me think there's more I can give."

"I'd say you've found it."

A few minutes later, he walked over as the gathering began to break up, parents corralled their kids, and goodbyes were being said.

"Hey, Jared!" Aiden called out. "Billie's a runner. We need to sign her up on our AL team for the Holiday Hope run."

He stepped close to her and caught her inquisitive expression. "It's our December fundraiser," he explained. "We get into teams, get the community involved, and have a fun race." He held his breath, hoping she would agree, indicating she'd still be here in another month.

"Sounds good," she said, her eyes bright. "I'd love to."

Letting out his breath, he hid his relief and offered handshakes to the men and cheek kisses to the women, noting that Billie was the recipient of many hugs. When the last vehicle finally pulled away, they walked back to the kitchen. Once they'd put the remaining food away, he stepped forward and placed his hands on either side of her, effectively caging her in against the counter. Her arms snaked around his neck as he leaned in for a kiss.

She pressed tightly to him, immediately angling her head so the kiss could go deeper. His tongue slid between her open lips, but she was ready, and they drank from each other. He swallowed the tiny moan that escaped from her.

Leaning forward, he pressed his front to hers from knees to chest, shifting slightly so her back wasn't digging into the edge of the counter. His hand dove into her hair, pulling out the hair tie and threading his fingers through her silken tresses.

Her chest heaved, pressing her breasts deeper against his chest, and he longed to explore every curve. His cock swelled painfully in his jeans, and the desire to take her upstairs almost overrode all other considerations.

Finally, with every ounce of self-control he could muster, he pulled back, his vision full of her kiss-plump lips and half-hooded eyes shining with lust. "It's getting late, babe," he managed to mumble.

"Hmm?" she murmured, still dreamy-eyed.

"As much as I love you being here and staring at me like that, I need to walk you back to your place."

"Oh." She blinked, pulling back. Her hand lifted to her lips as a blush covered her cheeks.

Hating the doubt that filled her eyes, he cupped her cheeks, holding her in place. "Simply because you're still recuperating, and I only want to take this further when you're one hundred percent."

"Oh," she repeated, her lips curving and her eyes twinkling again. "And I thought you just liked me for my painting skills."

He tossed his head back and laughed, willing his cock to stop hating him for the separation. "Come on, Daisy," he called, patting his leg. "Let's walk our girl back."

They made it to the top of the garage stairs, and she turned to ask, "Do you want to come in?"

He nodded slowly but said, "No way."

"You know your head and your words didn't match, right?"

Chuckling, he nodded. "Again, I want you well and ready for whatever we decide to do. And that's why we're taking things slowly." With that, he kissed her lightly and ushered her inside. Waiting to hear the lock click, he then jogged back down the stairs with Daisy on his heels. As he walked into his house, he could still feel her lips pressed to his.

18

By Monday morning, Billie was grateful to finally feel well enough to be back out on the water. She lifted her face to the morning sun and guided her boat along the coast, a wide smile battling for supremacy with a light heart.

At Jared's suggestion, she wore a knit cap as well as had her sweatshirt hoodie pulled up over her head. He insisted that she see Judith before going back out on the water. Unused to someone trying to tell her what to do, he'd been backed up by Rita, who also insisted.

In truth, she'd enjoyed talking to Judith, who was a fount of information about Baytown and the Virginia Marine Police. She even threw in a few tidbits about Jared. She'd declared Billie fit to go back to work with the usual precautions. "You'll have a lingering cough for a while, but if it or any of your previous symptoms gets worse, come in to see me."

She thought about kissing Jared, and the idea of

having a coughing spasm in the middle of their next kiss had her promise she'd take care of herself. Her cheeks heated at the thought, and she welcomed the fresh air as she boated along.

She'd relished the past few days with him. The care he'd shown had been a surprise, touching her deeply in the place where she'd buried her grief after her mother died. As she'd regained strength each day, she'd gone over to let Daisy run in the yard, and since Jared had insisted on her being able to use his kitchen, she'd not only fixed simple lunches for herself, she'd even cooked dinner for him when he got off shift.

The expression on his face when he'd walked in to find homemade spaghetti and meatballs, salad, and garlic bread sitting on his counter had been worth the fatigue of being on her feet for several hours. After he'd fussed, his words fell away to a groan when he'd taken the first bite.

He'd painted the dining room, insisting that he didn't want her to exert herself by helping but wanted her close by. She'd stirred the paint and scraped the old paint from the doors before he pulled up the counter stool and told her to plant her ass in it. Growing fatigued was the only reason she'd acquiesced without complaint. And the fact that she'd had the unadulterated view to ogle him as his muscles were on display made it easier to just sit and watch.

At first, she couldn't figure out why he was being so nice. If it was just because he felt guilty that she'd gotten sick from the ER trip, he could have checked on her, brought a few groceries, and that would be it. But he'd seemed to want her closer, occasionally touching her hand or shoulder when they moved about the kitchen area. She had no doubt that if she'd wanted him to back off, he would have. Instead, she'd craved each time their hands had met, or he'd tucked a strand of hair behind her ear.

And for the first time in a long time, she'd caught herself daydreaming of having a relationship with someone. Then they'd shared their first kiss. Holy moly… what a kiss. She'd felt the tingle right down to her curled toes. Hell, it wasn't like she was an untried virgin. But she'd never felt her entire body respond to a kiss like that. And when he ended it to walk her back to her place, she'd wanted to jump into his arms, wrap her legs around his waist, and not come up for air until the following morning.

And he'd said he wanted more when she was better. *I have to get better soon, or I'll spontaneously combust!*

Now, steering her boat toward one of the smaller oyster farm beds, she gave her head a little shake. *Time to pull out of dreamland and get back to work.*

Coming to a stop, she made sure to clearly have her identification lanyard around her neck since her last encounters with the vegetable farmers who'd made it known they didn't like her presence even if she wasn't on their land. The last thing she wanted was for an oyster farmer to take umbrage with her testing near their beds.

Bending to her task, she dropped her weighted line

for the water collection equipment down to the reef covered in oysters. Glad the day was not cold, she slipped her hoodie back but left her cap on.

"Hey!"

The shout rang out over the water, causing her to swing her head around, her braid slinging over her shoulder. Squinting, she observed an old, open-deck boat with a man standing inside, his narrow-eyed gaze boring straight into her as he held a long-handled oyster rake in a threatening position.

"Oh, sorry... I didn't know you were a girl," he muttered but kept his hand on his rake. "What are you doing? These are my beds."

She quickly held up her ID. "I'm from the Chesapeake Bay Foundation. I'm testing the water. I've been in the nearby inlets and seen a rise in toxins. I wanted to check the levels where some of the oyster beds are."

"Hmph," he groused but lowered his rake. "Fucking poisons get in the water through no fault of mine, yet I'll pay the price if you say my oysters aren't no good."

"Sir, I have no control over your oysters. The CBF is tasked to monitor the water in the bay, but we don't have any authority to tell farmers, either on the land or the water, what they can and can't do. I'm just a collector of information." Hoping to erase some of the suspicion in his eyes, she added, "My dad was a fisherman. Rockfish mostly. Up in Maryland."

"He no longer do it?"

"He passed away years ago."

The fisherman's shoulders slumped. "Sorry to hear

that." He looked away, his gaze moving over the water. "It's a hard life."

"Yes, it is. But he wouldn't have done anything else. He loved it."

The farmer's lips curved slightly. "Yeah. Same for me. Lou Akers, by the way."

Rubbing her lips together, she glanced down before pulling her testing equipment back up. "Billie Schmidt. Nice to meet you. Um… I'll be finished in just a few minutes and then can get out of your hair."

"Aw, you're not in my way once I discovered you weren't no poacher."

She chuckled and inclined her head toward the rake in his hand. "Glad you're convinced. I'm afraid the corn farmers nearby weren't easy to appease."

"Who? Old man Harper?"

"Um… well, there are several whose farms back to the inlets that run straight out here."

"Yeah, I know who you're talking about. Old Jed Harper and that rascal Porter Nevins. They've been farming the land out here since their daddies and their daddies' daddies. I'd say their bark is worse than their bite."

She thought of the rifles so casually held in their arms but kept that tidbit to herself. "Sometimes it's hard for people to see outsiders, thinking they're out for something. I just want to ensure the bay is healthy, including your oysters and all the other aquatic life. But I'm not here to make them do anything… that's not my job."

He nodded but continued to stare intensely, making

her want to hurry and finish. Looking down, she placed the water in various containers and marked them for identification. Finally finished, she offered a smile and said, "Well, I'll be on my way, Mr. Akers."

"You can just call me Lou. If you like oysters, drop by the Brewsters Aqua Farm. That's where I take my haul after I sell a few directly to some customers at the harbor."

"Thanks. I might just do that."

Starting her engine again, she moved to the next place for water testing, and then with fatigue pulling at her, she decided that working half a day was good enough after having the flu.

She maneuvered away from the shore, leaving him to his oyster bed, then decided to make a quick trip into the inlet to check the water since she had missed almost a week. If she had no more interruptions, it would be very quick. Twenty minutes later had proven her right, and she was back out on the bay. Passing the oyster beds from earlier, she didn't see Lou anywhere but assumed he had oyster beds all up and down the coast.

She kept her pace slow, enjoying the warm fall day and not wanting to create an extra breeze from rushing over the water. She closed her eyes for a few seconds, allowing the sun's rays to beam down on her, making her feel more alive than she had since she'd gotten sick.

A thump landed on the side of her boat, and she rocked perilously, immediately steering away so her small motor wouldn't hit whatever object had been in the water. *What the fuck was that?* She hoped it wasn't an injured sea turtle, having seen one earlier in the year on the Virginia Beach side of the bay.

She looked around in haste, instantly afraid she'd gotten too close to shore, but quickly ascertained she hadn't. Looking over her shoulder, she didn't see anything in the water that would've hit the side of her boat.

With her gaze circling the area, she slowed her engine to a crawl, leaning over the edge, trying to discern anything in the water. A murky blob appeared near the surface, and upon initial observation of the brown material, she wondered if it was a large duffel bag.

"Christ, people are such pigs," she muttered, thinking of the pollution and how it affected the bay. Looking in her boat for something she could drag it out with, she grabbed a heavy pair of gloves. Wanting to be careful in case it contained sharp objects or refuse, she gently reached her hand down into the water. As soon as she grasped the object, she pulled, surprised at its weight. When her hand broke the surface, she confirmed her fingers were clutching cloth. *What the hell is this?*

With another hefty tug, she was able to pull it upward a little farther. Her brain was several seconds behind her vision when reality slammed into her, and she jerked her hand back, gasping, as she scrambled backward, screaming, "Shit!"

A violent shudder slammed through her at the sight of the partially skeletal human body that began to sink into the bay again. But just as quickly, knowing she needed to do something, she leaned over the side of the boat and reached out. "Oh God! Oh God! Oh God!" she chanted, her stomach threatening to expel its contents at the idea of what she'd come across.

She had no idea what to do. She couldn't leave human remains. She couldn't let it sink back into the water, but she wasn't strong enough to haul it into the boat. Looking around, she grabbed a coil of rope near her feet and managed to loop it around the sleeve of the jacket. Pulling it up, the hand lifted into sight.

Another violent shudder hit her as she stared at the decayed, almost skeletal hand. Still holding the end of the rope, she leaned to the side and retched. She leaned back when her stomach was empty of what little she'd eaten. Her chest heaved as she tried to suck air into her lungs, but she felt as though she couldn't get enough. Light-headed, she knew she couldn't leave the body and couldn't drag it along with her.

Wrapping the other end of the rope around the seat on her boat, she grabbed her backpack, digging around for her phone. Her mind raced faster than her fingers could move. "Shit, shit, shit, shit!"

Dialing 911, she barked out, "I'm Wilhelmina Schmidt, and I'm a water analyzer for CBF in the bay. I've come across a dead body!" The dispatcher asked questions, but her mind raced ahead. "I'm about three miles north of Baytown Harbor, near the Wilder Pond inlet." Once she received assurances that the marine police and Coast Guard were on their way, she assured the dispatcher she'd stay there and lowered the phone into her lap.

Still sucking in air, she leaned all the way back to keep from looking at the body. Staring up at the blue sky, she remembered how she'd thought the day was beautiful just an hour earlier. Now, she was floating on the bay with a dead body attached to her boat. Jerking upward, she leaned over the far side and dry-heaved.

19

Jared reveled in being out on the water with the sun beaming down in the cloudless sky. The autumn temperatures kept the day perfect. Patrols had been easy during the morning, and the two vessels were almost ready to head back to the station for lunch.

The dispatcher radioed. "All units. A reported possible ten-eighty-two, three miles north of Baytown Harbor, near the Wilder Pond inlet."

He blinked before his eyes widened, his gaze jerking to Joseph, who was steering the boat he was on. "Copy that. Vessel four en route," Joseph radioed.

Looking behind him, he spied Andy and Callan following, hearing, "Vessel six en route."

"Call for the medical examiner," Ryan radioed before adding, "Vessel two en route."

"Be advised, Coast Guard is en route as well. ETA ten minutes."

He yelled over his shoulder, "We'll get there before the CG." With the VMP boats arriving first, he wanted to know if he was facing a fisherman or a vacationer. He radioed, "Who called in the report?"

"A water analyzer from the CBF," the dispatcher responded.

The air rushed from Jared's lungs. He only knew of one CBF water analyzer working in this area, and that was Billie. Changing frequencies, he radioed the other VMPs. "Shit, that's got to be Billie!"

"Steady," Ryan radioed.

Jared remembered when Ryan's wife and teenage daughter came across a dead man in a small boat while kayaking, but at least Judith was a doctor. *Fuck... Billie's probably freaking out.*

"I'm getting you there, man," Joseph called out.

The wind slammed into him as Joseph increased their speed. As they rounded a bend, he caught sight of a small, single-engine boat in the water, a lone figure leaning to the side as they appeared to hold something in their hands. Tendrils of white-blonde hair whipped about her head, and for some reason, it snagged his attention that she should have her hood up for protection. He winced at the incongruity of worry about her getting sick again when she was faced with discovering a dead body. Moving quickly toward the front of the boat, Joseph slowed to a crawl, and he just wanted to pull her into his arms.

Callan radioed, "Remember, Jared, by the book."

As soon as he got close, he called out, "Billie? Billie?"

She squinted with the sun reflecting off the water but didn't let go of whatever she was holding on to. "Jared?"

He'd seen her as a professional. He'd seen her when she was angry. He'd seen her when she was in a take-charge situation. He'd seen her when she was ill. He'd seen her being stubborn, funny, caring, and frustrated. But he'd never witnessed the expression in her glassy-eyed stare. He glanced down to see her shaking hands, clutching a rope that was obviously tied around whatever she'd come across.

"Billie, you're doing good. Stay calm. We'll come up next to you on the far side and tether your boat to this vessel." He glanced over his shoulder and saw Callan and Andy slowing as well. "As soon as we're secure, I'm going to bring you over to this boat, and we'll take care of everything."

She stared up at him, but he wasn't sure she comprehended who she was looking at. Finally, she shook her head. "I… I'm not sure I can let go."

He saw that she'd tied one end of the rope around one of her boat seats, but she seemed afraid the body might float away or sink if she didn't hold on. "We'll take care of that once we get you secure. Just stay where you are. You're doing great."

His words must have sunk in because she blinked several times, then nodded.

As Joseph slowly moved him closer, Jared leaned over the edge until he could reach her boat and pull her small vessel next to theirs. Attaching the tethering lines, he watched as Andy maneuvered the other vessel close without getting in the way of the body she was hanging on to. He could see a mostly skeletal hand, and his gaze flew back to hers, finding it pinned on him.

Knowing she needed to anchor to something emotionally solid, he wanted that to be him. Holding her gaze, he said, "Billie, I'm going to step over into the boat with you. You can just stay very still and don't do anything. Once I get into the boat with you, I'll take over, and you can make the transfer onto our vessel. Okay? Are you with me?"

She nodded somewhat jerkily, but at least he knew she was listening. He had no doubt she was in shock and wanted to get her off her boat as quickly as possible.

Looking behind him toward Joseph and receiving a nod, he then looked toward Andy and Callan, receiving affirmations of readiness from them as well. Ryan, Bryce, and Jose had arrived but kept their distance so their movements didn't rock her small boat. He heard another engine and knew the Coast Guard had arrived as well. They would take their cues from Ryan, so he focused on Billie.

Stepping one foot over into her boat, he balanced with precision to keep the boat from rocking any more than necessary before moving to where she sat. Once solidly in place, he sat on one of the seats and leaned over. With a quick assessment, he could see she hung onto the rope with a white-knuckled grip more out of fear and uncertainty than need, considering she'd lashed the end around one of the seats.

Squatting near her still-shaking body, he placed his hand on her shoulder, then rubbed her back gently. "You're doing great, sweetheart. You can let go of the rope, and I'll—"

"No, it'll sink! It did before, and I had to pull it back up!"

"No, it won't, sweetheart. You've got him tied right here. That was really smart, Billie. Now let's get you over to my vessel so we can take care of things here."

With his hand placed on hers, he gently pried her tight, frozen fingers away from the rope, relieved that the movement seemed to help snap her out of her stupor. Jose had moved from his vessel to Jared's and leaned over the side, ready to assist. "Billie, this is a good friend of mine, Jose. He's going to help you climb aboard."

Seeing she was wobbly on her feet, he held tight to her arms as she stood, relief spearing through him as Jose's hands reached out to close over hers. With their help, she made the transfer, her foot only slipping once, but with his hands on her waist, he held her steady until Jose could lift her the rest of the way onto their boat.

"I'm going to need my equipment," she said, suddenly turning back toward him. "Not right now," she rushed, "but before… um…"

"Understood. We'll take care of it. You go with Jose now." He waited until she turned away from the sight of her boat.

"Here we go, Billie," Jose said gently as he guided her to the wheelhouse, where Joseph waited with a bottle of water and a place for her to sit. His co-officers knew she'd had the flu, and Jared was grateful when Jose wrapped a blanket over her shoulders before making his way back to assist. The thought he'd like to be the one to wrap her in his arms and the blanket hit him.

Focus, man! With her safely off her boat, he knelt in the bottom and pulled on the rope to lift most of the remains to the surface. *Shit... fucking hell!* One look, and he knew he needed to get Billie away. Looking over his shoulder, he called out, "Jose, get her equipment. I'll hand it to you, and then I want Joseph to move you all back."

With complete efficiency, they unloaded her boat in less than a minute, and he untethered it from his vessel, allowing Joseph to pull away. Ryan now steered in to take their place.

"Medical examiner will meet us at the harbor," Ryan said.

"I wanted her out of here. It's bad. The body has been in the water for a while," Jared commented as Callan now tethered his vessel to Billie's boat.

"Do we know how much she saw?"

Shaking his head, he replied, "Enough to send her into shock."

"Fuck," Ryan cursed under his breath. "I'll call Judith when we get in to have her checked out."

"That'd be good. She just saw Judith early this morning about the flu, so she's familiar with her."

Once Callan was in place, he lowered a basket stretcher into the water, and Jared carefully maneuvered the remains into it, moving slowly and deliberately. He knew he needed to keep the evidence intact as much as possible for identification and investigation purposes. Unlike a body discovered on land where they could cordon off the area, a body in the water made it much more difficult to gather evidence. The current and tide could have carried the body a long way from the death site. The chemistry of the salt water, microbes present, light, and depth of the remains all worked to dissolve the flesh. Add in the aquatic creatures that would naturally feed on the body, and what was left would make their job of giving the person their dignity with a full investigation tougher.

Satisfied he'd kept the remains together, helped by the deceased's clothing, he held the basket stretcher steady while Callan covered and strapped the remains securely.

"Christ, the body must have been in the water for a couple of weeks at least," Callan groaned.

"The medical examiner will give us what they can," Ryan added, "but this may be more for the state forensic lab. Hell, maybe even the FBI."

Jared nodded but wondered if it would be enough for the identification or even the cause of death. All he knew was he wanted to get the collection of the remains completed so he could get to Billie.

They carefully hauled the basket stretcher up onto Callan and Andy's vessel. The CG boat came alongside Ryan's, and his chief talked with their commander. The CG would send divers down to search and gather more evidence as well as mark it for further investigation.

Jared checked the tie connecting Billie's small boat to Callan's, then climbed back into his, immediately going into the wheelhouse where she sat, her pale face staring up at him. Not caring what anyone thought, he opened his arms and welcomed her when she rushed forward, wrapping his arms around her. He pressed his face into her hair, offering support but gaining it in return as well.

"You okay?" As soon as the question left his lips, he winced at the ridiculousness. "I mean, are you hurt in any way?"

Her face pressed against his chest, but she shook her head, and he felt the motion against his heartbeat. She leaned back. "I'm fine. Well, as fine as I can be."

Her voice was once again hoarse, and it raked against his ears like shards of glass, so he imagined how it felt on her throat."You've been out in the weather too much. You're going to have a relapse."

Her brow furrowed slightly. "I was tired and on my way back to the harbor, but I think the hoarseness is from the scream." The lines on her forehead deepened as her gaze drifted to the side. "I think I screamed. It's weird. I remember hearing a scream, but now I can't remember if it came from me. But I was the only one out here, so it must have."

They continued to hold each other tightly, not speaking until they neared the harbor. His gaze occasionally met Joseph's, who offered a sympathetic frown. Joseph had gone through his own worries about the safety of his fiancée and would have an understanding of how Jared's protective nature wanted to roar.

She leaned back again and peered up. "I know I'll need to be interviewed. I'm not sure what I'm gonna be able to tell them."

"Shh," he murmured, shaking his head. "Just tell them the truth. Go through exactly what you saw and what you did. The Coast Guard and we will have the area marked, so you don't need to worry about remembering exactly where you found it."

She nodded again as Joseph expertly docked, then suddenly startled. "My boat!"

"It's being pulled behind one of the other vessels. Don't worry about it."

Jared looked to see an ambulance parked near the docks and then glanced over his shoulder to see that Andy and Ryan docked their boats close just behind him. Knowing the decomposing body needed to be transported to the morgue as fast as possible, but with the hospital almost forty-five minutes away, they needed to wait and let Ryan do what was necessary. "I want you to stay right here, and let's take care of—"

"Go, Jared." Determination filled her voice, and her eyes were now clear, although rimmed with dark circles from fatigue and stress. "I'll be fine, and you have things that need to be taken care of. I can take a few minutes to check my equipment while you all deal with everything that's time sensitive."

He kissed the top of her head, glad she was holding it together. "Okay, I'll be back as soon as I can." Stepping to the side, he watched as she moved out of the wheelhouse and to the deck where they'd placed her testing equipment bags. She bent over and opened several containers, busying herself in the best way possible for her attention to be off what was rolling down the dock.

Ryan stepped close to Zac Hamilton, the captain of the Baytown Rescue Company. "We'll need a body bag. We have to handle the remains carefully so as to disturb the evidence as little as possible."

Zac nodded and jogged back to the ambulance to retrieve what was necessary. He waved at the driver, who backed the vehicle to the end of the pathway, where the dock began to get as close as possible.

Sucking in a deep breath, Jared hopped onto the dock, trying to hold back the shivers at the sight. The clothing was mostly intact, although partially torn and covered with debris. It was evident the deceased wore a long-sleeved navy polo and khaki pants with a leather belt and large buckle. "Almost looks like some kind of uniform," he muttered to Joseph, who'd moved up next to him.

"You think male?" Joseph asked.

"From the size, I'd say yeah, but that'll be for the medical examiner to give us," he replied.

"As soon as we get something from the ME, we'll go from there," Ryan said, stepping closer. "Here comes Colt and Mitch."

Colt was the sheriff for North Heron County, and Mitch was the police chief for Baytown. Ginny MacFarlane was walking just behind Mitch, and Jared was glad Billie would have a familiar face. He offered a chin lift to Ginny before inclining his head toward the boat where Billie was still busy with her equipment. Ginny returned his acknowledgment. Looking over his shoulder, he called out, "Billie, I'm gonna have Ginny take you to our station."

Billie nodded and grabbed her backpack. Just as Ginny moved closer, Billie stepped onto the dock. In hindsight, he should have waited because, just then, Billie's eyes landed on the stretcher next to him.

A gasp bolted from her lips as her body jerked. "Oh my God! That… Oh God, he's… David—" Her words halted, and all eyes turned to her as she dropped to her knees, retching over the side of the dock, gasping for breath. And for a few seconds, he was too stunned to move.

20

Billie couldn't breathe, couldn't drag in enough oxygen to keep from passing out. Just from the little evidence she'd seen in the boat while waiting for the police to come, she knew the sight wasn't going to be pleasant, and when she'd stepped onto the dock, she hadn't planned on looking at the remains. But just like in a horror movie, when the teenager went down into the dark basement, her eyes moved to the stretcher.

But instead of the skeleton and gore, her gaze landed and fixated on the shirt. And while muddy, she recognized the logo over the breast pocket. And the oversized belt buckle. And instantly, her mind tumbled to her predecessor.

She had no contents in her stomach left to expel, but her body refused to believe that as she dropped to her hands and knees and began retching. Ignoring the humiliation of being surrounded by others and vomiting in front of an audience, she remained in place with her fingers gripping the wooden dock edge, unable to move.

Hands grabbed her shoulders, and she felt a solid presence bend over her back, pulling her to their front. "Breathe, sweetheart. Just breathe."

Jared's words were spoken softly by her ear, but the buzzing in her brain made it almost impossible to hear.

Someone placed their fingers on her wrist. "Heart rate is elevated. Let's get her inside."

She turned her head to see the man in the Baytown EMS uniform kneeling next to her. "No. I'll be fine. You need to—"

"You're the patient who needs attention right now," the man said. He twisted around and called out, "Ginny!"

Billie felt Jared place his hands underneath her armpits and gently lift her to her feet. With one hand on the back of her head, pressing her face to his chest, he murmured, "We're going inside."

"Hey, Billie," Ginny said softly, placing her hand on her back and walking along with them.

Stepping inside the station, she sucked in a deep breath of the cool air when the air-conditioning hit her, glad for its reviving properties.

"That's it. Deep breaths," Jared continued to encourage, guiding her into a room and settling her into a chair. He looked over at someone who'd walked into the room. "Can you see if Judith is on her way?"

A glass of water was thrust into her hand, and she drank gratefully, cooling her irritated throat. "No, please don't bother Judith," she begged, her foggy mind clearing.

"She's on her way. She was at the clinic, and she can easily come here," Ryan said.

He sat down at the table, and she was aware that others filed into the room. Some she recognized, but others were new to her. Jared reached over to take her hand in his. "Billie, you know some of these people, but let me make the official introductions, and then if you're up to it, you can tell us what you know."

She nodded to each person as he introduced Colt, Mitch, Ryan, Callan, and Ginny.

"Ms. Schmidt," Ryan began.

"Please call me Billie."

"Okay, Billie. I know this has been a shock, and normally we could put this off for a bit, but with what you said out there, you indicated you might know the decedent. That information would save a great deal of time in our investigation."

Swallowing, she gathered her wits, tamping down the sight imprinted on her brain. "The shirt." She pointed to the logo on her breast pocket and said, "This is what the CBF has on their new shirts, but I've seen some older employees with the logo that was on the… um… its shirt. And the belt buckle." Blowing out another breath, she cleared her throat. "I recognized it. David Bourne. He was assigned to the water evaluation here, but then our boss got a message that he had a family emergency and had to leave immediately."

She glanced to the side to see the others typing into

their tablets, but Jared kept his focus on her. Trying to offer him an expression that would let him know she was okay, she was sure it came out wonky. His hand squeezed hers, and his gaze remained pinned on her face.

"Is this him?" Ryan asked, turning his tablet around.

She stared at the pictures from social media of a smiling David standing on a boat holding a large fish he'd caught, and she nodded. "Yes. I don't… um… didn't know him well. I would see him a few times at department meetings. I knew he was from Texas, and he always wore that big belt buckle in the shape of a fish."

"He was employed with the CBF?"

"Yes. I was working the shores north of North Heron County, and I know he'd recently been down here. When he left, then I was reassigned." She glanced toward Jared. "That's why I needed a place to stay."

"Do you know what he was working on?" Ryan asked.

"It was the same assignment they gave me when he had to leave. We randomly test various sites on the bay for water quality. He had found high levels of toxins near the oyster beds at Wilder Pond inlet. Considering there are farms that raise corn and have runoff in the area, we were concerned."

"Does the crop make a difference?" Callan asked.

"Any land area can have runoff that leads to higher levels of toxins. But as you can imagine, pesticides can be one of the worst problems for the bay." Sighing, she lifted her hand and gently rubbed her forehead. "I know some people see what we do as just one-dimensional. That we only care about the water and our findings and don't understand anything else. But that could not be further from the truth. We need the crops that the farms produce, and we need aquatic crops, such as oysters, and crabs, and fish as well. Plus, the bay is a living, breathing entity, vital to the aquatic area. Of course, when we show up, farmers can get very concerned because my findings go straight to the EPA, but it can take years before the farmers ever get warned or fined. And they can alternate a few other ways to use pesticides to keep that from happening."

"Since you've been here, have you had any problems with the farmers?" Colt asked.

"No real problems. Concerns, yes. The two farms where I've had the opportunity to talk to the farmers would be the Harper farm, and I also met their farm manager. Tim… Tim… well, I'm afraid I can't remember his last name."

"Belvidere," Colt interjected. "Anyone else?"

"Um… Porter Nevins, also. And today, I had the opportunity to meet Lou Ackers, one of the oyster farmers."

"I'm familiar with all of those names," Colt said.

"We know Lou also," Ryan confirmed. "He's been an oyster farmer since taking over from his dad."

"That's where I was when…" She let out a heavy breath.

"Was Lou nearby?" Ryan asked, his gaze shooting at her.

"I'd left and gone to the inlet. When I came back, he

was gone. I felt… well, something bumped against the boat. I stopped to see what it was."

"Tell us about the farmers," Colt requested.

"When I met each of them, they wanted to know what I was doing, and I explained. The farmers weren't exactly conciliatory, but then they see us as someone trying to put governmental constraints on them. I've explained that I'm a water analyzer and have no say over how they run their farms."

"Would David have been in the same areas?"

"Yes. But I don't have his reports." Seeing the lifted brows, she continued, "When he left suddenly, he hadn't turned in any reports. I had to start over and didn't have anything to compare my results to."

"Do you know if David had any family in the area?"

"I'm afraid I didn't know him that well at all. My boss assumed that he went back to Texas."

"You said that he was going back for a family emergency. Where did that information come from?" Ryan asked.

"That's what Rita told me. Rita May, my boss at the CBF. I assumed she'd talked to him. I even asked her if she could message him about his testing." Jerking, she suddenly realized how much they were talking about David when there was no way she could be sure. "Please, don't go just on what I said. I mean… maybe it could be someone else… or maybe… I don't know." She twisted to peer into Jared's face, glad for his solid presence.

"Of course, until the medical examiner can give us a positive identification, all of this is conjecture," Ryan hastened to say. "But you've been a great help in giving us a place to start. Once we have a positive ID, and if we find out that it was David Bourne, then we'll be in touch with more questions for you and certainly your boss."

"Should I… well, I'm just wondering if I'm supposed to keep this a secret. I know that sounds like a foolish question, but one of my first thoughts was to call Rita. I barely knew David, but she would've known him better."

"At this time, Billie, we'll ask that you not speak to anyone other than us. We would rather not have anyone involved until we have the answers to a few more questions."

"My boss will wonder why I'm not working, although I can analyze the samples I took today, and that report should keep her satisfied for a couple more days." Sucking in a ragged breath, she felt her chest squeeze and tried to cover up more coughing.

"That sounds like my patient," Judith sing-songed from the hall.

Ryan smiled and nodded for Ginny to open the door, allowing Judith to come in. His wife smiled first at him, then immediately went to Billie. "Sounds like you've had quite the adventure, and you're not even completely well yet. If everyone here is finished, let's find an empty office and see how you're doing."

"You can use mine," Ryan said, gaining a nod from Judith.

Jared stood, and with his arm around Billie, they followed Judith down the hall. Once there, Judith listened to her heart and lungs and took her pulse and temperature.

"You sound pretty good, although I'm hearing a little rattling in your lungs. My recommendation is that you don't go back out onto the water. The activity, the cool wind, and the stress of the day can very easily set you back. The last thing you want is to end up with bronchitis or pneumonia. Your stomach is empty. I'm gonna recommend you take it slowly, but you need to hydrate and add food as you can."

"Thank you. I'll be fine." She tried to smile, but her face felt as though it would crack from the effort.

"She will be because I'm gonna make sure of it," Jared pronounced, shooting her a warning expression.

Too tired to protest, she nodded, thinking that if she fell into bed, she'd sleep for a week. They walked out of the station after Jared talked to Ryan and Callan for a moment. Andy and Joseph walked out behind them with her equipment cases in their arms, and she turned to take them. "Oh, thank you."

"You take it easy, darlin'," Andy said, his smile full of sympathy.

They loaded the cases into the back of Jared's SUV, said goodbye to his friends, and then he walked her over to the passenger side. She whirled around as thoughts flew through her mind. "My car is here. Oh, and my boat."

"Your boat will be fine at the harbor. But where'd you park?"

She pointed at the public lot on the other side of the harbor. "Over there."

"It'll be fine there, too."

"But—"

He stepped closer, pressing her back against the door. Her hands automatically moved to his waist as he placed one hand on the window next to her head and the other hand on the door beside her hip. Their faces were close, and his blue eyes held her mesmerized. For the first time in hours, her mind blanked of everything other than the man in front of her. Her heart pounded but not from fear. Her cheeks burned but not from the sun or a fever. Her breath hitched but not from being ill. His forehead gently laid against hers, and she finally closed her eyes and breathed him in.

"I'm taking you home, Billie." His whispered words puffed against her cheek, and she nodded.

The drive wasn't long but silent as fatigue weighed her down. He parked next to his house, and once she alighted, she started for the garage stairs. Her progress was halted as his hand clutched hers, and he directed her toward the main house.

"Come on, babe. You're staying here."

She tugged slightly on his hand, but it held fast. "Here? Why?"

Stepping closer, he looked down at her with an intense gaze, but she had no idea what he was thinking.

"Because I want you close by. I want you here with me. I want to take care of you. I want to make sure you're okay. I want to know that when I wake up, you'll be there. And when you wake, you can not only see me but feel me all around you."

Sucking in a hitching breath, she held his gaze. "That sounds really nice. Scary, but nice."

"Why scary, babe?"

She hesitated, terrified to put her feelings into words. "Because I've learned to be on my own. Because, other than James, I've learned that to rely on someone means you can hurt when it goes away."

21

When they entered his house, they were greeted by an enthusiastic Daisy, and Billie couldn't help but smile at the dog's shameless bid for treats. Ruffling her coat, she relished the smile considering it had been the first since earlier that morning.

While Jared let Daisy outside, Billie moved into the kitchen, plopping onto one of the counter stools, too tired to move, then proceeded to stare numbly into space. Startling as he returned with Daisy, she had no idea how long she'd been sitting there just vegging. When she shifted to get off the stool, he insisted she stayed seated while he heated tomato soup and made grilled cheese sandwiches. It only took a few minutes for her to decide that the soup and sandwich combination was the perfect meal, and she managed to eat every bite. By the time the warm meal was in her belly, she felt her shoulders slump with exhaustion.

He rinsed the dishes, still insisting she stayed in her seat, then took her by the hand and led her to the living room where the furniture was now in place and the TV fastened to the wall. With his arm around her, they settled on the sofa and watched mindless TV shows for several hours. Whenever her body tensed as visions of the day's horrendous events reared up, he rubbed his hand over her shoulder, down her arm, and back again before gently massaging her neck.

By the time the sun had set, she'd wondered what was going to happen next. She didn't want to go back to her place and be alone to face the thoughts, visions, memories, and musings. He must have felt the unspoken questions swirling in her mind because he stood, took her hand, and led her upstairs. They didn't stop until they entered his bedroom, and her feet stumbled to a halt.

"What are we doing, Jared?" she asked, her voice so low she was surprised he heard her.

He turned to face her, both of her hands held securely in his. "You're going to take a hot bath while I run to your place and grab a few things. Then you're going to settle into bed, warm and snuggly, while I take a shower."

Bypassing the idea of being warm and snuggly in his bed, she focused on him grabbing some things from her apartment. "What are you going to get at my place?"

"Do you trust me?" he asked instead of answering.

She nodded immediately without having to stop and think.

"Then trust that I'll take care of you."

A shaky breath left her lips before she pressed them together. She wanted to ask what came after that but decided that, at that moment, she didn't care. She watched as he bent over the tub to fill it with warm water, appreciating the view. And when he left the bathroom, she stripped, stepped in, and sank down until only her head was above the water, resting on a towel he'd propped on the back. She couldn't remember the last time she'd been able to have a long, soaking, hot bath and immediately felt her muscles relax.

She closed her eyes and blanked her mind as to what Jared might be collecting at her apartment, having decided her brain didn't have enough space for all the thoughts traveling through it. She trusted him, and that's all that mattered.

The water had cooled by the time she heard him return, and she quickly climbed from the tub and wrapped a thick towel around her body. Wondering about clothing, a burst of laughter bubbled forth.

From the other side of the bathroom door, he called out, "What are you laughing about?"

She opened the door, still wrapped tightly in the towel, and observed him holding some clothing. "I was just thinking about what you were bringing for me to wear and that you've already seen me without clothes on." Her cheeks heated as she shook her head.

He held up his hands, showing that he'd brought pajamas and clean underwear. "I want you to be comfortable, but I just have to say if you think that I've forgotten that I've seen you without clothes on, you'd be greatly mistaken. That image is burned on my brain forever."

Her blush deepened as she reached out to take the

items from him. They passed each other in the doorway, and she stopped to peer up at him. They stared, silence stretching as electricity sparked about the room. Blowing out a breath, she whispered, "Thank you."

He offered a sweet smile, lifted his hand to cup the back of her neck, bent to place a kiss on her forehead, then disappeared into the bathroom, shutting the door behind him.

She stared at the closed door for a moment, then blew out another long breath. Looking down at the clothes in her hand, she smiled at the pajama bottoms and panties but didn't recognize the T-shirt. Dropping the towel, she slid on her panties and the bottoms, then shook out the folded shirt. Her lips parted at the sight of the VMP T-shirt. Hearing the water from the shower shut off, she quickly jerked the shirt over her head and thrust her arms through the sleeves. It hung to her mid-thighs, but her fingers clutched the worn, soft material, feeling surrounded by the scent of Jared. Suddenly, tears pricked her eyes just as the bathroom door opened.

He stepped out, and once again, her breath hitched. Drawstring pajama bottoms slung low on his hips was the only thing he wore. His chest and biceps were clearly defined by muscles and tattoos. Each individual piece of him was gorgeous, but the entire package together was drool-worthy. But as her gaze moved from the top of his head down to the floor, his naked feet, peeking out from the bottom of his pajamas, made her grin. She had never noticed it before, and maybe it wasn't true with all men, but with Jared, his bare feet were sexy. Lifting her gaze, she found his sky-blue eyes staring at her.

He stepped closer and cocked his head to the side. "When I opened the door, I thought you were ready to cry. And now you have a grin on your face."

She nodded. "Are you asking a question or just making an observation?"

"I guess both."

"I was touched that you got some things from my place to make me comfortable. But putting on your T-shirt just made me feel… not just comfortable but comforted. I can't explain why that brought about tears other than to say that after such an emotional day, comfort is a nice thing to feel."

His hand reached out to hers, holding them between their bodies. "I always want you to be comfortable, Billie. And I want to be the one to comfort you."

"When… when my dad died, my mom and I clung together, but we were both grieving. We offered comfort, but each needed so much. Then when Mom died, James and I did the same. We comforted each other, but our grief was so consuming that I never allowed myself to just *accept*. Surrounded by your shirt made me just accept what you were offering." She shook her head and scoffed. "I'm not sure that makes any sense."

"I think it makes perfect sense. You've had to be strong. But you don't have to be strong now. Not for me. All I need is for you to let me take care of you."

She glanced down, then allowed a small grin to curve her lips. "I really like this shirt."

He chuckled. "As I grabbed some things for you, all I could think about was wanting to see you in my T-shirt." Inclining his head toward the front of the faded logo across her chest, he added, "That was the first VMP shirt I got after I was hired. But seeing it on you has given a whole new meaning to that being one of my favorite shirts."

Her lips curved again, and his eyes twinkled as he then prodded, "And the smile? What was that for?"

"When you stepped out of the bathroom, I wasn't sure what part of you to look at first. Everything looked good, but all together, you look amazing."

He stepped closer, wrapped his arms around her, and pulled her in tight. Instead of pressing her face against his chest, she leaned back to hold his gaze as he peered down. He whispered, "I could say the same thing about you." He bent and kissed her lightly, her lips tingling as he gently moved his mouth over hers.

Her short fingernails lightly scraped over the warm skin of his back. When he ended the kiss, she sighed, instantly missing his lips.

"As much as I would like to keep this going and even take it further, I want you to rest."

The temptation to tell him to take *it* further died on her lips from a combination of fatigue and nerves. "I'm exhausted," she admitted. "But I have no idea how I'll be able to sleep tonight."

"You're going to sleep with me right here in my bed. You'll be warm, snuggled, and just like with my T-shirt, you'll be comforted and safe. And if you can't sleep, we'll talk. If you need to walk around, I'll get up with you. If you need a snack in the middle of the night, I can take care of that too."

"You might just be too good to be true, you know that?" she mused aloud.

He grinned and bent just enough to kiss the end of her nose. "Come on, let's get in bed. It's been a shit-kicker day, and I want you to rest."

She hesitated, waiting to see which side of the bed he wanted to sleep on. He took the one closest to the door, which didn't surprise her. Crawling in, she immediately groaned in pleasure at the firm mattress, reveling in the soft sheets and the warmth of the comforter as he pulled it over them. As soon as he turned off the light on the nightstand, he scooted toward her, pulling her in close to him. They lay quietly for several minutes before the thoughts in the dark began to creep in.

His arm squeezed her gently. "I can tell you're thinking."

She nodded, gathering strength from his hold. "Do you know what bothers me the most about today?"

"What, sweetheart?"

"The… the remains that we saw were unpleasant, but that's nothing compared to the fact that someone died. And whether or not that someone was David, it was still someone. Maybe someone's husband or father. Someone's son or brother or uncle or friend. And I can't help but think how they ended up there. Did they suffer? Was it natural? Were they afraid? Did they know they were dying?" She shivered, and his arms tightened around her.

"I haven't come across anything like this in my career so far, although I've dealt with death. We've been called to accidents on the water where someone died, and it doesn't make it any more tragic than thinking of this person today. You have an analytic mind, honey, so you automatically want to know what happened. But you're also very caring, seeing humanity in the middle of the tragedy. That makes it hard for you, yet it's part of your beauty."

He pulled her in tight, and she allowed his words to ease over her. Now, with her cheek resting on his chest and his arms wrapped around her, she closed her eyes with the sound of his steady heartbeat lulling her to sleep.

22

Billie blinked her eyes open slowly, the thick fog of sleep still warmly blanketing her. She inhaled deeply, but her lung expansion was constricted as a heaviness pressed down. She lifted her hand and discovered a muscular arm lying across her chest. Blinking more to force the fog to lift, she realized the heat was not just from the bedcovers but from the hard body curled around her back, completely cocooning her in its embrace.

Consciousness brought back memories, but instead of horror, she simply *felt.* Felt warm. Felt safe. Felt cared for. The sting of tears hit the back of her eyes, and she wrapped her fingers around the arm holding her tight. What she'd told Jared last night was true—she hadn't felt comforted just for herself in a very long time. Her mother held her when her father died, but her mother's needs were even greater than hers. And James loved her mother so much that their shared caring during her illness and death was needed, yet she felt the need to give more than she'd received.

And to have Jared's care made her realize how much she craved the connection with someone special.

Filled with the desire to see his face, she twisted around gently, hoping not to wake him. Successful in her task, she stared at his sleep-relaxed features. Thick lashes that many women would love to have. Slight crinkles emanated from the corners of his eyes, indicating frequent smiles. His skin was not dark but tanned from working on the bay. His brown hair was short but long enough on top that she wanted to run her fingers through the strands. Stubble covered his jaw, just waiting for his next shave.

From here, she could see the sleeve of tattoos and air-traced her finger over the swirls, desperate to touch him but not willing to disturb his sleep.

He stretched, opened his eyes, and grinned. "How is it that I can feel you touch me when you're not actually touching me?"

A smile spread unbidden across her face. "I don't know. I was trying not to wake you, yet couldn't help but just stare."

"Baby, you can stare as much as you want. For that matter, you can touch as much as you want."

They lay pressed together, and she could feel his desire, creating a pool of need deep in her core. Drawing strength and courage from his embrace, she whispered, "What comes next?"

His hand slid from her back to cup her jaw, his thumb sweeping over her cheek as his fingers threaded through the hair at the back of her head. "Whatever you need. Whatever you want."

"I have no idea what I need," she admitted, "other than to forget the images of yesterday. But as far as what I want, I know that with complete certainty."

His intense gaze held hers, and the air grew thick. His voice lowered, and the sounds pulled from deep inside. "And what do you want?"

Speaking the one word she felt more than any truth she'd ever spoken, she replied, "You."

"Thank fuck!" Faster than she imagined he could move, he rolled on top of her, his thighs parting her legs as his hips pressed into hers. His thick arms bulged as they kept his weight off her chest, his forearms bracketing her shoulders.

Their gazes held for a few seconds more before he angled his head and took her lips in a searing kiss. Fireworks exploded behind her closed eyes, and she could only imagine if this was her reaction to being kissed in his bed, her body might combust if they took it further. *And please, let this go further!*

Filled with the need that was tied to her expectations, she gave in to the sensations assaulting her as she opened her mouth to welcome the velvet touch of his tongue as it glided over the roof of her mouth, danced with her tongue, and explored and plundered. She clutched him tighter as she wrapped her legs around his waist.

Suddenly overheating, she was desperate to get out of her clothes. He must've felt the same because his hand slid over her breasts and down to the bottom of the T-shirt. His fingers glided under the material and branded her skin as he pushed it upward, his fingers skimming lightly over her stomach. He shifted to the side so he could continue lifting the material over her breasts and then over her head. After dragging it off her arms, he tossed it to the floor.

Now, with no barrier between their torsos, the feel of his muscular chest rubbing against her sensitive breasts only made the sparks brighter. The sight of the thick ropes of muscles in his biceps tempted her to snake her hands up to feel them move and contract underneath his warm skin. His hand held her face as he lowered his head again, plundering her mouth.

He dragged his lips along her jaw, down her neck, and sucked along the way toward her breasts. He sucked one nipple deeply, his tongue rolling over the bud until her hips undulated upward as the nerves that connected her breasts and core were electrified with need.

Giving her breast a nip with his teeth, he then kissed along her stomach, swirling his tongue around her belly button, eliciting a giggle and squirm from her. The sound caught in her throat as he continued lower, dragging her pajama bottoms and panties down as he went. Desperate to get them off, she wiggled her hips and kicked her feet to send them to the side. He kissed over her mound, and she let her knees fall open, welcoming him with a gasp as his mouth clamped over her clit.

His talented mouth worked wonders, and her hips bucked upward again. It didn't take long once he slid a finger inside to find the spot that made her entire body quiver.

"Oh God," she cried out, her fingers dragging through his hair as fireworks crackled behind her eyelids once again.

His cock swelled painfully as the vibrations of her release hit his tongue. Her legs fell open as though boneless, and he grinned while kissing over her mound and back up toward her breasts, eagerly latching onto one taut nipple before moving to the other. Working her body caused his cock to swell even more, and the desire to sink inside her sweet body knocked all other thoughts out of his mind.

Settling his thighs between hers, he surrounded her body as his forearms pressed into the mattress on either side of her shoulders. He was a big guy and never wanted a woman to feel overpowered, but with Billie, his heart soared as she stared at him as though he were a superhero and all he wanted to do was protect and defend.

Her fingers hadn't left his hair, and she pulled him down for a kiss. He dove in as a man starved, but she drank her fill as well. Their finesse was gone as noses bumped, lips smashed, and tongues tangled in an uncoordinated battle for dominance. Her taste was intoxicating, and he was drunk on the honor she bestowed by being in his bed.

He wanted her. Not just a willing woman, but her.

Needing her to know how he felt before they went further, he lifted upward to peer down into her eyes and gave voice to his thoughts. "I'm honored, babe. Seriously honored that you're here with me. And if we stop right now, I'll be fine. I just want you taken care of."

She kept her eyes pinned on his face, her chest barely moving with her light breaths. Her fingers clutched his shoulders, then glided upward to cup his face as her thumbs trailed over his lips before moving through his stubble. "I'm right where I want to be." Her lips curved slowly, and her eyes sparkled. "What I really want is to feel everything you have to offer." She pressed her hips upward again against his aching cock. "Please, Jared. I want it all."

Grinning, he rolled his hips, and his cock dragged along her clit, eliciting a hiss from her lips. At that moment, that was the sweetest sound he could imagine hearing. Heart pounding in his chest, he leaned to the side and jerked a condom from his nightstand drawer.

As he shifted up onto his knees, ass to his heels, he ripped open the condom packet, catching the smirk on her face.

"What are you thinking?" he asked.

"I remember seeing that woman leave your place after my first night in the apartment. In my mind, I described her hair as sex hair. I was wondering if I would have a chance to walk out of here with sex hair tomorrow, too."

He hadn't thought of any other woman in weeks, certainly not Stephanie. Rolling the condom on, he didn't miss the way her pupils dilated as she stared at his erection. But the last thing he wanted was for her to think she was just another woman in his bed. Leaning forward, the tip of his cock rested against her sex, and he planted his hands on either side of her head so he was the only thing she could see.

"We've got to get something straight right now, babe. What she was, was a fuck. Nothing more. It was never gonna be more. I was an idiot for bringing her here that night, and I guess that was pretty evident by the way you saw things go down the next morning."

She sucked in a deep breath and shook her head slowly. "Jared, this doesn't have to mean anything. I'm a big girl and can enjoy being here for now." She huffed, "I've had promises that were worthless. If all we have is a chance to wipe out yesterday, I can do that."

"I'm not that man," he growled, leaning down to nuzzle his nose along her neck. "Not with you."

"What makes me different?" she challenged, her gaze intently holding his.

He pressed his hips forward, his cock now teasing. Her eyes rolled back into her head, and a small gasp left her lips. Pressing down once more to gain her attention, he continued. "What you are, Billie, is not a fuck. The first time I saw you standing on the island, I saw your beauty. But I was so fucked in the head that day I pushed down any thoughts I had of you and was an asshole. I sure as hell wasn't expecting you to be my renter. And Stephanie's bitchfest in my yard in front of you only made things worse. But ever since we pushed past that, I've wanted to get to know you. And the more I do, the more I want to be with you. So this"—he pressed his hips forward again, the tip of his cock now just at her entrance—"is no fuck. No one-time thing. No hit-and-run. I want to take this and see where it can go, but I need to know we're on the same page."

It took every ounce of self-control he could garner to keep from thrusting deep inside her, but he refused to give in to his urge until they came to an understanding. A small crease settled in her brow, and his breath halted in his throat as he waited to see what she would say.

"Jared, life holds no guarantees."

"I know that, babe. And right now, I'm not asking for a lifelong commitment. I just need to make sure you understand that this means something to me. I don't want to just have sex and then both walk away. I want to see where this goes between us. Doesn't mean I'm running out to buy a ring, but it means I want to make a commitment to you to take us as far as we can."

"Exclusive?"

"Abso-fucking-lutely," he bit out, pressing his hips forward again. "We don't have to slap a label on us yet. But I want to spend time with you. Get to know you more. I already like everything I know about you, and I have no doubt that will grow. Unless we both agree to end it, then I want to be exclusive with you."

A smile graced her face, and his arms began to shake with the exertion of holding him up and nerves shooting through his body as he controlled the desire to take her.

"Then I guess I only have one question," she said.

Uncertain he could speak any more words, he waited.

"Think I can finally find out what sex hair from you looks like?"

A growl erupted, and she laughed, her fingers digging into his shoulders. "Babe, with you, I have a feeling it's going to be the best we've ever had. What do you say?"

"I say hell yeah!"

As if the dam broke and the water rushed forward, all the air left his lungs, and he thrust deep into her core, his cock nearly weeping in relief.

She gasped, and his eyes stayed on her, making sure it was a gasp of pleasure and not discomfort. He halted, but her gaze immediately flew to his. "If you don't move, I think I'll die of need."

"I'm not gonna leave you wanting, babe," he vowed. He began to thrust more, driving deep each time. Her thighs widened as she wrapped her legs around his back, her heels pressing his ass forward. Her short fingernails scratched along his back and dug into his shoulders.

A wildness exploded at her touch, and he reached down to grab one leg, lifting it higher as he pistoned his hips, dragging his pelvis along her clit at the same time. Her body began to vibrate, but considering that tingles zipped through his body, he wasn't sure who was more affected. Wanting to make sure she was taken care of, he shifted slightly and bent, pulling a tight nipple into his mouth. Sucking hard, he nipped and licked the sting away as his hips continued to thrust as deep as he could go.

Her face was tight, and her eyes squeezed shut. Her head leaned further back against the pillow, exposing the long expanse of her neck. Reluctantly, leaving her breast, he planted his lips against her fluttering pulse as it beat wildly against her pale skin. Her body tightened, and then she suddenly cried out as her inner core gripped his cock. And he could've sworn he saw fucking stars.

She was meeting him thrust for thrust with enthusiasm. This beautiful woman made him feel like he was the only man in the world who could do this for her. He felt like a fucking king.

Her eyes blinked open as her chest heaved, sucking in air. Feeling his balls tighten and every muscle in his body tense with exertion and need, his orgasm exploded. He came harder than he ever remembered, pumping until he was wrung dry.

He panted as though he'd run up a mountain, swam across the ocean, and soared on eagle wings. Blinking his eyes open, he stared at the beautiful woman whose gaze never left him and knew she'd altered his life. And he never wanted to go back to the existence he had before.

His thick arms shook with the exertion, and he managed to scoop her closer as he fell and rolled, dragging her to lay on top of him, clamped to his chest. They lay together for long moments, allowing the air to cool the sweat from their bodies and their lungs to regain the ability to breathe steadily. His heartbeat slowly returned to normal, but he wasn't sure it would ever beat exactly the same way again. Somehow, it seemed to need to beat in time with hers.

She finally pushed up and looked down at him, a perfect smile on her face. She bent and kissed him lightly, then mumbled against his lips, "How's my hair?"

He barked out a laugh and shook his head. "It looks like something I want to be spread across my pillow every night, and just that messy from being with me."

Her bright smile met his. *Yeah, I could get used to this woman in my bed... and in my life.*

23

Jared waited as Bryce steered their vessel to the dock at the station the next day, anxious to see what information the medical examiner had given to Ryan. He'd left Billie in his house, reluctantly kissed her goodbye, and come to work wishing for nothing more than to sleep in with her.

Thinking of last night, he grinned. The sex had been phenomenal, and knowing he was with a woman he cared about made all the difference. As the boat gently bumped against the dock, he was startled into action, glad that his fellow officers were busy and not noticing him being lost in thought.

Walking into the conference room, he discovered Colt and Hunter there as well. Hunter was one of Colt's detectives, having come to the North Heron Sheriff's Department from the Virginia State Police. His wife, Belle, was a nurse, and it struck him that he'd like to introduce her to Billie sometime. As the other VMP officers filed in and sat at the table, they gave their full attention to their chief.

"Okay, first things first," Ryan began. "We will assist with the evidence gathering and the investigation, but it will fall under the North Heron's homicide department as the lead in the case. Hunter Sims is the lead detective. It's taken most of today, but with Billie's observation and information as a starting place, the medical examiner was able to obtain David Bourne's dental records. He has made a preliminary determination that the remains were indeed David Bourne."

Blowing out a breath he didn't realize he'd held, Jared wondered how this information would hit Billie. She indicated that she and David weren't friends and had only met a couple of times, but he knew how disturbing the news could be since she'd seen the remains. Hearing the others ask questions, he jerked his attention back to the meeting.

Continuing, Ryan added, "He was forty-one years old. Not married. No children. Has a condo he rents in Virginia Beach. Has worked for the CBF for eight years in various departments."

"Any ideas about the cause of death yet?" Joseph asked.

"The ME is also giving a preliminary determination that the cause of death was blunt force trauma to the head. The skull was severely cracked, but there were discernible holes in the back of the skull."

"That rules out gunshot," Hunter said, leaning forward with his arms on the table, looking at his tablet with the ME photographs and report displayed.

"Yes," Colt agreed, nodding. "It was much larger. He hasn't determined the weapon yet but said it was cylindrical and sharp-pointed. No wooden, glass, or plastic shards found."

"So metal?" Ryan asked, flipping through pictures on his tablet.

Hunter nodded. "That's what he's looking at now. Looks like there are particles of rust around the edges embedded in the skull. The diameter is about one centimeter."

"Some kind of tool? Sure as hell doesn't sound like something someone would carry in their pocket," Andy said, his brow furrowed.

"Hit from behind," Ryan commented, his dark scowl looking at the photographs from the ME.

"What about the location of death?" Jared asked, his gut clenching as he thought about Billie out on the water. He was glad she didn't go out today, agreeing to a day of rest, but she'd be back on her job tomorrow, insisting she had work to do. *"Jared, it's not like people are just dropping dead out there on the water!"*

"Right now, we don't know. He's sent the clothing as well as soil samples to the state lab for further analysis. Due to the decomposition, no internal organs were left to determine whether he was dead before or after entering the water."

"And the motive?" Callan asked. "What do we know about him?"

"That's what we're going to start on," Hunter said. "I've spoken to Rita May, who was his supervisor. She confirmed he was working on the water samples, particularly looking at the inlet near the Harper farm. She stated that he had not sent in any reports yet, but they talked on the phone twice before he left the area. She got a text from him that said he had to leave for a family emergency."

"If he didn't actually leave because of a family tragedy, are we assuming that someone killed him and then used his phone to send a message? And if so, how would they know to text her?" Jared asked.

"When I asked her that question, she had no idea but said they sometimes communicated by text about work. Since we don't have his phone, I've had her forward the texts to me."

"If someone went through his phone messages, it wouldn't be hard to see who his boss was."

"Christ, that still seems so random," Andy said.

"Did Ms. May have any idea about the motive?" Jared continued to press.

Hunter shook his head. "She said he was likable. She didn't know a lot about him, but he was reliable, on time, and did his work."

"Billie has mentioned the farmers in the area. It seems like they don't take very kindly to the water analysis, saying that they end up getting letters and fines based on what's found," Jared reported.

"Jared, I'd like you to come with me to talk to them and follow up on that," Hunter said. "We'll find out if they've seen David and interacted with him. Also, we'll find out the last time they saw him in the area."

Colt said, "If it turns out we need a search warrant

for farm implements as possible murder weapons, we'll get it."

Jared nodded, then turned back to Hunter. "So if we're going on the assumption that someone local killed him, got ahold of his phone and wallet, then dumped his body into the water… where is his boat?"

"Good question," Ryan said. "I want everyone searching for his boat. Ms. May reported that it would be similar to the one Billie is using now. Small, single manual engine."

"Does this make sense to any of you?" Jared asked. "If it was a farmer, would that indicate a less planned attack? Someone like that would panic, not think to get a phone and send in a message."

"We look from all angles," Colt said.

"If someone killed him in a rage and then had time to get his phone and wallet, he didn't immediately drop into the water. It would have been on land or on a boat," Jared continued.

"I want everyone looking for that boat," Ryan said. "Start interviewing those on the water. Others would have seen him. Talked to him. Taken note of him. Gather everything you can while we wait on the rest of the ME's report."

With that, the meeting ended, but Jared headed down the hall and out the front door, needing to hear Billie's voice. He looked at Hunter and said, "Be with you in a moment." Hunter offered a chin lift and walked toward the parking lot.

"Hey, Jared. Are you okay?" Billie said as soon as she picked up.

He dropped his chin, shaking his head as he stared down at a crack in the sidewalk. "You don't need to worry about me, babe. I'm good. It's you who I'm worried about. How are you feeling?"

"I'm okay," she admitted, not playing down anything, which he appreciated. "A bit of a cough. My plan was to rest, but I have some company."

"Company?"

"Yeah. It seems news travels fast, and a group of women has been stopping by to check on me."

He grinned, knowing she needed a posse, something she hadn't had before. "You okay with that?"

She laughed. "Yeah. At first, I was stunned by how many people showed up, but they all brought food, and we've settled in for me to get to know some of them. There's Judith and Sophia and Shiloh. Then more came. Tori, Jillian, Belle, Lia, and Madelyn, who's a counselor in town. A few more dropped by, but their names run together in my mind. But it seems they all belong to the AL Auxiliary, so they said they'll see me at the Holiday Hope run."

"I'm really glad they came, babe. You needed this."

She chuckled, and he loved the lightness of the sound. Then she sighed heavily. "Jared, how about you? Any news?"

He wanted to tell her what he'd learned, but the investigation was ongoing, and he preferred to give her as little as possible until he knew more. "Some. I'm going out with a county detective to talk to a few people. I'll talk to you when we get in this evening."

"I'll be here. I'll fix dinner."

"Babe, you don't have to—"

"It's got nothing to do with what I *have* to do, Jared. It's what I want. Plus, I won't have to do much with what the others brought!"

He sucked in a deep breath and spied Hunter at his sheriff's department vehicle. "Sounds good, sweetheart. I hate to go, but I'll see you this evening." Disconnecting, he jogged over to Hunter's vehicle.

Once on the road, he filled Hunter in on Billie's experiences with the farmers along the edge of the water analysis area where the CBF was focused.

"You're now dating the woman from CBF who took David Bourne's place after he disappeared?" Hunter asked, his brows shot upward to his hairline. "Shit, man."

"Yeah, tell me about it."

It didn't take long to arrive at the Harper farm. Climbing from their SUV, they walked down the lane past the house where they could see Jed and JC at the fence near the barn, working on a tractor that had seen better days. A young woman hung sheets on the clothesline, her eyes following them as they continued toward the barn.

As soon as Jed saw them approaching, he elbowed his son and inclined his head toward them. Pulling off his ball cap, then wiping his brow with a bandanna before stuffing it back into his pocket, Jed offered a hard stare. "Officers," he growled, planting his booted feet wide with his beefy arms crossed over his chest. JC adopted his father's stance.

Hunter stepped forward, dipping his chin. "Mr.

Harper," he greeted the elder. "Mr. Harper," he repeated as he shifted his attention to JC. "I'm Detective Hunter Sims with the North Heron Sheriff's Department. This is Officer Jared Dobson with the Virginia Marine Police."

"What can we do for you?" Jed asked, his narrow eyes darting between the two.

"We're investigating the death of David Bourne. He was an employee of the Chesapeake Bay Foundation and doing water testing in the area."

"'Fraid I don't know him," Jed replied.

"No," JC added, shaking his head. "Me neither."

Hunter held out his tablet with a photograph of David.

Jared carefully watched as recognition dawned in both farmers' eyes. "Seen him around? On the inlet at the edge of your farmland, perhaps?"

"Yeah, we've seen him but not for weeks now. It was..." Jed shook his head slowly. "Hell, it must have been back last month."

"And you haven't seen him since?" Hunter asked.

"Not me? You, son?"

JC shook his head. "Not for weeks. Last time I saw him, I just waved. I'd talked to him the previous week, wanting to know what he was doing." He glanced toward his dad, adopting a hound-dog expression. "I was kind of rough 'cause we don't like people trying to tell us how to run the farm."

"Can you define *kind of rough*?" Hunter rumbled.

JC's eyes widened as he jerked back. "No, no, not like

that. I was just talking to him." He ducked his head and made a side-eye toward his dad.

"Why don't you tell us what happened?" Jared prodded. "And when it happened."

"I was down in the back field, near the bottom. A man stood at the edge of our land, bending over the water. I just asked him what he was doing." JC hefted his shoulder, then sighed heavily. "He stood up and turned around. Said he was doing water testing. I told him he needed to move on. Hell, a couple of years ago, we had someone from the EPA come by and want to talk about the fertilizer we use 'cause the report had gone in that it was running off in the water." He turned to his dad. "Remember?"

"Hell yeah, I do," Jed grumbled, his expression hardening. "They had all these suggestions on how to keep that from happening. We did a few things, like add some plants at the edge of the fields, but changing our fertilizer was too damn expensive. But then we can get slammed with fines. We get hit no matter what we do."

Looking back at JC, Jared asked, "What was Mr. Bourne's reaction when you told him to move on?"

"He just told me he was taking more samples, and he'd be on his way, but I'd probably still see him around a bit." Shuffling from one foot to the other, he ducked his head as he admitted, "I told him that he was gonna find people who didn't take too kindly to trespassers."

"And?" Hunter prodded.

"And nothing! I saw him in his boat a couple of times, but he wasn't standing on our land, so that was all."

"Can you remember when this was?"

JC scrunched his face and looked upward as though the answer would fall from the sky. "I saw that pretty lady that's now on the water taking samples a couple of weeks ago. I haven't seen him since she was around." Suddenly jolting, he grinned. "Hey, maybe she did it. She might have killed him so she could have his job!"

Jared's eyes bugged as he forced a silent count to ten to calm his irritation.

"Let's just stick to what you know?" Hunter advised. "Did you ever see him with anyone else? Either on the water or in the area?"

"No, not me," JC replied.

"Me neither," Jed agreed. "Mind you, I never actually saw him. JC just told me about him."

JC swung his head around to stare at his dad and opened his mouth. Then as Jed shot him a glare, JC clamped his mouth shut.

"Anything else?" Hunter asked.

The two men shook their heads in tandem. "Okay, if you think of anything else, give me a call," Jared said, handing them a card along with Hunter's.

"Hmph. Sure thing, officers." Jed offered a curt nod.

Turning, Jared and Hunter walked back down the drive, not speaking until they were out of earshot. "Did you see the garden rake leaning against the side of the barn?" Jared asked. The metal prongs at the end of the long wooden handle had drawn his gaze, and he recognized the prongs to be about three inches apart.

"Yeah, and there was another one by the vegetable garden at the back of the house."

"Fuck me. I missed that one. Hell, every farm and house around here probably has one. A shit ton of other implements could be the murder weapon, but I swear, I looked at that and could just imagine someone swinging that toward the back of his head."

"They're hiding something," Hunter said. "Might just be about the farm, but whatever it was, Jed wanted JC to stop talking."

"Yeah, that's the feeling I got, too."

The woman was no longer in the backyard, but as they came to the front of the house, she was sweeping leaves from the front porch. Dressed in worn jeans and a flannel shirt with her dark hair pulled back, she was pretty in a wholesome, girl-next-door way.

Hunter and Jared detoured to approach. "Ma'am, we were just checking to see if anyone here had seen this man." Hunter held out his tablet with David's picture displayed.

She looked at it, then shook her head. "No, sir."

"And you are?"

"Melissa Harper, but everyone just calls me Missy."

"Is your mother around? She might have seen something," Jared pressed.

"Mom passed about three years ago. Since then, I'm the one who does all the housework here. If I'm not at the farm, I'm working at the grocery down the road. And if he came into the store, I didn't notice."

Her voice held a bitter quality, and Jared could imagine that staying at home to help take care of Jed and JC would undoubtedly not be the job of choice for any young woman. Hunter thanked her and gave his card before they walked over to the SUV and climbed inside. As they pulled away, Jared looked back to see Jed on the porch speaking with Missy. Her eyes widened just before her shoulders sagged.

The SUV turned onto the road and hadn't gone far when they looked to the side to see a man repairing a fence on the Harper property. Without Jared having to say anything, Hunter flipped on his blinker and pulled to the side of the road.

The man caught sight of them and stopped working, resting his arm on the fence post. With his forefinger, he tipped up the brim of his cap and watched them approach.

"Tim, how're you doing?" Hunter asked.

"I'm doing okay. How's your wife and little one?"

"She's as pretty as ever, and he's growing like a weed."

Tim laughed before his eyes cut over to Jared, and Hunter made the introductions. "Tim, this is Officer Dobson from the Virginia Marine Police. And this is Tim Belvedere, longtime farmhand here at the Harper place. Tim belongs to the American Legion, and you might see him at one of the meetings."

"Nice to meet you, Tim," Jared said.

"Likewise. Saw you all come from up at the barn. Figured this must be official."

"We're looking into the death of one of the CBF water analyzers—"

"Not that pretty young woman?" Tim asked, his eyes widening.

Jared tried to keep from rolling his eyes at the oft-heard description of Billie. *Did everyone see her?* A thought slammed into him, jarring his gut. *Did the murderer see her?*

"No. Her predecessor. Man named David Bourne." Hunter once again showed the photograph on his tablet.

Tim scratched the whiskers on his neck. "I remember him. Never met him formally, mind you. But I saw him out and about on the water at the back of the property."

"You never talked with him?"

"No, but I heard JC complaining about him one day. Said he was getting too close to the land." Tim snorted and shook his head. "I told him just to mind his own business because that man had a job to do just like we do. JC… well, you know he ain't the sharpest tool in the shed."

Jared thought the analogy was apropos, considering they had their eyes on some of the tools. "You're not offended by someone coming in and checking to see if there's too much farm refuse and fertilizer running into the water?"

Tim propped both forearms on the fence post, resting his body on the thick wood. "I've been a farm-hand all my life. My granddaddy and daddy own some land up in Acawmacke County. But eventually, the economy went to hell, my daddy gambled some of the lands away, and by the time he died, there wasn't much to farm. Only time I left the area was when I did a stint in the Army, then came home and went back to doin' the only job I knew. Except instead of running my own place, I work for others. But you know what? That's fine by me. Somebody will always hire an experienced farm-hand, so I get a paycheck without all the headache."

Jared could tell the man was in for a story and rested his stance, knowing Tim would tell it in his own time.

"I've been with the Harpers for about eight years now. Good people. But like most, they're trying to scrape out every dime they can from the dirt to make a living. It was real hard when Jed's wife died, but their daughter stayed around to help out."

"Missy?"

A soft smile curved Tim's lips. "Yeah, Missy. She deserves a lot more than what Jed and JC dish out, I can tell you that. Not that they're bad, you understand. But I imagine she had dreams to do more than just care for her dad and brother." He shook his head slightly, then continued with his story. "Around here, tomatoes used to be the king crop. Hell, a farmer around these parts was known as the tomato king at one time. He kept snapping up other smaller farms and had contracts with big companies that do tomato soup and ketchup. Imagine that!"

He chuckled and shook his head. "He died. Younger people don't want to go into farming, and the big farm broke up. The name of the game is to keep growin' crops so that you can sell them at the best price, hoping you can just hang onto your farm and not lose your shirt. Now it's corn, potatoes, and cotton."

"Is that what the Harpers do?" Jared asked.

"That's what they're all doing, Officer," Tim replied. "The Harpers are no worse or no better than anyone else trying to earn a living from farming. You use more fertilizer to get more crops and, in turn, can make more money. You use every inch of your land that you can. But then, a lot of that fertilizer washes straight down into the water. Flows out into the bay and then messes with all God's creatures who live in the water. Makes it hard for the fishermen to make a living."

"You seem to have a good understanding of the water analyzer's job, so you didn't resent him being here?" Jared asked.

"That's one of the beauties of being a farmhand, Officer. I come to work every day, do what I do best, and then go home at night. It's not my worry about how much fertilizer somebody uses or if somebody's checking to see if it's too much. I can respect both sides as they're just trying to do their job."

"Considering you know everyone around here, Tim, can you see anyone wanting to harm Mr. Bourne?" Hunter inquired.

Tim sucked in a deep breath through his teeth and let it out slowly, his gaze drifting over the land before bringing his attention back to Hunter and Jared. "It doesn't make any sense to me because just like when one farmer dies or sells out, another one comes in. One government person goes away, and another one comes in." Chuckling again, he added, "Of course, the new one who came in is mighty prettier than the man who was here."

"There's nothing in particular that you can give us?" Jared asked, irritated to hear Billie having attracted attention just by her beauty.

"I've lived long enough to know that I wouldn't put

it past any man to do what they think they've got to do to protect themselves. I guess the Army taught me that. Anybody can fight for what they believe in."

"And kill?" Hunter growled.

"Oh yes, Officer. If someone believes what they're fighting for, they can kill."

24

Billie had been steering her small watercraft slowly along the coastline, finding it difficult to concentrate on her job as her mind continually churned the possibilities. She'd enjoyed the previous day despite the circumstances that had her staying home. The women who descended on Jared's house had engulfed her in immediate offers of friendship. She knew Judith and had met Samantha at the AL meeting. But she loved meeting Shiloh and Sophia as well since their significant others were coworkers of Jared's.

Tori Evans and Jillian Wilder were hilarious and appeared to hold the unofficial "first ladies of Baytown" titles since their husbands were on the police force and had been part of the original Baytown Boys with Callan. They talked of having her and Jared over to their beach cottage for one of their summer parties. And somehow, they made her feel included even though it appeared most of the women had been friends for years.

Madelyn Hamilton, the wife of Zac from the rescue

squad, took the opportunity to offer her business card from the local counseling center. Just from looking into her eyes, Billie knew she could talk to Madelyn any time she needed and appreciated the offer.

The day had been fun, but exhausting, and she'd been surprised when the women left as soon as they noticed how fatigued she'd become.

Now, she was back on the water the next day, trying to focus on her job with great difficulty.

"Had some excitement around here, didn't they?"

At the sound of the voice calling over the water, she jerked her head around, amazed that she'd been so lost in thought that she hadn't even realized she was nearing the oyster beds. Seeing Lou standing in fishing waders in waist-high water next to his flat-bottomed boat, she lifted her hand and waved, slowing even more so as not to disturb the water near him.

She didn't respond, figuring no response was necessary, and hoped he didn't know she was the one who *discovered* the cause of the excitement. The report of the death had hit the news, but thankfully, her name had been kept out of the press. Jared called her earlier that morning to tell her that the medical examiner had determined the decedent was David, and the detectives had talked to Rita to begin gathering information. Her phone rang not long after that.

"Billie! What the hell? I just heard... holy shit... I can't believe it! Oh God, I can't imagine. It's crazy! How are you doing?"

"It was horrible, Rita. I'm just trying to wrap my mind around it, but I can't. I'm back on the water today, trying to

stay busy but even being here makes it all come back. Did they tell you who found the body?"

"No, just that he had been discovered. Don't tell me it was you?"

"Yeah... it was."

"Oh my God! I can't imagine! Billie, you shouldn't be alone now. Why don't you come back here? You can stay with me and just travel over each day that you need to be there. I can even swing it so you can be in the lab here for a while."

"Well, I'm not really alone. Jared... he's my landlord... um... the one with the Virginia Marine Police... he's taking care of me."

There was silence before her boss erupted, "That sounds suspiciously like a relationship that goes beyond landlord and tenant, girl. We definitely need to get together. I want details on your personal life, and you can let me know what's going on with this crazy situation with David."

"I don't know anything about the investigation, Rita. I don't know if they have any suspects."

"Well, someone had to send that text to me from his phone. Who would do that?"

She hesitated, then added, "Someone hiding the fact he was going to be missing."

"Christ, Billie. My mind is blown."

She rubbed her head. "I know. I just know that out here, all I can think about is him being alive and doing his job, and then he's gone. And I feel guilty as hell because I was complaining about him leaving before sending in his reports."

"Hey, that's not on you, so don't go there. I was bitching just as much." There was silence again before Rita added, "I'm serious about you coming here. We can go out for a drink or

just hang out at my place. Although, if you've got something going with a hot cop, then you probably don't want to leave."

"Why don't you make a trip over to the Eastern Shore?"

Rita sighed loudly. "Because I have some meetings coming up with the EPA liaison. But maybe soon. It would be nice to get over there."

They'd disconnected, and while she'd been glad to talk to Rita, it had done nothing to dispel the mind muddle she was experiencing. The undulating water that she always loved appeared more gravelike than filled with life.

Now, she offered a polite smile toward Lou while feeling ill at ease being all alone, so near where she discovered David.

"Couldn't believe it when I heard the news. I came out here the other day, and the police had this whole area sectioned off right to the dunes and all over my beds. I don't mind telling you that I told them they'd better not tramp all over my oysters."

She knew that the CG would have sent divers down to go over the bay bottom, including the oyster beds below, in an effort to investigate for any clues as to what happened to David. Politely nodding again, she aimed her boat to go around him.

"Damn government. Farmers pollute the bay, and it seems nothing happens to them. Then my oysters have too many *toxins*," he complained, rolling his eyes at the last word. "Then I can't sell them at the cost I should be able to, if at all. Someone's always got their hand in my pocket, you know?" He jammed the long handle into the water and shifted it around before bringing up a clump of oysters lying in the basket.

He looked up and grinned. "You like oysters?"

"Not raw… but fried? Yeah. My mom used to cook them whenever we could get them fresh."

"Aw, you should try them raw." He slipped on a shucker's glove and pulled out a knife.

She tensed, her gaze never leaving his hands.

With practiced ease, he cracked open the oyster and stared down, a wistful expression on his face. "When I was a kid, we'd eat them straight from the bay. Some raw and some my ma would cook over an open firepit on the beach."

Not wanting to see if he was going to slurp the oyster, she mumbled her goodbyes and added a little hand toss as she aimed her boat farther into the bay to go around him. The back of her neck prickled, and she tried to ignore it until she finally gave in and looked over her shoulder only to find Lou back on his boat, his gaze pinned on her. Swallowing deeply, she jerked back toward the front and kept going, not stopping until she arrived at the harbor. No longer trying to avoid Jared, she wanted to dock close to where he was and looked with longing toward the VMP station, seeing Jared's now-familiar SUV in the parking lot.

"Hey, Billie."

Turning, she smiled as one of the VMP officers walked toward her. "Hi. Um… Andy, right?"

"Yeah," he said, nodding while offering a smile of his own. He jerked his head toward the station. "Jared's not there now. He's out with one of the county's investigators."

"Oh, thanks. I was just getting off the water."

Concern filled his eyes. "You doing okay?"

"Yeah, I'm fine. It's… weird…" She let her sentence fall away, suddenly self-conscious.

He ducked slightly to catch her eyes. "Hey, you're right. You're hit with the realization that your life continues when someone else's isn't. On top of that, you're out there where he'd been. Someone you'd known. When it's personal, it makes it much more real."

She let out a breath, glad he seemed to understand. "That's exactly right. Thanks. Well, I need to analyze my samples."

"I'll tell Jared that I saw you. I know he's worried."

"Worried?"

Andy grinned another panty-melting smile. She was immune but had no doubt many women all over the Eastern Shore were desperate to have it aimed toward them.

"Yeah, he's worried about you. What you went through was the stuff of nightmares, but you hung in there and did what needed to be done."

She snorted and rolled her eyes. "I seem to recall tossing my cookies over the side of the station's dock."

"Hell, Billie, you had good cause. Don't think a few of us didn't struggle to do the same. Anyone would." He visibly shivered at the memory. "But you managed to take care of business without losing your shit. Made it a helluva lot easier on us." He cocked his head to the side. "You know, I've never found it… well, what I mean is that it was hard to imagine that Jared had fallen so quickly. But meeting you, I can see how you're good for him. Take care of yourself."

He waved and then turned to walk away before she could come up with a response. But as she walked to her car, a smile crept over her face.

25

Hunter pulled onto another farm lane, this time on the opposite side of the inlet, across from the Harper farm. "The man who lives here would also have had the opportunity to be impacted by the CBF testing. It's a smaller farm owned by Porter Nevins. The farm has been in their family for years."

"I didn't think you were from around here," Jared said, impressed with Hunter's knowledge of the area.

"I'm not. Porter has been known to drink until he passes out at one of the local bars. The deputies have had to haul him in for bar fights numerous times. I never had to deal with him, but I've read the records."

"Great. Thanks for the insight," Jared said, exhaling a heavy sigh. "We know this guy has a temper that gets away from him."

"Yeah." They pulled to a stop and walked to where they could see the farmer tossing tools onto the back of a pickup truck.

Walking up, Hunter went through the introductions,

then informed Porter why they were questioning the landowners who might have seen David.

"You been over to the Harpers? Hell, they got more reason than me to want to off someone."

Jared's chin jerked back. "*Off* someone? Who said anything about that? We're just investigating the death. Do you have information that would indicate you know how he died?"

Porter dropped his gaze, but his eyelids blinked several times. "Naw, I was just figurin' that he got killed since you were asking about him. I mean, it was in the news that he was found in the water. So, um… I just figured… you know?"

"Why don't you tell us what you *do* know," Hunter suggested in a way that gave no doubt that it was an order and not a request.

"I don't know anything. I saw him a couple of times. Told him the same thing I told that new girl who took his place."

Jared felt his insides clench and had to work to keep his jaw from cracking his molars.

Porter continued, "I don't like anyone poking around my farm. But then I know I don't own the bay, so they ain't on my property. I ain't got no cause to go after them." He rubbed his chin and grinned. "Saw him once, though. He was drinking with some woman."

"Where was this ?" Jared asked.

A deep crease formed in Porter's brow as his face scrunched. "I don't… well, I don't recall. I have a couple of places I like to go to."

"When did you see him?"

Porter blinked, a blank look settling on his face. "I don't remember. Must have been sometime when he was over here."

Fighting the urge to roll his eyes, Jared nearly snapped. "Really? I think we can assume you saw him when he was here."

Hunter questioned him further, but they weren't able to get anything else from him. After tossing out thanks and goodbyes, they drove back to the station. Once there, Ryan called a meeting again, and Jared offered a chin lift toward the others in attendance. Settling around the table, they gave their reports on what they'd learned, starting with Porter.

Colt spoke up. "His granddad was a part-time preacher besides being a farmer. A real hell-fire and brimstone preacher. Porter's dad died of cirrhosis a year ago, and his dad was known to have a heavy hand with the discipline, and Porter's had a trigger finger all his life." He looked over at Ryan. "You probably remember him from high school also. The rumors were that the preacher grandpa probably had a heavy hand as well."

Ryan nodded his agreement, and Jared respected their local insight from having grown up in the area. They discussed the Harpers, but other than the farm implements that might have matched the ME's description of the murder weapon, they had very little to go on.

The other VMP officers reported that they'd questioned the fishermen they came across, but no one had any new information. And much to Jared's frustration, no one had found David's boat.

"What about Porter saying he'd seen David at a bar

with a woman?" he asked.

Ryan replied, "Andy has been working with Colt to check David's credit card usage for the time around when he disappeared." He nodded to Colt, who sent the information to the screen on the wall. "Most of the transactions were at restaurants and gas stations near here during the daytime hours when he would have been working. The others are for the Virginia Beach area where he lived."

"He probably used cash at a bar," Callan surmised.

Jared nodded in agreement, then sighed.

"But," Andy interjected, "we found a few at a small hotel up the road. I figured he spent the night occasionally to keep from driving all the way back over the bay. But now that you said that Porter saw him with a woman… think maybe he didn't spend those nights alone?"

"One way to find out," Jared suggested, looking at Ryan.

His chief nodded. "You two head over with Hunter and see what you can find out. Then tomorrow, I want everyone on the lookout for his boat. It has to be located since that could be the murder scene."

After the meeting was dismissed, Jared, Andy, and Hunter walked out together. Since it was nearing the end of the day, they decided to take two vehicles so Hunter could go directly to the sheriff's station.

He and Andy climbed into Jared's SUV. On the way to the hotel, Andy said, "Meant to tell you that I saw your girl earlier when she got back to the harbor."

"Billie?"

Laughing, he asked, "Do you have another girl I don't know about?"

"No, I guess it was just weird hearing you refer to her as my girl."

"Is that not the right description?"

Jared couldn't help but grin. "No, that's right. I just didn't expect you to tumble to that conclusion so quickly."

"I might not be ready for the same thing, but you're transparent, man. You fell. Fell hard and fell quickly."

Nodding, Jared felt the warmth build inside his chest at the thought of her. "You know, it's weird. My old man once told me that he saw my mom from across a room, and that was it for him. He was at the Naval Academy, and she was visiting for one of their dances. No doubts. No question. Just her. I believed him but figured that only happened to some people."

"No way are you going to say that happened with you and Billie! Not the way you two met!"

Chuckling, he shook his head. "No, you're right. I noticed she was beautiful, but I was an ass, and she was a smart-ass. Hardly a match made in heaven. Then I told you about her seeing Stephanie leave, and that was about as fucked up a situation as it could've been. I still looked like an ass, and she made it clear that avoiding me would be her life's pursuit."

Andy threw his head back and laughed. "Yeah, and then you went and fell off a ladder. I guess it's a good thing she's a caring person, or you could've lain there broken and bleeding!"

"Don't remind me. But you're right, she's not only

beautiful, but she's a really good person. I guess once we got past being an ass and a smart-ass, we had the chance to find out more about each other. And everything I found out just made me want to know her more."

"Well, I'm glad for you, brother."

"I'm worried about her."

"I know. I told her that."

Jared jerked his head around quickly. "What did she say?"

"She said she was doing fine but admitted the situation was weird. I'm sure you know today was the first day she was back on the water."

Jared winced as he nodded. "Yeah, and I've only been able to send her one text. As soon as we get this over with, I'll drop you back at the station and head home."

"She's tough. She'll be fine."

Jared remained quiet, holding on to his fear.

Andy cocked his head to the side. "There's something you're not saying."

Sighing heavily, Jared nodded. "Truthfully? I'm worried about her, and not just because she went through a trauma. I guess I'm worried because until we know who killed David and why, there's always the threat that someone killed him because he was out here testing."

"Holy shit," Andy said. "And you think she could be next?"

"It's occurred to me. I mentioned it to her, but she said she had a job to do. I just wanna find out what happened to David before anything happens to her."

They pulled into the hotel parking lot, and as they

alighted, Andy clapped him on the shoulder. "You know everyone's working as hard as they can on this case. But at the same time, we'll all keep an eye out on her."

Nodding his appreciation, they walked inside the reception area of the cheap hotel with Hunter in the lead. There weren't a lot of hotels along the Eastern Shore, but some catered to tourists traveling through. A few others, like this one, seemed a little seedier, and he wondered why David would have stayed here. But then, according to Billie, they didn't have much reimbursement for expenses, so maybe it was an occasional indulgence he could afford if the cost was low.

A young, bespectacled man sat behind the desk, his gaze pinned on his phone. "Just fill out the registration form." He spoke without looking up.

"I don't think that'll be necessary," Hunter said, slapping his badge on the counter.

The man's gaze jumped to the badge before shooting his now-wide eyes up to Hunter, then Jared and Andy. "Oh, sorry!" Crinkling his nose, he said, "Whatcha need?"

"Let's start with your name?"

"Tommy," he squeaked. Clearing his throat, he added, "Thomas. Thomas Stockley."

"Okay, Tommy. Were you working when this man stayed here last month on the seventeenth?" Hunter asked, turning his tablet around to show him a photograph of David.

Tommy pushed his glasses up on his nose and leaned in closely before nodding slowly. "Yeah, I've seen him. Not much, mind you. Maybe two or three times. I could look in our book if you'd like me to." He looked at Jared, a hopeful expression on his face.

"Did he ever come in with a woman?" Jared asked.

Tommy blinked, his mouth now hanging open. "Huh?"

"A woman. Did you ever see him with a woman?"

"Naw, man… uh… Officer." Then Tommy chuckled and leaned forward, lowering his voice. "But, you know, he could've had someone outside, and then he just came in to pay and get the key. Happens all the time."

"Any security cameras here?" Andy asked.

A bark of laughter erupted from Tommy as he slapped his hand down on the counter. "Here? Look around this place. First of all, the owner is some dude from Maryland who never comes down here, and he isn't about to spend any money if he doesn't have to. Plus, we get some… um… short-term customers, if you get what I mean."

He winked, and it took all of Jared's patience not to slap his hand on the counter next to Tommy to jar some sense into him. "Was this man one of those short-term customers?"

Tommy went back to blinking. "I didn't see him leave, so I couldn't say. But if he had a woman, she didn't come in here with him." Shrugging, he added, "But that's not unusual. She could have been waiting in the car."

Hunter gave him his card, telling him to call if he remembered anything else. Walking outside, Jared swiped his hand over his face. Turning to Hunter, he asked, "Any ideas about a bar around here?"

Hunter planted his hands on his hips and stared off into the distance for a few seconds before jerking back around. "You know, I just might. There's a small place about two miles up the road. Not too many locals hit it during the tourist season, but this time of year, it could be where Porter ended up since he's gotten kicked out of a few of the other bars."

They followed Hunter to the small yellow building just off the main highway. Again, Hunter took the lead as they approached the bartender, a young woman whose heavily lined eyes widened when she saw them.

She leaned on her forearms, pressing her elbows together in a practiced maneuver to deepen her cleavage. Popping her gum, she grinned widely. "Howdy. What can I get you boys?"

"Some information," Hunter said, tapping on his tablet.

Jared almost laughed at the loud huff from the woman as it dawned on her that she'd get no drink order, tip, or phone numbers from them.

She stood straighter and took a swipe at the bar with a dirty rag. "Kinda busy here, you know."

"Won't take a minute. Have you seen this guy?"

Her gaze dropped to the tablet, and recognition shot through her eyes. "Oh, uh... yeah." Her renewed interest seemed to pique with the idea of talking to the police. "Hey, is this where I can help solve a crime like on TV? I've always loved those shows. You know, where the police don't know what they're doing, and somebody comes along and—"

"What can you tell us about him?" Hunter

interrupted.

Her brow lowered as her lips pursed.

Andy stepped forward, leaning one elbow on the bar. "Yeah, this is just like on TV. I like those shows, too. What's your name?"

Her eyes flashed as she bent forward again, her gaze raking over Andy, a slow smile spreading over her face. "Tara."

"Well, Tara, whatever you can tell us will really help."

Jared could hear Hunter growl but kept his expression neutral.

"Really?" Twirling one long strand of hair, she bit her bottom lip. "Maybe you and I can talk about it sometime."

"If I'm ever in here again, we can certainly do that. What can you tell us and keep it to just the facts, okay?"

"Sure, sugar. Well, he's come in a couple of times. Nice enough. Decent tipper. Usually just got a drink and made small talk."

"Did he ever come in with a woman?" Jared asked.

Her brow creased, and she nodded slowly. "Yeah… once I saw him with someone, but I wasn't working that night. I'd come in to get my pay." She rolled her eyes. "If I don't come in, Terrance is likely to make me wait, so I'm always in here as soon as he's got payroll ready."

Andy nodded, making a sympathetic noise. "That sucks. But did you notice anything about her?"

Warming to her story, she nodded. "Yep! He was right over there." She pointed, and Jared gazed to see the closest booth.

"Did you recognize her? Can you describe her?"

Andy prodded.

"Never seen her before. Um... dark hair. About to her shoulders. Kind of thin. She had a black turtleneck on. Only reason I noticed was because she had a silver chain with a starfish charm around her neck. I remember thinking it was nice. I've always liked starfish, you know."

"How old do you think she was?"

"Oh, she was old– at least forty!"

Hunter sighed heavily, and Jared began to wonder if they were on a TV show that was more comedy than reality.

"Sure, sure," Andy continued. "Was it just the one time that they were here together?"

Tara nodded. "In fact, that was the last time I saw him here."

"What was the date?"

She cackled. "How would I remember that?"

"It would have been when you picked up your pay."

Blinking, she laughed. "Oh yeah. That would have been on the fifteenth of last month."

A few minutes later, they walked out of the bar, Hunter still growling about being too old to deal with flirty witnesses and Andy laughing. Jared just shook his head, tired and ready to get home to Billie.

"The fifteenth was the last time anyone saw him, and he was with a woman wearing a starfish necklace," Jared said. "Now, if we could just find out who she was, we might be closer to finding out what happened."

With waves goodbye, he drove Andy back to his vehicle and headed home. Home to Billie.

26

Billie had gone to her apartment to shower and change clothes, then headed over to let Daisy out into the yard. Checking Jared's refrigerator, she pulled out the ingredients for dinner, then hesitated. *What am I doing? Playing house in someone else's house?*

She sighed heavily, her thoughts tangled. Deciding on spaghetti, she gathered the ingredients and started the sauce before boiling the water for the noodles. Once everything was ready, she turned the heat down to let the flavors mingle as it stayed warm.

Lost in mundane tasks, she jerked when her phone vibrated and smiled in relief when she spied the caller. "Hey, Rita."

"Hi, Billie. I wanted to see how you were doing."

She must have waited for a half second too long to reply when Rita jumped in and said, "Okay, what's going on?"

Snorting, she leaned her hip against the counter.

"I'm at Jared's place and was just thinking about if I should be here or not."

"Well, technically, his place is your place."

"No... my place is the apartment I'm renting. The one that I haven't spent much time in recently." She scrunched her face, glad her boss couldn't see her expression, considering how cringe-worthy her words were. "God, I'm sorry. That's so stupid. He's out investigating the murder of a coworker, and I'm creating drama where there isn't any."

A few seconds of silence passed before Rita said, "What's going on, Billie? I'm worried about you."

"Don't be. I'm fine, really."

"You know when someone says they're fine, and then add the word *really* after it... they're not."

She huffed despite Rita being right. "Maybe it seems like things are just going too fast. I came over here to do a job and got a tiny efficiency to live in for a few months to keep from the wear and tear and expense of going back and forth across the bay each day. Now, my predecessor is dead. I'm practically living with my landlord in his house. And he's investigating the murder of David. I can't seem to wrap my head around everything."

"Has he introduced you to his friends?"

Squinting her eyes closed, she knew what Rita was implying, and the heat of shame hit her.

"Since I already know the answer to that, I'll just remind you that not everyone is Patrick."

"I know. But it makes me wonder if I'm going too fast."

"There's no fast or slow in how you feel, Billie. We fall for who we fall for. God knows, most women fall for an asshole every now and then. It just makes you realize a prince when you find one."

"Sounds like you've been there."

Rita barked out a high-pitched laugh. "Girl, I've been there, bought the T-shirt, and then burned it along with him at the stake!"

Mood lighter at Rita's description, she laughed. "I'll let you tell me about it sometime."

"Oh, some tales aren't worth bringing back to life. What else is going on with you?"

"Other than that, I was going to tell you that I'm about finished with the constant water monitoring of Wilder Pond inlet. To be honest, I'm going to start widening the expanse to see how far along the bay the toxin levels have changed. Plus, I want you to come over here to visit sometime. I can treat you to lunch and introduce you to Baytown."

"Just Baytown?" Rita asked with an added lilt to her voice.

"Well, maybe to Jared as well."

"We'll see. Going across the long bay bridge isn't one of my near-planned activities. I'll treat you to lunch the next time you're here for a staff meeting, which should be next week. You can fill me in on everything then."

Disconnecting, she jumped at the sound of Jared's SUV on the driveway and Daisy jumping against the door, desperate to get to him. Letting the overexcited dog outside, she laughed. "I know how you feel, girl."

She followed along, her heart warming at the sight

of him kneeling while giving Daisy a generous rubdown before lifting his gaze to peer toward her. Her skin felt singed by the intensity of his smile. Suddenly nervous, she waited at the end on the patio for him to come over.

Stalking forward with Daisy rushing about, she inhaled deeply as his arms banded around her. He always smelled of the outdoors—fresh, with a touch of briny air and pine. It was a strange combination but made her feel as though they were standing on the edge of the bay with sea grass and pine trees nearby. Comforting. Much like the home she'd come from. So much like the home they had. *He had...* she reminded herself... *the home he had.*

Pulling back, she turned and headed into his kitchen, calling over her shoulder, "I'm fixing something simple if that's okay."

His footsteps, along with Daisy's nails clicking on the patio, hustled after her. He caught up to her at the counter and, leaning forward with his hands resting on the edge of the sink, boxing her in, he bent to capture her gaze. "Hey, babe. Are you okay?"

She stared at his neck, avoiding his eyes. "I'm fine." As soon as those words left her lips, she was reminded of what Rita said about the word fine. Shaking her head slightly, she scrunched her nose. "In truth?"

"Always."

"I went back to the efficiency to take a shower after work."

He leaned to the side and flipped off the stove. "Okay," he said, dragging the word out.

"Then I came over here to let Daisy out and was

trying to figure out what to fix for dinner. Then I suddenly realized I don't even know if that's what I should be doing."

"Billie, you're not here to fix dinner for me. You should never feel like that's what you have to do."

"No, no, Jared, that's not what I'm talking about. If I'm home first and fixing food, fixing for one more is easy. It's just, well, it made me think that maybe here isn't where I'm supposed to be."

Now, his brow shot upward. "I can tell you've got something on your mind, and I can tell you're trying to let me know what it is, but I'm gonna need you to be a little more clear."

She leaned forward and rested her forehead on his chest, feeling his chin settling against the top of her head. She reached out and clutched his shirt around his waist and breathed him in, trying to gather her thoughts.

Leaning her head back, she focused on his beautiful blue eyes. "I just came in and made myself at home in your place."

"Yeah," he said, nodding. "I thought we established that was okay."

"It just seems like we're going awfully fast, Jared."

"How fast is too fast?"

She snorted, "That's what Rita said."

"You talked to your boss?"

"She's kind of the only thing close to a girlfriend that I have, or at least had, until I started meeting a few people here."

"Well, I have nothing against your boss, but I'd love

it if you could have some girlfriends on this side of the bay. But let's get back to us going too fast. I don't think feelings have a timeframe, do you?"

"I didn't use to."

"Sounds like there's a story there."

Pressing her lips together, she nodded.

"I'd like to hear it."

Glancing to the side, she said, "Maybe we should eat first—"

"Stove's off. Let's talk first. I don't want anything between us, babe. Especially if it's something that's putting doubts into your head."

He took her hand and led her into the living room, where they settled on the sofa. She hated that she'd put fear in his eyes. Causing him anguish was the last thing she wanted.

"It's hard for me to trust." As soon as the words left her mouth, she knew they were inadequate. They barely hinted at everything she felt. "The last relationship I had was almost two years ago. We dated for six months, and I thought we were heading in the direction of... well, not ring shopping, but at least talking about the possibility of something more permanent down the road."

"What happened, sweetheart?" Jared asked, holding her hand between his and gently rubbing her fingers.

"He'd already gone ring shopping."

Jared's head tilted slightly. "I don't understand."

"He wouldn't be going ring shopping with me because he'd already done it with someone else four years earlier." Sucking in a deep breath, she blurted, "He was married."

Jared's chin jerked back, surprise slamming across his face. "Fuckin' hell, Billie. What a piece of shit!"

"I know I should've known. That it should've been instinctive that I knew he was lying to me. I should've seen the signs. Yet, when I look back, I'm not sure that I could have. I never met his family because he told me his parents had passed away. It was something that he and I had in common. He didn't have a social media account because he didn't believe in posting everything about his life for anyone to see. That was another thing he and I had in common. And I only met a couple of his friends, but when we were together, I thought we all had a good time. He told me he loved me, and I loved him. But looking back, there were things I should have noticed."

"Tell me about them, babe."

"He never asked me to any of his work functions. His apartment was in the next town, and he always drove to my place, saying he didn't want me on the roads too much after dark. I thought he was just being sweet, but of course, I later realized he didn't want me over to his house. He never spent the entire night with me, saying he had an older cat he needed to get back to."

"You've got to be kidding me."

She shook her head and sighed. "There was never going to be a good way to find out, but the way I did was worthy of bad TV drama." She closed her eyes and grimaced even though the memory was several years old, but the emotions always cut straight to her heart. "My doorbell rang one day, and when I opened it, there was a beautiful and very pregnant woman standing outside. Before I had a chance to ask if I could help her, she wanted to know if I knew Patrick Wilson. I said no, and then she held up her phone with a picture of my Patrick. I told her that it was Patrick Dalton, my boyfriend. She croaked a rather unearthly sound and told me that his name was Patrick Dalton Wilson, her husband and father to their child."

The air rush from Jared's lungs, but he kept her fingers clutched in his, and she relied on the lifeline he'd thrown her.

"I won't go into more sordid details, but suffice it to say I was devastated and mortified. Devastated that the man I thought I'd be with was a liar, cheater, and horrid human being. But that was nothing compared to the mortification I felt. I was the other woman! I was the one her husband was cheating with! Me!"

"Babe, you have to know that's not on you. It wasn't your fault. You weren't knowingly dating a married man… you were dating a man who you thought was available."

"That's what my head said, but my heart ached for what hadn't been real and for the pain that poor woman was going through."

"I'm so sorry," he said, still holding her hands tightly.

She blew out a breath, puffing her cheeks out. "There was a massive argument that occurred between him and me. He was contrite, but I was never sure if it was more because he got caught. He admitted he didn't know she was pregnant when he met me, and they had discussed separating. Then after he and I dated for a couple of months, they found out they were expecting.

Of course, who knows if that was true. I hurled accusations and asked questions, none of which he could give a response worth a shit. I took everything he left at my place and everything he'd ever given me and tossed them over my apartment balcony."

"Was that the last time you saw him?"

She snorted while nodding. "The last time I saw him, the last time I spoke to him, and in some ways, the last time I thought about him. Yes, I cried, threw a few things around my apartment, went for long runs, where I tried to pound out my frustration onto the pavement, drank copious amounts of wine, and ate gallons of ice cream. And then, I moved on from being the other woman, something I never thought would be a label slapped on me."

"Billie, honey, you can't blame yourself for that. You were in a relationship, and he was the one cheating, not you."

"I was so hurt and angry that when I walked away from him, I walked *away*! No conversations. No phone calls. No regrets about not having him in my life and no looking back… but it did a number on my ability to trust my gut."

"And because of that, you don't trust what you feel now?"

Her shoulders slumped as she groaned. "That sounds so petty, doesn't it? You're not him. I'm not comparing you to him. It's my fear about *my* judgment."

They sat in silence, and with each second that passed, her heart beat faster. She wanted what he had to offer. She wanted to take what he was giving. She wanted to race headfirst into the rush of feelings and accept the blush of love that was growing. And she wondered if she'd dashed it all to hell with her admission.

"Do you remember the first morning in your apartment?" he asked, drawing her gaze to him. "The argument between Stephanie and me?"

A dry laugh left her lips. "Um... that was kind of hard to forget."

He winced, and she felt an instant pang of regret. "I'm sorry—"

"No, you're right. My past was here, right in your face. And I fucking hate that."

She waited, knowing he had a lot more on his mind than that morning with Stepanie.

"I once thought about going ring shopping. Years ago. A girl I met in South Carolina when stationed there. Like you, after six months of dating, getting to know each other, and growing closer, I thought we had a future. I thought we were on the same page. I knew I had a temporary assignment coming up and thought about asking her to marry me when I got back. I even hinted that's what I wanted to do, but she learned I wasn't the one while I was gone."

"I'm almost afraid to ask how you learned that," Billie said.

"I came home to find out that she'd gone out with a coworker and decided that staying in one place and being with him was what she wanted."

"Oh, Jared, I'm really sorry. It's hard, isn't it? When

you think you trust another person only to find out they aren't at all who or what you thought they were."

"Yeah. Only I realize that with your story, you pulled back. If you doubted yourself and others, you didn't even want to put yourself out there for it to happen again. I did the opposite and decided to just date for fun. Keep it light. Keep it easy. No expectations and nothing but physical fun with no messy emotions to get in the way."

"Hence, the Stephanie parade began?"

Now it was his turn to bark out a laugh. Nodding, he reached over and tucked a wayward strand of hair behind her ear. "Never thought of it that way, but yeah." He sighed, shaking his head slightly. "It wasn't a big parade. But whenever I did meet someone, I made my expectations clear. Occasionally, someone thought they could bend me to their will and try to make me fall for them. Since I was never interested in them that way, there was no chance. I never realized Stephanie held any thoughts that we were more until that morning."

"What's different now? With you and me? How are you sure?"

"A lot of things."

Rolling her eyes, she said, "You're gonna have to break it down for me, Jared."

"Okay, first of all, it's what I feel for you. And before you say that I felt it for someone else, you'd be right. But just because love doesn't work at one time doesn't mean it doesn't work out with someone else. Second of all, I never started anything with you based on physical. What we started with was based on true admiration and friendship. To me, it was at the perfect starting point for deeper emotions."

"Deeper emotions..." she repeated, liking that description.

"I know we're not ready to label what we feel. But I like you being here in this house. You feel right here. You understand what this place has been and what it means. And having you here makes it complete. Do you still want your own space for now? Keep the efficiency and keep some of your things there. But I hope you'll spend most of your time here. And as far as being too soon, like I said, there's no timeline on what you feel for someone or when you feel it. Just don't keep yourself safe by holding back. And don't keep me at arm's distance because of what someone else did."

She stared into his eyes as his words swirled around her like an embrace, warmth sinking into her pores and filling her being.

He smiled and squeezed her fingers. "Can dinner wait a little longer?"

Pressing her lips together, she tried to stifle her grin but was unsuccessful. "Yeah. What did you have in mind?"

He stood, drew her to her feet, and wrapped his arm around her shoulders. "How about I show you instead?"

Laughing, they walked tightly together up the stairs. And as they slipped into the bedroom, she was right where she wanted to be. In this house, with him.

27

When Jared walked up the stairs of his house, his fingers linked with Billie's, he had no grand plan of seduction. Sex? Yes. Taking care of her? Absolutely. Trying to solidify in her mind that they were right and deserved to have a shot at happiness together? Hell yeah.

But it wasn't until he reached the top landing and glanced toward the bathroom straight in front of him that the idea hit him. Instead of leading her into the bedroom, he detoured them straight into the bathroom. The slight pull on his hand gave evidence of her hesitation. Looking over his shoulder, he grinned. "Don't worry. I haven't forgotten the layout of my house. This is just the place we need to be."

He released her hand and bent over the tub, starting the water. Turning back to her, he moved closer until barely an inch was between their bodies, and she had to lean her head back to hold his gaze. Closing the scant distance, he rested his forehead on hers before gliding his nose along the side of her cheek and whispering in her ear, "Let me take care of you, sweetheart."

She held his arms, and at his words, her fingers clenched. "My dad always called my mom sweetheart and me his little sweetheart. I love hearing you say it as well."

Her words seeped inside, and he knew what a gift she was giving him. "I love saying it." His hands moved to the bottom of her shirt, and he lifted it, grinning as she raised her arms into the air, making it easier to strip the material from her body. Her bra was next to be discarded, freeing her breasts. His fingers made quick work of her zipper, and with his thumbs hooked into the waistband of her pants, he slid them slowly over her hips and down her legs. As he knelt on the floor, her hands rested on his shoulders as she stepped carefully out of her pants and panties.

Standing slowly, his hands trailed from her ankles, up her legs, and over her delectable ass. He breathed in deeply, the scent of her arousal making his already erect cock twitch even more. His hands continued their path over the dips and valleys of her waist to the fullness of her breasts, where his thumbs circled her nipples. With great reluctance, he finally took her by the hand and assisted her over the side of the tub, where she settled into the warm water.

She peered up at him, a questioning specter in her eyes, and he smiled. Reaching behind him, he stripped off his shirt, shucked his pants and boxers after removing his boots, and stood in the middle of the bathroom, naked, preening as her appreciative gaze devoured him.

"Scoot up a little bit, babe," he requested. She immediately acquiesced, and he stepped into the tub behind her, leaning his back against the porcelain, his knees cocked on either side of her body, and guided her back to his front.

He couldn't remember the last time he'd taken a bath and had never had one with a woman. Suddenly, it was important to him to let her know that, wanting her to claim something that no one else had ever had.

His hands dipped into the water and trailed droplets over her shoulders. Since his shared bath was spontaneous, he was glad her body wash was within grabbing distance. Squeezing a generous amount of the sweet floral scent onto his hands, he glided them over her arms, neck, and back, then massaged her breasts, eliciting moans from her as her head fell back onto his shoulder. Dipping the clean washcloth into the warm water, he gently followed the same path, rinsing away the suds.

She appeared almost boneless as she relaxed against his body, but he was anything but at ease. With her perfect ass nestled against his erection, he battled against the desire to drag her out of the tub and plunge into her waiting warmth.

"This is a first for me. When I redid this bathroom, I wanted the soaker tub, but I've always taken a shower. I've never taken a bath with anyone before."

She twisted slightly, her cheek now resting against his shoulder as she held his gaze. "I've never shared a bath with anyone either." Her smile was steady but almost shy.

He bent and kissed her lightly, not wanting to rush anything. "Then this is ours." Seeing her still focused on his face, he continued. "I've never shared a meal with anybody in this house until you. I've never worked with anyone in this house who wasn't just helping me out as a friend. But you actually understand what I'm trying to do. I've never bathed with anyone, so this is another first."

"You're giving me first memories."

"Sweetheart, I want what we have to keep growing. And if it goes the way I want it to, then you and I will have a lot of firsts in this house. Here, there's no past. There's just going forward."

Wrapping his arms around her, he kissed her ear and nuzzled her neck as one hand played with her breasts before tweaking her nipples, and the other hand slid lower. His thumb pressed against her clit as he inserted his forefinger deep inside. She groaned and arched her back, pressing her tits deeper into his palm. She was like a fine instrument that needed to be savored as well as played. As the maestro, he applied just the right pressure to find the right spots before her hands gripped his arm, and her body shattered through her release as she cried out his name. Her head fell back against his shoulder, and he kept his arms around her as her body slowly recovered from her orgasm.

When her breathing slowed to normal, she tipped her head back and kissed the underside of his jaw. It was the softest touch and sent tingles reverberating throughout his body.

With a little splashing and not much grace, Billie maneuvered around so that she was on her knees facing him. Her brilliant smile shot straight through him, and catching him by surprise, she reached to the side and grabbed his soap, lathering it in her hands. Her palms massaged his chest and abs, shoulders and arms, and she even had him lean forward slightly so she could slip her fingers down his back.

Each touch sent shock waves of need through him, but he was struck with the realization that it was more than just sexual. It was the need for intimacy. The need for tactile care. It was the need for comfort. It was the need to explore each other's bodies.

Her hand slipped to his cock, finding it erect and ready, and he grinned. *Oh yeah, it's this need, too.*

He'd wanted it to be all about her, but she shushed him when he opened his mouth. "You're going to tell me this is about me, and I'm here to tell you it's about us."

He laughed at the accuracy of her statement, but with her hand wrapped around his cock, it came out as more of that garbled, strangled sound. Not masculine at all, but with the other sensations zinging through his body, he didn't care what he sounded like.

Her hand stopped as a crinkle formed along her brow. She looked up and sighed. "I know I should be creative. I know I should figure out a way to make this work in the bathtub, and I'm sure in a romance novel somewhere, couples are doing this right now. I just have no idea how."

This time, his laughter rang out loud and true, loving how real she was. "Babe, since I've never had a bath with a woman, I can't give you the benefit of any experience. And I can't figure out a way to have sex in the bathtub right now without it hurting or straining you in some way, so we're not gonna do it. In the next room, we've got a big bed. Our bed. How about we finish this bath and take it in there?"

"God, yes," she gushed, standing quickly, keeping her balance with her hands gripping his shoulders. That put her sex right in front of his face, and mesmerized with the droplets of water sluicing down her curves, he missed taking advantage of the delight presented to him. But she was too fast, and he barely had time to grab her hand to help her out of the tub. Once she was out, he followed, taking the thick towel from her hands and gently patting her body dry. His gaze devoured each inch of skin, loving how she glowed pink when he finished.

He made quick work of drying himself off, then scooped her up into his arms and carried her into the bedroom. Stalking over to the bed, he grinned just before he tossed her, watching her bounce on the mattress, her eyes wide in surprise. An interrupted laugh erupted from her, and he wiggled his eyebrows as he crawled over her body, licking, nipping, and kissing from her knees upward. He nuzzled the small strip of curls at the apex of her thighs, the scent of her arousal once more filling his nostrils. With the flat of his tongue, he licked her slit, finding her wet and ready.

Continuing to kiss his way up her body, he

caressed the underside of her breasts before circling her nipples with his tongue, then drawing one deep into his mouth. Surrounded by the scent of her body wash, he settled between her thighs, his cock nudging at her entrance. As his lips found hers once again, an explosion of desire for this woman made it hard to think rationally. But he managed to lift up long enough to grab a condom from the nightstand and roll it on.

With her body welcoming, she lifted her hands toward him, wiggling her fingers as she beckoned him in. For just a second, he halted, memorizing the smile on her face, the light in her eyes, and her silky blonde hair spread over his pillow. Then with his massive arms cradling her and his hands clutching her cheeks, he drove his erection upward, filling her. Bound together, it was like coming home.

Billie gasped with fullness as his cock stretched her inner core, sending shards of light flickering behind her closed eyelids. Her fingers dug into his warm skin, the feel of his muscles moving underneath her hands, giving evidence of the power and control in his body.

"Look at me, sweetheart," he ordered gently.

She knew it wasn't an order of dominance but a request to make sure she was okay. She snapped her eyes open, still smiling. "You feel amazing, Jared, but it would feel even better if you'd move."

His smile spread over his face before he chuckled

and dipped his head to trace her lips with his tongue, mumbling, "Whatever the lady wants, she gets."

As his hips pistoned, they moved together with each thrust until nothing existed in the world but their bodies, their hearts, and the sounds of them coming together.

Just when she thought she couldn't take any more, he pulled out, and she gasped again, this time in an unpleasant surprise. "What—"

Before she had a chance to finish her sentence, he shifted back, grabbed her hips, and flipped her over. With his palms smoothing over her ass, he pulled her hips upward. "You okay, babe?"

She tossed her hair over her shoulder as she turned and looked at him, smiling. "Oh yeah."

He plunged into her once again, filling her just as much yet touching every nerve so differently. Her breasts bounced in rhythm with his thrusts, and he bent over her back, his hands filled as they teased and tantalized her nipples.

She wasn't going to last long, and soon her body began to shatter as she cried out her release, flinging herself over the precipice into an abyss that sparked brilliant shocks throughout her core. He groaned along with her, fingering her clit with one hand and her nipples with the other. He grunted, then his release pulled a long groan from him as his body shuddered around her.

As the last vibrating ripple left her body, she slumped forward, feeling his weight pressing against her back. He was heavy but not burdensome. She felt cradled. Surrounded. Protected. And it struck her that she'd never felt that emotion before. And following on the heels of that thought, she realized she could trust what she felt for him.

He rolled to the side, shifting her so they faced each other, arms wrapped and legs tangled.

"Are you okay, sweetheart?"

Clinging to his bicep, she whispered, "I trust you."

His chin jerked slightly. "What are you saying?"

While holding his gaze, her heart pounded against her rib cage as his blue eyes held her captive. She blinked at the moisture gathering. "I trust you. I trust us together. I trust what I'm feeling. Because what I feel is nothing like what I've ever felt for anyone else before. When I'm with you, it's like coming home."

The smile he bestowed surrounded her with warmth, emotions so choking it was hard to breathe.

"Christ, babe, I was just thinking the same thing. You and me together—we make home."

A tear escaped, dropping over her nose and onto the pillow. He captured the trail with his thumb. "What're the tears for, sweetheart?"

She swallowed deeply, uncertain of her voice. Finally, dragging in a breath that didn't hitch, she said, "Home. It's been a really long time since I've felt at home."

28

The next day, Billie was in the apartment using the floor space to spread out her reports. She heard Jared coming down the driveway, and a smile slid across her face at the same time she jumped up from sitting on the floor. Opening the door, she stepped out onto the landing and called down to him. The greeting smile on his face struck her. *I could watch this scene play over and over for years.*

"Hey, what are you doing up there?"

"I'm working on some reports. Come on up. I'm almost finished."

He bounded up the steps, his boots clomping on the wood, and once he was at the top, she threw open her arms, welcoming him with a kiss. He grabbed her around the waist and lifted her feet off the ground, his lips still devouring hers. Stalking inside the apartment, he kicked the door shut with his boot before setting her down on the floor.

Pulling back, she laughed. "Wow, that was some greeting."

"Well, I was glad to see you. Plus, I have good news."

Curious, she dragged him over to the small sofa, making sure to step carefully over the papers scattered on the floor. Once seated, she gave him her full attention. "Okay, let's hear the good news."

"The North Heron Sheriff's Department brought Lou Ackers in for questioning, and they might have enough evidence for suspicion of the murder of David Bourne."

The words took a few seconds to sink in before her head jerked, and she blinked. "What? Are you kidding? Wait a minute… Lou? That doesn't make any sense! Why?"

"Hang on." He chuckled. "Let's do it one question at a time. First of all, there are some things I can't say since the investigation is ongoing, but I can tell you that the medical examiner determined the weapon was some type of metal instrument with prongs, like a rake. The deputies gathered some of the farm and garden rakes with the farmers' permission, but none fit the medical examiner's exact parameters. Then when Joseph and Callan were out and had stopped Lou for a routine check, they noticed the type of oyster rake he used."

Billie gasped, jerking again. "I've seen him with his rake, or at least one of them. But as an oysterman, he'd hardly be the only one with a rake! There must be a variety of oyster rakes out there."

"He admitted he had several near the dock where he

keeps his boats. It was kind of weird because he told the deputies they could check whatever they wanted."

"If he's guilty, he must not have realized how accurately they could check."

"We figured the same thing. We found one that when the deputies took it to the ME, it matched and had traces of blood and brain matter."

She slumped back against the cushions, thinking of how Lou could've killed David. Shaking her head slowly, she said, "My mind is whirling." She pressed her lips together tightly for a moment as she sorted through the information he had given. "Doesn't it seem rather strange that he would use one of his own rakes and then just leave it out with a bunch of others he had near his dock?"

"Sweetheart, if you only had any idea how many dumb mistakes criminals make, which certainly helps law enforcement apprehend them."

"I'm sure you're right." She nodded, still turning the information over in her head. "What was his motivation?"

"My guess would be that he may have come across David and thought he was a poacher."

Another gasp slipped from her as she asked, "He would kill somebody poaching his oysters?"

"It could have been spur of the moment. He may have just been angry. He may have just been swinging the rake to knock him back. It could've been an argument that got out of hand, and he reacted."

"What does he say?"

"From what Hunter told Ryan, he denies that rake

was his. He'd seen David, but he didn't do anything once he found out who he was."

"Kind of like with me," she murmured, her mind traveling back to when she'd first met the oyster fisherman, her heartbeat now pounding. "Jesus, he thought I was a poacher at first."

Jared swiped his hand over his face. His mouth pinched in a tight line. "Fuckin' hell."

She blew out a breath and shook her head. "He was suspicious, thought I was a guy at first, but then talked a little bit once I identified myself."

Brows lifted, Jared leaned in for a kiss. "I'd never mistake you for a guy."

She laughed in the middle of the kiss, shifting closer, wanting to dispel the tension from Jared at the thought she had been in danger. "Mmm, I'm glad." Leaning back, she reached up to sweep her fingers over his jaw. "Is the investigation over?"

"Not at all," he said, sucking in a deep breath before letting it out slowly. "He hasn't been formally charged... just held for questioning right now. They'll check the rake for fingerprints. Keep looking for David's boat. And there are a few other leads they'll continue to investigate."

"Those are the ones you can't talk about, right?"

He nodded, then looked down at the messy floor. "Do I even want to know what the hell all that is for?"

"Ugh. I told Rita I was finishing the Wilders Pond Inlet water analysis today and was pulling together my reports."

"What's next for you?"

"Oh, there are lots left to be done on the bay. In fact, next, I'm going to go several miles north of the inlet where the natural preserves are. I told Rita that when I finished the reports tomorrow, I would start a comparison study of that water with the water on the edge of the overfertilized farms. I just need to compile these papers, and then I'll start at the new location tomorrow."

"Rita isn't going to assign you to the farthest regions of the bay?"

Shaking her head slowly, she smiled. "Nope. I'm here in this area to stay."

"Good."

Her hand flew to her chest, and she batted her eyes in mock surprise. "Good?"

He dragged her over his lap and surrounded her in his embrace. "Yeah… good. Good for me to keep you close."

Feeling as light as air, she grinned. "No… good for us."

He stood with her still in his arms and gently settled her feet to the floor. With his knuckle under her chin, he lifted her face to his and kissed her lightly. "You told your boss that you wouldn't have the reports ready until tomorrow?"

Following his meaning, she grinned while nodding. "Yep."

"That means you have the rest of the evening free?"

"Absolutely, positively, unequivocally free for whatever I want to do."

Bending, he nibbled around her lips before licking

the seam, giving her just a taste before pulling back. "And what would you like to do?"

Throwing her head back in laughter, she replied, "Anything with you."

Brows lifted, he confirmed, "Anything?"

"Absolutely, positively, unequivocally anything with you."

It was his turn to laugh as he linked his fingers with hers and led her to the door. "Then let's leave this mess and head over to our place."

With those words now replacing all other thoughts, she danced beside him, anxious for whatever the evening would bring.

Billie was thrilled to be back out on the water in an area where she didn't have to worry about farmers glaring at her with the guns in their arms, being near oyster beds with fisherman wielding a rake viciously. In fact, the idea of being out on the bay near one of the preserves where there were no houses around and few boats in the late fall on a cool day filled with sunshine was one of her favorite activities. It barely felt like work as she breathed in deeply and appreciated the view from her small boat.

Her mind rolled to last night's activities with Jared once they made it back to his place, and she laughed out loud. The lighthearted sound reverberated over the water. *Okay, so today is great, but last night was definitely the best!*

Coming to the shore area of the three-hundred-acre preserve, she looked toward the maritime forests and bird habitats that lay just beyond the beach and dunes. She was also aware of the population of northeastern beach tiger beetles, the endangered species that kept the beaches along the bay from becoming overrun with hotels and condos. Offering thanks for such a tiny creature that allowed the Eastern Shore of Virginia to remain unspoiled, she aimed her boat toward the area she was most interested in.

She made several stops close to the shore to test the water, moving in a pattern that she thought would give her the best readings. There were several inlets around, and as she moved into a smaller one, she was immediately struck with the thick underbrush that grew close to the marshy edge of the water. *So different from the farms that extend all the way to the water without a vegetation barrier.* She couldn't wait to see the results of her water testing in this more natural environment.

Deciding to follow the inlet to its end, the shorelines on either side of her narrowed until she was almost in a creek. Light reflected through the trees nearby, and a glint of something metallic buried in the marsh vegetation caught her eye. She moved her boat closer, glad it was high tide, or she would never be able to make it to the object. Cutting her engine, she used her paddle to maneuver closer, pushing the limbs and grasses to the side.

Upon closer inspection, she could see a small boat. The back was submerged in the thick mud, and as she leaned over, it was evident the boat was empty. A dark stain covered part of the seat and bottom that she could see. Using her oar to push away a few of the reeds near the front, she stared dumbly at the faded CBF insignia. *Oh shit! David's boat!*

Her heartbeat stumbled at the idea of the dark stain being his blood. A shiver wracked her body, trying to force her thoughts to settle on what she should do. She knew Jared and the other investigators had been searching for the missing watercraft, and having watched enough TV dramas, she knew not to touch anything.

Another stream of light through the trees hit a sparkle in the bottom of the boat, partially under the seat. Leaning to the side, it appeared to be a glint of gold. Maneuvering closer, she bent over carefully, wanting a closer look. A small golden charm in the shape of a starfish lay on the bottom of the boat. She didn't see a chain, but the gold pendant was distinguishable. *But... how...?*

Scrambling, she dug into her backpack for her phone, desperate for her fingers to wrap around the case. Pulling it out, she dialed Jared first, then grimaced as it went straight to his voicemail. Next, she dialed the dispatcher at the VMP. As soon as she answered, Billie blurted, "This is Wilhelmina Schmidt. I was trying to get ahold of Jared, but I couldn't. I found David Bourne's boat."

"What is your location?"

Giving the best description she could, she listened as the dispatcher radioed her location to the others.

"Billie? I know you don't remember meeting me, but

I talked with you when you called before. Jared and Chief Coates are out together, along with several of the others. I've sent your information, and he's just radioed back that he's getting ready to call you. I will disconnect so you can lead him straight to where you are."

She barely had time to think before the dispatcher disconnected, and Jared was calling. Connecting, she didn't give him a chance to speak. "Jared? I think I've come across David's boat. It's hidden, half in the mud. I'm not touching anything, but I can see that it's empty except for—"

"Bille, hold on. Give me your exact location," he ordered, his curt voice cutting through her racing thoughts.

"I entered Smith inlet. Part of the preserve—"

"I know where that is. There are smaller inlets as you go. Which one are you in?"

"I kept following the main one until I ended up near a creek. I'm almost to the point where my boat wouldn't go any farther. I don't know that you can get all the way in here with your vessel—"

"Don't worry about that. We're on our way, and the sheriff's department will be coming by and through the preserve as well."

"Jared, I can see a gold necklace part… um… the charm lying in the bottom under a seat."

"Don't touch anythi–, Bi—"

His voice cut out. "What? What did you say?"

"Shit, Bill–Le– everythi– I'll be th– in– few—"

They no longer had a connection and wondered how long it would take before he arrived. She debated whether she should stay close to David's boat or push back a little bit to give them more room. She had no idea how the large VMP vessel would get to where she was, but she knew he'd take care of everything.

Sucking in a deep breath, she let it out slowly as she tried to steal her tumultuous thoughts, but her eyes stayed on David's boat, and thoughts of him dying there filled her mind. She would later wonder why she hadn't immediately tumbled to the obvious, but the bizarre mix of evidence facing her seemed incongruent at the moment.

She pulled up her phone's GPS and looked at the map, wondering how the sheriff's department would get to her location on land. While the preserve was uninhabited, there were walking trails and dirt roads for maintenance and preservation caretakers throughout. Looking up, she couldn't see a road from where she was, but according to the map, there was a dirt road just on the other side of the tree line.

The sound of muffled cursing and thrashing met her ears, and she watched in stunned, open-mouth, wide-eyed silence as a female burst through the vegetation, stopping on the other side of David's boat.

The woman looked down, focusing on the boat before her attention snagged upward. Her mouth hung open as she stared at Billie. "Oh God," the woman murmured.

29

"Rita!" The name came out strong, without a hint of surprise, which was amazing, considering Billie's body quaked.

"You weren't supposed to be in the area until later," Rita said, her wide-eyed gaze pinned to Billie's face.

"I finished my reports early and decided to get back out on the water." It was as though they were in the office, not standing in the marshy wilderness near a murdered coworker's boat. Looking down into the boat again, the gold starfish charm twinkled, taunting her. And so did the truth. *It was her... it had to be her.* Another shiver sliced through her, and she pressed her hand against her chest to still the pounding of her heart. "Why, Rita? What... why?"

Rita opened her mouth, then snapped it closed, heaving a great sigh. She appeared so calm Billie almost expected her to ask about the reports. If Billie had been on land with her boss, she would have shaken her, looking for some emotion. "Why David? Why kill him? You barely knew him!"

Those words snapped something in Rita, and her lips curved upward on one side in a sneer. The clouds of understanding parted, and Billie's lungs expelled air with a rush. "Oh. You did know him well, didn't you? Oh God, you never said anything." Her chest heaved again. "But that still doesn't tell me why?"

"I guess maybe he was more like Patrick than I thought." Rita scoffed, then dropped her chin and stared down into the boat, slowly shaking her head. "It shouldn't have ended this way."

"You two were… dating?"

Rita's eyes flashed, and her face screwed into a grimace. At that moment, Billie didn't recognize her friendly, easygoing boss at all.

"It was more than just dating."

"O…kay." Billie agreed as fear slithered through her.

"We started dating months ago and quickly fell in love. We agreed to keep it quiet since I was his boss. That wasn't too hard since he was already working on this side of the bay, and I'd come over here to be with him. We'd usually go to a small out-of-the-way restaurant or bar, just the two of us, then find a small hotel. Sometimes we'd go out in the motorboat and watch the sunset over the bay. He'd pull some oysters from a local bed, and we'd go to the beach, start a little campfire, and roast them. He gave me the starfish necklace, and I took the meaning to heart. Eternal love. But I got tired of hiding. I was ready to let the world know."

Rita's face tightened, her grimace taking on a vicious

scowl. "I was stupid. I didn't see the signs. We never saw each other in Virginia Beach. He never invited me to his apartment there. I didn't meet his friends or any family. I fell for a man I thought I knew, and I really didn't."

Rita's words echoed deep inside Billie, remembering learning that Patrick was married. *But I never thought of killing him...* Watching her strong boss crumple in front of her, Billie struggled to understand. "What happened?"

"I came over for one of our dates, and we met at a bar, then he planned for us to roast oysters while watching the sunset. We went out in his boat, and he harvested some oysters and started talking. I thought I had found the most amazing man, and he said he had something to discuss. I thought he was going to propose. Then he told me this would be our last date, and he wanted to make it special."

Billie's mouth opened, then closed quickly, uncertain what to say. It was just as well since Rita was on a roll.

"Because he was moving away to pursue his former ex-fiancée. He said they'd been together before, but her job took her to another state, so they ended it. But he'd decided he wanted to move to where she'd gone and pick up where they'd left off. He had the gall to tell me that dating me gave him the bravery to decide to pursue the one who got away!"

"Oh God, Rita," Billie breathed, seeing the disaster playing out in front of her with the agonizing words spewing forth.

Rita's hands jerked upward to the side, her fingers making air quotes. "Special! He wanted this last date to be special. Jesus, how stupid could he be?" Her words guttural, she added, "And then all I could think of was how stupid could *I* be?"

Billie was filled with a strange mixture of sympathy at her situation and fear of what she'd done.

Rita's voice now became unemotional, as though she were reciting a recipe. "We were sitting in the boat, and he told me there was no future for us. That it had been fun, that he loved getting to know me, but he had made his choice." She snorted, the barking noise sharp. "I guess that's all I was to him. Fun… and an entanglement he no longer wanted."

"What did you do?" Even as the words left her lips in a whisper, Billie already knew the answer. She felt torn between wanting to hear the story and desperate for Jared to arrive. A bizarre emotion hit her, tangling with all the other thoughts going through her head. A part of her wanted to climb out of her boat and go to Rita, wrapping her arms around her and telling her that no man was worth that agony. After all, Billie had that experience and had made it to the other side of that pain. Yet the evidence of what Rita had done was like a lightning bolt, keeping Billie rooted to the seat of her boat. She repeated, "What did you do?"

Rita heaved her shoulders in a slight shrug. "I… I don't know. I was angry. He wasn't even regretful. Or apologetic. He didn't act like it was any big deal for us to part ways. My heart was being ripped open, and all I could think of was that he just sat there with a stupid smile on his face as though we'd been nothing."

She squeezed her eyes tightly shut, and Billie could tell Rita was lost in her thoughts and memories.

"I wanted to lash out. I wanted him to feel part of the pain slashing through me. I don't know… the oyster rake was lying in the boat next to me, and I grabbed it. I swung because I just wanted him to hurt." Her face scrunched, and her hands gripped into tight fists as though she were holding the rake in her hand. "I swung blindly and hit him. I didn't even know what part of him I hit, but my whole body jarred. When I opened my eyes, I saw that the rake prongs had… Oh God, there was so much blood. And I panicked. I dropped the rake into the bottom of the boat, and rolled him over the edge, and dumped him out into the bay. I took the boat back to one of the docks, where I saw other oyster rakes around. I dragged it through the water, hoping to get off any blood, and then dropped it among all the others."

Seemingly exhausted from her tale, Rita heaved a great sigh.

"The boat? How did it come to be here?"

Rita stared dumbly at her for a moment, her scrunched expression giving evidence she was struggling with remembering. "Um… we were parked near here. It was a place he knew, and we could come and launch in a secluded area. I tried to scuttle the boat, climbed through the marsh and brush, and hurried along the path until I came to my car. I had his keys and drove his car into some brush at the preserve."

"Why did you come back? Today. Why did you come back here today?"

"Because you told me you would be working in this area. And I was afraid you might find the boat."

"It wasn't the boat, was it? You were afraid of what was left inside."

Rita's gaze jerked downward, and she nodded. "He'd given me the necklace. In the struggle, it had broken. I thought it might be lost forever, which was fine by me at the time, but when you said you would be in the area, I knew the boat might be found. And if it was, I needed to be sure you didn't find the necklace." She looked up again, offering a sad, barely-there smile. "You were the only one who'd ever seen the necklace. I kept it under my blouses, but you noticed it one day when we moved equipment in the office."

Billie nodded slowly, remembering her remark about the lovely necklace, only to have Rita tuck it back inside her shirt and keep working. She jerked at the sound of a motor in the distance, closing her eyes in relief for a second. A gasp caused her to look up, seeing realization flit across and then settle on Rita's face.

"They're coming," Rita said, resignation dripping from her words.

Swallowing deeply, Billie nodded. "I called them when I found the boat. I'm…" She'd almost apologized, then halted, anguish spearing through her.

The engines grew louder, and she chanced a glance over her shoulder to see two VMP vessels having come close and recognized Callan, Jose, Joseph, Andy, and Ryan. Another smaller boat launched from one of the vessels toward them, Jared at the back with his hand on the motor handle. Her gaze held his from the narrowing distance, and her heart squeezed in her chest. *He's coming for me.* In spite of the fucked-up situation, her lips began to curve upward, then froze as the men in the boats raised their guns, and Jared's eyes were no longer on her.

"Ma'am, drop your weapon!" he called out.

She blinked, her world now in slow motion as she turned around to see Rita with a gun drawn and pointed right at her. "R… Rita?"

30

Jared's heart pounded as a cold sweat broke out over his body. Billie's gaze had registered relief when she'd spied him arriving, and his heart leaped. Then the woman standing on the mucky edge of the water near the boat had reached into a bag and lifted a gun, pointing it directly at Billie's back. His breath was now held captive, burning in his lungs.

Shouting the order to drop her weapon, he caught the sudden jerking of Billie's body, and her eyes widened before she turned toward the woman.

"I'm sorry… but I… I… don't know what to do…" the woman proclaimed, her face contorted as tears streamed.

He moved closer, hoping to get to Billie before the woman discharged the weapon, even by accident. His boat bumped gently against hers, and he whispered, "It's me. Stay calm."

Billie's chest heaved. "This isn't the right thing to do, Rita. I know you're upset. I know what he did was hurtful. But, honey, this isn't right. Please… drop the gun. Let them help you."

Rita? Her boss? Speaking softly into his radio, he murmured, "Rita May. Billie's boss."

"Copy that," Ryan radioed just as softly. "North Heron deputies are approaching by land."

Though he was trained to read and defuse situations, all he could do was stare at the back of Billie's head, the woman in front of her with the gun, and try not to lose his shit and make things worse. "Billie." He kept his voice low, and her shoulders slightly stiffened as she sat up straighter, her head cocked slightly to the side. "Stay very still." She gave an almost imperceptible nod, and he shifted his focus to Rita.

"Rita? You're Billie's boss, I believe. And her friend. She's spoken of you. She doesn't need to be part of this. Let's have her move out of the way."

The gun wavered in Rita's hand, and he could see her chewing on her bottom lip. Ryan's voice over the earpiece radio indicated that Colt, Hunter, and several deputies coming up behind Rita were apprised of the situation.

"Let's get you out of this cold, Rita. And you can tell us what's going on. You can let us know what's happened so we'll know how to help."

"H… help?" she stammered. "I think it's gone far beyond helping." A wail left her lungs as tears continued to stream down her face. "He's dead. David's dead, but I didn't mean to kill him. I just wanted him to hurt. I wanted him to hurt as he'd hurt me." The gun wavered again as she squeezed her eyes shut, shaking her head as though to dislodge the memories.

"Rita," he continued, "You don't want to point the gun toward Billie. She hasn't done anything to you, and we don't want anyone else to get hurt. We've got some people who can help you that are gonna come up behind you, so I don't want you to be surprised. But first, we need you to lower your weapon."

Hunter and two deputies slipped behind her, their guns trained on her as well. Billie whimpered at the sight, and he wanted nothing more than to keep her out of the line of fire and not a witness to whatever was going down. Billie spoke up just as he opened his mouth to issue another warning.

"Rita… look at me, honey." Rita's gaze jumped to Billie, and the gun wavered again. "Please, please give up. Let them help you. Whatever happened before, you don't want to make it worse. I know you don't want to hurt me."

Pressing her lips together as her head jerked side to side, Rita's face crumpled. "I don't want anything to hurt again."

She turned the gun away from Billie, and Jared let out a quick breath and then sucked another one in again as she aimed the gun toward herself.

"No!" Billie screamed, her body lurching forward, hands out as though she could stop the horror from happening.

Two shots rang out, and Rita fell backward, her scream echoing over the water, instantly joined by another scream bolting from Billie's lips. Jared reached over, grabbed Billie around the waist, and dragged her to his small boat, pushing her down while his gaze raked over her, assuring she was unhurt. "Christ, babe, fuckin' hell. Christ, Jesus…" he groaned, his body lying over hers for protection. Lifting his head, he watched as the deputies rushed to Rita, who was bleeding from a head wound, but it appeared to be superficial.

Another smaller boat bumped against his. Twisting around, he spied Andy's concerned expression peering at him. "She's okay, she's okay, she's okay," he chanted, pulling a shaking Billie closer to him.

Billie clutched him tightly, then leaned her head back and gasped, "Is she—"

"She's injured but alive. She'll be fine," he assured.

Shaking her head slowly, she choked down another raspy breath. "I don't know if she'll ever be fine."

"Maybe not," he agreed, but he didn't care about Rita at that moment. All he cared about was the woman he'd fallen in love with and thanking God she was safe.

"Let's get her to our vessel," Andy said, cutting into the fog in Jared's mind. "Then we'll get her and David's boats in as well."

Billie sat up quickly. "Wait! There's a necklace at the bottom of her boat. It belonged to her, but she lost it when she and David argued."

"I have an evidence bag, babe. Show me."

She pointed. "It's under the front seat."

He assisted her into Andy's boat and then crawled through her boat to lean over to retrieve the starfish charm from its hiding place. Once bagged, he turned. "Got it. Now let Andy take you to Callan, and we'll deal with these boats and get you back to the harbor as soon as we can."

She quickly acquiesced but not before casting a wobbly smile his way. He knew she was trying to let him know she was okay and that she understood he had to deal with the crime scene. That smile said everything. Everything he was feeling, too.

Jared wasn't sure his heart had returned to normal after seeing a gun pointed at Billie's head. After Rita was transported under guard by ambulance to the hospital and the VMP and North Heron deputies secured and investigated the area, he was crawling out of his skin to get back to Billie. Colt and Ryan decided to have David's boat taken from the muck and transported by land to the sheriff's department station for processing. The VMP transported Billie's boat back with them to the harbor, where Colt and Hunter met them to get Billie's statement. He'd entered the station, uncertain what state he'd find her in, but per usual with his girl, she was calm, if not pale and exhausted.

Now, they sat at the conference table they'd been at before, surrounded by the VMP, Colt, and Hunter. Most importantly, Jared sat beside her with his hand resting on her arm, desperate to maintain contact. The others probably thought the physical touch was for her, but in truth, it kept him grounded.

"And that's what she said." Billie glanced over at him after giving her statement, carefully reviewing everything Rita had told her. He offered a small smile, hoping it was encouraging while hiding his still heart-pounding nerves.

Shaking her head, she sighed heavily. "Rita fell for David—thought they were going to be together. He'd given her the starfish necklace." Looking around the table, she asked, "Do you know what the starfish symbolizes?"

At the shaking heads that answered her, she replied, "It's a celestial symbol. It represents infinite, divine love." Dragging in a shaky breath, she blinked away the gathering moisture he spied in her eyes. "I know it probably makes no sense to you. But she loved him, and when he told her it was over, she just snapped. She said she hit him with what was on hand, never meaning to kill him. But when she realized what she'd done, she acted quickly to cover everything up."

"Billie, we realize how difficult this has been for you," Colt said. "We appreciate your candor, knowing this is devastating with Rita being your boss and someone you knew. As soon as you found the boat, your actions were perfect, allowing David's death to be understood. And Rita is under medical as well as psychiatric care while she's under arrest. The county attorney is being apprised of her needs and the investigation."

Jared squeezed her arm as the others stood and started leaving the room. He slid his hand down to link his fingers with hers. Leaning forward, he whispered, "Let's get you home, sweetheart."

She nodded and stood. He unlinked their fingers

only long enough for him to wrap his arm around her shoulders and pull her into his side. When they stepped outside, he found his friends waiting for them.

Ryan moved in first, stooping slightly to hold Billie's gaze. "You did real good, Billie," he said. "If you need anything, anything at all, or even just someone to talk to, give Judith a call."

Jared released his hold on her, giving her a chance to move forward to offer Ryan a hug.

She offered a gentle smile. "Thank you. I will."

As Ryan walked down the hall, Callan, Joseph, Jose, Bryce, and then finally Andy stepped up, each hugging her as well. Andy leaned in close and whispered into her ear. Jared's attention came into sharp focus as he zeroed in on his friend, wondering what the hell he was saying. But Billie's wider smile eased his own tension, figuring Andy probably cracked a joke.

She was quiet for most of the trip to their house, and once there, she headed into the kitchen while he let Daisy out. When he came back in, she was still standing with the refrigerator door open, staring into the abyss as though wondering if dinner would grow wings and fly out at her. Stepping forward, he placed his hands on both of her shoulders and pulled her back against his chest, pushing the door closed.

"We're ordering. Pizza, Chinese, or Mexican?"

"Would it sound bad if I said I wanted to order Chinese?"

He turned her around and held her gaze. "Sound bad?"

"You know, the *my only friend just got arrested after*

holding a gun on me and finding out that she murdered her boyfriend, and I'm asking for Chinese food kind of bad."

Unable to stop and not really wanting to, he barked out a laugh. Pulling her close, he kissed the top of her head. "No, I'd say all of the above equals Chinese delivery."

While he pulled out his phone and ordered their favorites, he glanced over his shoulder to see her standing in the middle of the still-unfurnished dining room, a lost expression on her face. After disconnecting, he walked over, wondering if he should call Judith or maybe Zac's wife, Maddy, who was a counselor in town.

She startled as he neared and wrapped his arms around her. Without saying a word, she pressed her cheek against his chest, and he felt her swallow deeply several times as though battling back tears. At a loss for how to help, he just held her, glad her arms encircled his waist, holding him close as well.

Without lifting her head from his chest, she whispered, "That could have been me."

Of all the words she could have spoken, those were not what he expected. He wanted to question, deny, object, but somehow found the strength to remain quiet and allowed her to keep talking through whatever was going through her mind. Squeezing her a little tighter, he waited.

"I was so angry to discover Patrick's subterfuge. To realize I was his side piece. That everything I thought was going to happen wasn't even on his radar." She leaned back, and her haunted ice-blue eyes stayed pinned on him. "Jared, that could have been me. Angry. Lashing out. Then desperate to cover up the horror." Swallowing deeply again, she winced. "I'm not making excuses for Rita. It's just that I realized how all humans are capable of doing unspeakable things when our rational minds are overtaken by emotions." Her fingers tightened as she gripped his waist. "Don't you see? That could have been me. Am I so different from her?"

"Babe," he finally said, knowing she needed more than just understanding silence from him now. "You're not Rita." When she started to speak, he shook his head. "Let me finish." He waited until she pressed her lips together and nodded.

"While it's true that we're all capable of things we don't want to imagine, we don't all do them. We get angry, frustrated, and upset, and the urge to hurt someone can be real, but we don't act on them. Do you remember what you told me that you did when you found out about Patrick? You said that you cried, threw a few things around your apartment, went for long runs, drank wine, and ate ice cream. And then, you moved on. See, sweetheart, you are not Rita. You have coping skills that she didn't have. Honestly, she didn't seem contrite. She just seemed resigned that it happened, and now she got caught. But you… you found ways to move on that were good for everyone. You are *not* her." He squeezed her a little tighter. "Got it?"

Her lips were still pressed together, but they now curved ever so slightly. "You really listened, didn't you?"

"I've listened to everything you've ever said."

"Well, you didn't get it all completely right. I believe I said I drank *copious* amounts of wine and ate *gallons* of ice cream. Then I moved on."

Chuckling, he rocked their bodies back and forth, then kissed her forehead. After another moment, he sighed. "Scared the shit out of me, Billie. I've never been scared like that before."

"Me, too." Looking up, she bit her lip, her eyes filled with tears. "That's my fear. Loving and losing."

His heart jumped, and he wondered if she even realized what she'd said. "Then we just need to hang on tight to each other. Emphasize the loving part."

Her lips parted slightly, but before she could take the words back, he grinned. "And for the record, I've fallen in love with you, too."

A tiny gasp slipped out, and she grinned. Lifting on her toes, she kissed him, mumbling against his lips, "How much time before dinner is delivered?"

Laughing, he scooped her up into his strong arms. "We'll always make time, babe!" With her beautiful smile glowing, he carried her upstairs.

31

Billie ran alongside Jared, the wind coming off the bay cooling her body, heated from the five-mile Holiday Hope run for the American Legion's fundraiser. She was shocked at how many people showed up, both to run and to cheer. The course had traveled along back-roads, cleared by the sheriff's department deputies, and finished with a circle around the historic district of Baytown, ending at the town beach.

Each runner had sponsors, and when she'd asked at the CBF, she'd been amazed at how many coworkers and volunteers had donated to the cause. A new boss had taken Rita's place, and a month later, it still seemed strange to walk into the office that had once belonged to the woman she'd considered to be a friend and find someone else sitting there.

Rita had been charged with second-degree murder but was still undergoing her psychiatric evaluation. Billie hadn't talked to her since that day out on the water, and while Rita had held a gun on her, she still felt the loss of the friendship.

But Jared had been determined to fill Billie's life with new friends, often having his coworkers over for impromptu gatherings and becoming more active with the American Legion. She'd developed relationships with a number of women, finding it strange at first to be part of such a large sisterhood but loving the growing closeness and camaraderie.

"There's the finish line," Jared called out as they ran down Baytown's Main Street past the throngs of cheering spectators.

Her gaze focused on the town pier and beach up ahead, and she grinned. They soon passed the banner and slowed to a walk to stretch their muscles on the beach as friends surrounded them.

"Good run, son. Billie."

She smiled at the distinguished man walking toward them and the beautiful woman tucked next to him. Jared's parents, Robert and Sally, had come for a visit, wanting to meet the woman who Jared had moved into his house. She'd been nervous, but it didn't take long to discover that her no-nonsense personality meshed perfectly with Robert. And Sally declared that she trusted her son to know his mind, and if Billie was the one for him, she was thrilled. Robert was impressed with the work they'd completed on the house, and she and Sally had spent time shopping for a few items to make it seem more homey.

She hugged both of them, then turned to see another loving face. "James! You made it!"

He'd come to visit a few weeks ago to give his stamp of approval on her relationship with Jared, and she'd invited him back for the race weekend, not realizing Jared's parents would be visiting, too. But with them in the apartment over the garage, James in the guest room, and she and Jared in the primary bedroom, they had all managed just fine.

"I know you're still cooling down. We're heading over to the pub with James," Robert said. "We'll save you a place in the booth."

Waving goodbye, she turned to Jared, wrapping her arms around his waist. He inclined his head toward the pier, and she nodded. They walked down the long wooden pier until they got to the end. She could tell something was on his mind, so she silently waited, her hands resting on his waist as he peered down at her.

"I wanted to get you something," he began. "Something that would signify how I feel about you. But..."

She rolled her lips inward as a crinkle formed along her brow.

"But after what happened with Rita, it didn't feel right to give you a piece of jewelry that signifies feelings. Instead, what I want to give you is right here."

He took one of her hands and placed it over his heart, and she felt the steady beating underneath her palm.

"I know you were afraid we were going too fast, but no time limit has to be met before you know what you feel. Billie, I love you. I want to wake to your face each morning. I want to know everything about you. I want to help you achieve your dreams and slay your fears. I want to curl up with you every night. Your smile is all I need to be happy. I don't have a piece of jewelry right now to commemorate my declaration of love. Just know that my heart beats for you. And when you're ready, we'll find a ring to seal what we already know we feel."

She blinked, feeling a tear escape as it ran down her cheek, and for a moment, his face was blurry through the moisture. Swallowing past the lump in her throat, she smiled. "I love you, too. I don't need any jewelry. I just need you."

Laughing, he said, "Just so you know, sweetheart, when the time is right, we'll go jewelry shopping together… for a ring."

She gasped, then lifting on her toes to meet him halfway, she clung to him as they kissed. The warmth from his lips quickly sent heat throughout her body, and she pressed tightly to him. There, in her hero's strong arms, sure that their hearts were beating as one, she didn't want the kiss to end.

For Andy's story next, click here!
Needing A Hero

ALSO BY MARYANN JORDAN

Don't miss other Maryann Jordan books!

Baytown Boys (small town, military romantic suspense)

Coming Home

Just One More Chance

Clues of the Heart

Finding Peace

Picking Up the Pieces

Sunset Flames

Waiting for Sunrise

Hear My Heart

Guarding Your Heart

Sweet Rose

Our Time

Count On Me

Shielding You

To Love Someone

Sea Glass Hearts

Protecting Her Heart

Sunset Kiss

Baytown Heroes - A Baytown Boys subseries

A Hero's Chance

Finding a Hero

A Hero for Her

Needing A Hero

For all of Miss Ethel's boys:

Heroes at Heart (Military Romance)

Zander

Rafe

Cael

Jaxon

Jayden

Asher

Zeke

Cas

Lighthouse Security Investigations

Mace

Rank

Walker

Drew

Blake

Tate

Levi

Clay

Cobb

Bray

Josh

Knox

Lighthouse Security Investigations West Coast

Carson

Leo

Rick

Hop

Dolby

Hope City (romantic suspense series co-developed

with Kris Michaels

Brock book 1

Sean book 2

Carter book 3

Brody book 4

Kyle book 5

Ryker book 6

Rory book 7

Killian book 8

Torin book 9

Blayze book 10

Griffin book 11

Saints Protection & Investigations

(an elite group, assigned to the cases no one else wants…or can solve)

Serial Love

Healing Love

Revealing Love

Seeing Love

Honor Love

Sacrifice Love

Protecting Love

Remember Love

Discover Love

Surviving Love

Celebrating Love

Searching Love

Follow the exciting spin-off series:

Alvarez Security (military romantic suspense)

Gabe

Tony

Vinny

Jobe

SEALs

Thin Ice (Sleeper SEAL)

SEAL Together (Silver SEAL)

Undercover Groom (Hot SEAL)

Also for a Hope City Crossover Novel / Hot SEAL...

A Forever Dad

Long Road Home

Military Romantic Suspense

Home to Stay (a Lighthouse Security Investigation crossover

novel)

Home Port (an LSI West Coast crossover novel)

Letters From Home (military romance)

Class of Love

Freedom of Love

Bond of Love

The Love's Series (detectives)

Love's Taming

Love's Tempting

Love's Trusting

The Fairfield Series (small town detectives)

Emma's Home

Laurie's Time

Carol's Image

Fireworks Over Fairfield

Please take the time to leave a review of this book. Feel free to contact me, especially if you enjoyed my book. I love to hear from readers!

Facebook

Email

Website

ABOUT THE AUTHOR

I am an avid reader of romance novels, often joking that I cut my teeth on the historical romances. I have been reading and reviewing for years. In 2013, I finally gave into the characters in my head, screaming for their story to be told. From these musings, my first novel, Emma's Home, The Fairfield Series was born.

I was a high school counselor having worked in education for thirty years. I live in Virginia, having also lived in four states and two foreign countries. I have been married to a wonderfully patient man for forty-one years. When writing, my dog or one of my four cats can generally be found in the same room if not on my lap.

Please take the time to leave a review of this book. Feel free to contact me, especially if you enjoyed my book. I love to hear from readers!

Facebook

Email

Website

Made in the USA
Coppell, TX
28 February 2024

29549847R00204